DUSTY ROADS

Ghost Highway

R.N. Harscher

BOOKS BY R.N. HARSCHER

DUSTY ROADS SERIES:

Dusty Roads: First Highway Taken

Dusty Roads: Ghost Highway

COMING IN 2026:

Dusty Roads: Broken Highway

DUSTY ROADS

Ghost Highway

R.N. Harscher

Copyright © 2024, 2025 by R.N. Harscher.

All rights reserved.

ISBN- Paperback: 979-8-9923669-4-5

ISBN - eBook: 979-8-9923669-5-2

Library of Congress Control Number : 2025928062

First Edition : August 2024

Second Edition : October 2025

Second Edition—Updated and Expanded

Printed in the United States of America.

For more information, or to book an event, contact :

Bookings@rnharscher.com

https://www.rnharscher.com

Book and Cover design by RLA Publishing

This book is dedicated to all of the people in my life who showed up when the times got tough.
Thank you, from the bottom of my heart.
~Dusty

PROLOGUE

Family has always been the compass that guides Dusty—even when the highway and new cases beckon her.

She came from a family stitched together by faith and stubborn love. Her father, Myron, taught her that justice was worth standing up for even when it left scars. Her mother, Armindia, taught her that strength could be soft-spoken and still unbreakable. Her siblings—Layne, Rocky, and little Milo—were the ones who taught her how to fight and forgive.

Those lessons had carried her farther than she ever dreamed—through danger, loss, and the ghosts she couldn't outrun. But in this life, lessons haven't come easy. Every mile has had a price, and every case took something she couldn't get back.

The First Highway Taken had tested her courage and her faith. The Ghost Highway will test her soul.

Now, with the open road stretched before her again; the hum of the tires is a rhythm she knows better than her own heartbeat. She is following clues and something unseen but calling her name all the same.

Her shoulder still ached from the last case; her spirit still bruised from the things she couldn't change. Yet something inside her burned brighter—knowing that every shadow she walked through brought her closer to understanding why she was here at all.

Wampachaw had warned her: "Your help is needed, little one. Listen carefully."

And he was right. Some hauntings lived in memories. Others waited on winding desert highways, in towns like Jerome—where time itself seemed to stand still. Dusty had faced danger before, but never like this. This time, the spirits weren't just whispering from the past—they were guarding secrets that refused to stay buried.

Every story has a beginning.
Every ghost has a reason.
And every road, no matter how haunting, must eventually be traveled.

This is where the next highway begin.

CAST OF CHARACTERS

Dusty Roads: Now a seasoned investigator, guided as much by spirit as by instinct, Dusty faces darkness with hard-won grace.

Armindia Roads: Quietly resilient, Dusty's mom remains the family's moral compass and Dusty's touchstone of faith.

Myron Roads: Dusty's dad continues to provide the steady principles that steer Dusty's sense of justice.

The Roads Siblings: Layne, Rocky, and Milo – Each unique yet bound by loyalty: Layne's reason, Rocky's courage, and Milo's wisdom keep Dusty grounded no matter how far she roams.

Iola Abrams: Dusty's sharp-minded mentor whose faith in her grows deeper with every case..

Officer Ryan: A young cop whose admiration for Dusty has matured into steadfast respect.

Elizabeth Sherwood: Elegant mistress of the Bask Estate, haunted by secrets she can't bury.

Charles Durant: Devoted butler and secret keeper, torn between love and loyalty.

Clint Walker: A principled FBI agent whose calm strength mirrors Dusty's resolve.

Michael Yoder: A grieving rancher from Overgaard drawn into mysteries beyond reason.

Sven Johanson: His loyal friend and ranch hand, pragmatic until the impossible becomes real.

Eunice Thorman: A lost woman seeking redemption whose story intertwines with Dusty's.

Heidi: Iola's no-nonsense housekeeper whose wit and warmth steady even the darkest days.

Wampachaw: Dusty's ever-present spirit guide, his lessons now woven into her every breath.

1

A GIRL AND A GHOST STORY

The highway stretched ahead of Dusty like a ribbon in the sun. She had just passed Black Canyon City and was taking in some of the most beautiful views in Arizona. She loved this drive—whether she was heading to Prescott, Sedona, or Flagstaff, she always looked forward to the peace and tranquility this stretch of Interstate 17 offered.

Dusty was ready to leave Phoenix behind and move on to a new case. Until this moment, she hadn't realized just how keyed up she was. As the tension left her shoulders, she was surprised by how stiff her muscles felt. Her left arm was still in a sling from the gunshot wound that wasn't healing as quickly as she would've liked, and doing most things one-handed had become a real pain.

She was sick of the sling, but her arm hurt so badly without it she wasn't about to take it off. Her sister, Layne, had warned her that if she didn't start using the arm more, she could end up with a frozen shoulder. Dusty knew Layne was probably right, but she hadn't been keeping up with the daily exercises the doctor had prescribed—and her arm reminded her often that she needed to get with the program.

She hoped her mom and dad were getting a brief reprieve from worry while she was gone. She had been through one ordeal after another, and her family's worry never eased. Dusty took a few moments to count her blessings and thank God for her wonderful family.

She planned to return to Phoenix by the end of the week—her brother Rocky would soon be off to San Diego for six grueling weeks of Navy boot camp, and she wanted to make the most of their time together.

Dusty found it hard to believe her little towheaded brother was old enough to join the military. It scared her, and she couldn't help but think about all the dangers that came with going to war. Vietnam was brutal, and the thought of him being sent over there terrified her. She could only imagine how her folks were handling it. Their children were turning out to be a handful of drama. She just hoped it would all work out—for all of them.

Since Dusty had taken on the P.I. work for Abrams Investigations, she had put her family through hell. Her parents, Myron and Armindia, her sister Layne, and her brothers Rocky and little Milo had all been worried and stunned by the volatility of her job. She had been shot twice, and the fact that she had shot and killed several people in self-defense, had furthered their worries.

She prayed that her spirit guide, Wampacha, would not only guide her and keep her safe but also help her protect her family from the many dangerous situations she continued to face. Her prayers and thoughts remained focused on those wishes—during all her waking hours and much of her sleep.

She had met many new friends, and the investigators she worked with had broadened her experiences greatly. Iola Abrams, her boss, was becoming very special in her life, and Dusty was grateful to have her as a friend.

She reflected on how much had changed—including herself. These were changes she never would have imagined just a year ago.

As she made the turn at Cordes Junction and headed west through the town of Mayer, the weather began to turn. The wind picked up, and sprinkles of rain dotted her windshield. The sky turned hazy, and broken pieces of a rainbow flashed through the motion of her windshield wipers. It all felt surreal.

She wasn't quite sure what she was feeling, but the atmosphere held an ominous weight, charged with an unknown energy. The best she could guess was that the universe was showing her a balance between good and evil. She was approaching it ill-equipped, and—like the storm around her—she realized she was not in control. Lightning flashed every few minutes. Suddenly, the sun disappeared, and heavy black clouds descended over Prescott Valley. Rain came down in buckets, and she could barely see the road ahead.

Dusty came to a dirt road on the north side of Highway 69 and pulled off to wait while the storm raged. She found herself closing her eyes when a voice spoke to her.

Little one, it is good to see you. I am here to give you guidance about the next turn on your road. Listen to your inner guides—things are not what they seem, and you may be in the middle of a deception beyond your comprehension. Remember, when in doubt, say my name.

When she opened her eyes, the sun was bright against the wet earth. She stretched and thought about the dream she had. She knew that Wampacha was with her—and it did not sound like this would be an easy client.

She turned around on the dirt road to head back to the highway and nearly got stuck in the mud. To make matters worse, she had lost two hours of time. She must have been more tired than she realized, and the rain had likely lulled her to sleep.

She was losing daylight and wished she had something to eat. Her first stop in Jerome would be food—something to ground her. At least, she hoped it would.

She made the turn onto 89A, and the view was spectacular. She loved the smell of the air, the way the sun cast shadows across the lower hills, and how the drive felt like something out of a dream. It was as if she were in a movie—unable to fully grasp the breathtaking landscape that God had created.

Arizona had always seemed beautiful to her. Whether she was in the valley or the mountains, she'd admired the terrain. But this felt entirely different. She had never experienced emotions like this from Arizona's landscape—an overwhelming mix of joy and dread.

What the hell was going on?

She needed to get a handle on herself before speaking with Lizzy Sherwood. Maybe she should call her first, just to let her know she was stopping for supper.

As she approached Jerome and began ascending Cleopatra Hill, a long, hard shiver ran up her spine and down again. So it begins.

Dusty pulled into an old gas station called The Outpost. She spotted a pay phone and pulled out her file with Sherwood's number. After locking the car, she walked over to the phone—only to find it was out of order.

She went into The Outpost and asked the cashier if there was another phone nearby. He told her there was one in the back, near the restroom. She walked to the back of the building, spotted the phone, dropped in a dime, and dialed the number.

Lizzy Sherwood answered on the first ring.

Dusty told her she had just rolled into town and was going to grab a bite to eat before heading to her home.

Ms. Sherwood replied with an air of snootiness, "I have arranged for you to eat dinner here tonight. Though you may not *grab* it—you may *sit down* and eat it."

Dusty assured her there was no need to provide a meal, but Ms. Sherwood insisted. She explained that Dusty was expected to take all of her meals with her while in Jerome. Eating at the local café would only alert the townspeople to her presence.

Sherwood was firm. Dusty relented and said, "I'm on my way up the hill."

Back in the car, Dusty took a deep breath and whispered a prayer that she could handle this one. Give her a truck stop any day over a formal meal in front of someone—especially a client.

She meandered through Jerome's narrow streets, looking for the Bask house—or should she say, mansion. It looked out of place. She wanted to see it as stately and beautiful, but the Victorian house looked dark and intimidating. If only it had been painted like the "Lady" it was meant to be.

Normally, she loved the architecture of homes from that era, but this one felt downright spooky.

It was starting to get dark. As she pulled into the circular drive with its lion-head gate, she noticed a light in the upstairs window flicker on and then off.

She wondered what she was about to walk into in this eerie old house. Maybe a ghost from the past with an unsolved mystery?

As a child, she had gone through a phase of night terrors and would only sleep in a room with her mom.

Gosh, she hadn't thought of that in years.

Dusty parked, took out her bag and briefcase, and retrieved the pager from the glove box. She hadn't missed any pages, so she stuck it in her back pocket.

She walked up to the front door and rang the bell. Within seconds, a gentleman in a suit answered. Dusty introduced herself and asked for Ms. Sherwood. The man led her into the hallway.

"Let me take your bags to your room. The first door to your left is the powder room. Ms. Sherwood asks that you wash up and proceed to the dining room. I'll be right back to take you to dinner," he said.

She went into the bathroom and took her time. When she went to wash her hands, she noticed for the first time how elegant the little room was. Boy, she hoped the food was as good as the décor.

When she stepped out of the powder room, he was already waiting for her. She looked up at him and said, "I didn't catch your name."

He smiled. "I didn't throw it. My name is Charles. It's nice to meet you, Miss Dusty."

He opened the double doors to the right of the foyer, revealing the dining room. A small, middle-aged woman with faded red hair stood at the head of the table. She looked at Dusty and said, "My God, you're just a baby."

Dusty took her seat and smiled.

Lizzy didn't miss a beat. "I thought I hired the cream of the crop after all the hoopla in the paper, and what do I get? A child—dressed for Rodeo Days and disabled to boot."

For some reason, it struck Dusty as funny. She burst into one of those laughing spells where you can't stop and teeter on the edge of hysterics. She laughed like a hyena for several minutes. When she finally regained some semblance of control, she looked as seriously as she could at Lizzy and said, "You want the office to send someone else? I don't think it would be a problem. Just say the word and I'm outta here."

Lizzy looked mortified. "You can hardly blame me for being shocked. You are certainly not what I was expecting."

Just then, Charles entered with a tray and placed a plate in front of each of them. The aroma was mouthwatering—roast, potatoes, and carrots in a rich, savory gravy.

"It looks delicious," Dusty said, ignoring the look of utter disgust she was getting. "May I eat before you throw me out? I love pot roast and gravy."

"It's beef bourguignon, not pot roast—for God's sake," Lizzy said with an appalled look on her face.

She sat down and placed her napkin on her lap, all the while staring at Dusty. If looks could kill, Dusty would be having her last meal.

Lizzy began eating in a very sophisticated manner. Dusty tried to mimic her, but she was just too hungry. After the first bite, she thought she was in heaven. The food was so wonderful—and she was so hungry—that she couldn't contain herself for the sake of good manners.

She ate with her mouth closed, didn't talk, and kept her elbows off the table. That was about as much as she could manage. She wondered if seconds were out of the question.

Looking up, she saw Charles standing in the corner, smiling like he was thoroughly enjoying the interaction between the two women. Dusty swallowed hard and asked if she might have a little more.

Lizzy gave her a stern look—then suddenly burst out laughing. "Feed the girl, Charles. She acts like she hasn't eaten in days."

Dusty let out a sigh of relief. "I'm sorry for acting so ravenous, but you're right—I haven't eaten all day, and it gets me a little edgy. Thank you for the wonderful dinner. I really do appreciate it.

"If you need to replace me, I understand—I'm not everyone's cup of tea." Dusty said, "But I'm a good investigator, and I tend to get to the bottom of things quickly. I have a sixth sense about how things happened, and if you'd give me the opportunity, I'd really like to help you with your situation."

Lizzy motioned to Charles, and he quietly left the room. She turned in her chair and said, "A sixth sense? You mean ESP? Do you believe in ghosts? After dinner, I'd like to take you on a little tour of the house and then have a drink and talk about your ESP."

Dusty smiled. "That would be great. I'd love to see the house. Is the furniture in this room original? What year was the house built? Do you have a chocolate pie in the kitchen?" She asked with a grin.

Lizzy raised an eyebrow. "What would make you think I have a chocolate pie?"

"I just keep thinking about a big piece of pie. Chocolate's my favorite—and I love the crust. Just thought I'd ask." Dusty said hopeful.

The door to the dining room opened, and another plate was set in front of her—along with a large cake stand bearing a chocolate pie.

She looked up at Lizzy, smiled, and said, "Ask and you shall receive."

Lizzy smiled too, and they continued eating. The second helping was just as amazing—and the pie was unbelievable.

Charles cleared the table, and the two women got up and moved into the foyer.

Lizzy began telling the history of the house as if she were opening a murder mystery.

"Building of the house began in 1882." She said, "It stood alone at the top of the hill. Nathaniel Bask wanted to build an impressive home to attract the 'right kind of people' to the town, which he hoped would flourish."

Lizzy continued, "Copper mining began in 1876, and the town quickly sprang up to support it. By 1883, a post office had been established, followed soon after by shops, hotels, a bank—and even brothels—typical of the rapid development that follows a major copper discovery."

Lizzy leaned against the banister, her voice steady but tinged with old emotion. "Nathaniel, who was married with three children, moved to Jerome in 1884, just as soon as the house was completed. Within a year, two of the children died from fever. After that, Mrs. Bask packed up their surviving child—Elizabeth Anne—and went back to San Francisco."

Dusty frowned. "That must've been devastating. Losing two children like that?"

"I believe it was," Lizzy said quietly. "But Nathaniel didn't follow. Instead, he stayed here, and as the town began to grow, he became one of its most prominent figures. He filled the home with servants and potential investors. When the narrow-gauge railroad came through—connecting Ash Fork to Jerome Junction—the town really began to boom. New York money poured in."

She started walking slowly toward the parlor, her hands clasped behind her back.

"He never returned to San Francisco," she continued. "But in 1895, he sent for his daughter. She was sixteen by then. He hoped she'd want to stay in the house and take her place in his world. As the story goes, Elizabeth only came because her mother asked her to—to see if she could secure money for schooling."

Dusty raised an eyebrow. "And I'm guessing that didn't go as planned?"

Lizzy gave a tight smile. "Not quite. While she was visiting, Elizabeth—named after her mother—met an eighteen-year-old bank worker named William Preston.

Billy, they called him. Nathaniel saw an opportunity and encouraged the relationship from the very beginning. He wanted her rooted here. And within a short time, they were married."

Dusty tilted her head. "Was it love or something else?"

Lizzy's expression sharpened. "According to the story, she was pregnant. Nathaniel forced the marriage. And apparently, that wasn't exactly what young Billy had bargained for."

She paused before adding, "Nathaniel gave him a large sum of money to open a mercantile in town. But before the baby was even born, Billy vanished—along with the money. He was never seen again."

Dusty shook her head. "That's... cold. For all of them."

Lizzy nodded, her tone clipped. "That's how it started, Dusty. And that's just the beginning."

Lizzy paused. "Elizabeth fell into a deep depression that lasted the entire pregnancy."

Lizzy moved toward a nearby side table, tracing her finger along the edge as she continued. "When the baby—a robust little boy named Randolf, or Rand for short—was just two months old, Elizabeth left him. Abandoned him, really. Nathaniel took over, raised the boy himself. He hired the best nurse he could find, kept a full household staff, and made it his mission to teach Rand everything he believed a young man ought to know."

Dusty frowned. "Left her baby? That's heartbreaking. I guess she never came back?"

"Not once," Lizzy said, her tone sharp. "Nathaniel did his best. He was strict, proud, but devoted. Still, it was the Wild West—there was only so much even a wealthy man could control."

She stepped toward a nearby portrait and glanced up at it. "In 1915, Rand was badly hurt in a riding accident—nearly died. There wasn't a hospital nearby, not even a decent clinic. That changed everything. Nathaniel poured money into building one, staffed it, supplied it, and practically willed it into existence. He knew how many lives it could have saved."

Dusty nodded slowly. "He sounds like a complicated man. Harsh, but maybe trying to make things right."

"Complicated is a gentle way to put it," Lizzy replied dryly. "Then, in 1921, Nathaniel was shot. Right here in the house. No murder weapon, no suspect, no arrest. Just... dead."

Dusty blinked. "Wait, what? Murdered?"

Lizzy met her eyes. "Shot in his own home. They never solved it. Some say it was a business deal gone wrong. Others say it was a revenge killing. I say..." She shrugged. "Jerome has a way of swallowing truth whole."

She walked toward the staircase, gesturing for Dusty to follow. "Rand inherited everything at just twenty-five. A fortune. The estate. But he wasn't like his grandfather. He didn't want responsibility—he wanted adventure. Travel. Romance. Escape."

Dusty raised an eyebrow. "Let me guess... that didn't end well either?"

Lizzy gave a tight smile. "Before he left, he turned this house into something of a hostel. Repainted, modernized the seven bedrooms with indoor plumbing— quite forward-thinking at the time. Kept the staff. Tried to make it a respectable stop for visitors interested in Jerome's mining history."

She paused on the steps. "Then in 1922, he left. Traveled the world. Gone nearly ten years. And when he came back, he brought with him a young wife, Anika, and their one-year-old daughter, Matilda."

Dusty smiled faintly. "At least that part sounds romantic."

"On the surface," Lizzy replied. "Anika was from Virginia. Grew up on a tobacco farm. Tough stock. She fell in love with Jerome the moment she arrived—unusual, considering most people don't. She saw it as a challenge."

"She sounds like someone I'd get along with," Dusty said, trying to lighten the mood.

Lizzy nodded. "She wanted to build something lasting. Started a social club so local families wouldn't have to travel to Prescott or Phoenix to find community. She thought she could change the town."

"But let me guess," Dusty said. "Jerome had other plans?"

"Exactly," Lizzy replied. "The town was wild. Greedy. Dishonest. It didn't matter how noble your intentions were—Jerome chewed people up and spit them out."

They reached the top of the stairs. Lizzy stopped and turned to face Dusty.

"No one knows how Rand lost his money. But by 1935, it was gone—suddenly, completely. Rumors started flying. Some said he went mad. Others swore he robbed banks. It was hard to say what was true."

Dusty tilted her head. "You think he really did it?"

Lizzy's eyes darkened. "In 1940, a gold shipment from the Prescott mine vanished on its way to Phoenix. $400,000—never made it onto the trucks. Disappeared without a trace. So did Rand."

Dusty stood still, taking it all in. "So... he just vanished?"

Lizzy nodded slowly. "Vanished—like the fortune. Like the truth. That's the kind of legacy Jerome leaves behind."

Lizzy's voice grew softer as she continued, her eyes fixed on a spot in the distance as if she could still see the events unfolding.

"Anika eventually had Rand certified as deceased and, in 1948, married a man named Homer Helm," she said. "But not long after they married, Homer suffered a heart attack down in the lower basement level of the house... and died."

She exhaled slowly. "Anika stayed in this beautiful old house and watched it fall apart piece by piece."

Dusty remained quiet, the weight of the story settling heavily between them.

"The mine closed in 1950," Lizzy went on, "and Jerome was all but abandoned. Anika did what she could—she opened the house as a boarding house for a while. But then..." She paused, swallowing hard. "She was murdered. A vagrant broke in. He stabbed her—thirteen times."

Dusty's eyes widened, horrified.

"Matilda—Anika's daughter—was twenty years old at the time," Lizzy said quietly. "She grabbed a shotgun and shot him in the back. Killed him. That's how Matilda came to own the house."

"My God," Dusty said. "This house has had its share of heartache. Where is Matilda now?"

Lizzy turned and looked at her. "I am right here. Matilda Elizabeth Sherwood. I've been trying to set up a trust for the house and its future."

She paused before continuing. "I left the house for almost a decade, but since returning two years ago, I've uncovered some interesting things. I've been working to restore it and turn it into a bed and breakfast. I'm also trying to establish a trust for my charities, but as you'll see... it's turned into a can of worms."

Dusty kept looking at her and realized she was in for quite an experience. "So... does that mean I'm staying or going?" she asked.

"Let's get you settled in the guest house," Lizzy replied. "We'll meet for coffee at 8:00 a.m. tomorrow and discuss the rest—unless you'd like a drink before bed. Wait... are you even old enough to drink?"

"Not quite. I'm mostly a coffee and root beer girl," Dusty said, snorting with laughter at the look on Sherwood's face.

"I'm sorry I came across so snooty earlier," Lizzy said with a sigh. "It's my best defense for my own insecurities. But tomorrow is a new day. We'll be refreshed and start it with the most beautiful view from the front porch. It overlooks the Verde Valley—it's quite spectacular."

She glanced back at Dusty. "Do you have any questions at this point?"

"Just one," Dusty said. "Who does the cooking here, and how many staff are on the premises?"

"At this time," Lizzy answered, "there are four staff members: two maids, Charles, and myself."

Dusty looked baffled. "You consider yourself staff?"

Lizzy smiled. "Yes—I'm the cook."

She gave a small nod to Charles. "Go ahead and show her to the guesthouse."

2

THE PAINTED LADY'S SECRET

The guest house sat about 100 feet behind the main house. Dusty figured it had once been a carriage house— she loved it from the moment she stepped through the door.

"Wow," she said to Charles. "This is perfect. When did she convert the carriage house?"

Charles looked at her oddly. "What makes you think it was the carriage house?"

She shrugged and winced as a sharp pain shot through her shoulder. Damn, she thought.

"I just assumed it was," she said aloud.

She sat down on a chair near the door and took a deep breath.

"You alright?" Charles asked.

"Yeah, just my shoulder acting up," she replied.

"How did you hurt it?" he said.

"I was shot." she said, looking at him for some kind of reaction.

Charles turned abruptly and walked away.

"Goodnight," Dusty called after him, but he didn't answer.

She slept like a baby and woke up feeling rested and ready for coffee. After taking a long, hot shower, she put her hair up, made her bed, and prepared for the day. She left her new .38 tucked away in her travel bag but slipped the boot pistol her dad bought her into the ankle holster she wore.

At 7:45 a.m., she headed up to the main house to use the phone and grab some coffee. As soon as she stepped through the back door and into the mudroom, the delicious aroma hit her—something more than just coffee.

The first person she saw was Charles.

She smiled and greeted him. "Good morning."

He smiled back. "Ms. Sherwood is out on the porch, off the side of the dining room," he said. "How do you take your coffee?"

"Black," she answered.

"Why does that not surprise me?" he said with a smirk.

She took her cup and inhaled deeply—it smelled wonderful, just as she knew it would.

She walked out onto the porch, and as promised, she was greeted by the most beautiful view of the Verde Valley. Sparse clouds cast early morning shadows across the landscape.

"Stunning," she said, walking over to a porch rocker. "Mind if I sit down?"

Lizzy smiled and glanced back at the newspaper in front of her.

Dusty turned the chair slightly to face the hillside and the buildings of Jerome. It was an interesting view, and she let stories of all kinds flash through her mind.

What must it be like to live here now? She wondered. *Nearly a hundred years since the town's beginning, and it still looked like it was the 1870s.*

The hospital above them was now a hotel of sorts—supposedly haunted.

She sat quietly, gazing intently at the valley below. There was a peaceful calm about it all—until the hair on the back of her neck began to bristle. She knew that feeling well. Slowly, she turned to look behind her.

Nothing appeared out of the ordinary, but she felt the breeze stir around her and knew a pair of eyes were on her. She hoped it was Wampacha.

She glanced at Lizzy, who was also looking in the same direction.

"We have company, it seems," Dusty said quietly.

"I feel it too," Lizzy replied. "Let's have breakfast at the kitchen table."

"Sounds good to me. Something sure smells good, and I could use more coffee," Dusty said.

"By the way," Lizzy added, "do you like dogs?"

"I love dogs! Do you have one?" Dusty asked.

Lizzy smiled and headed into the house. "I'll meet you in the kitchen."

Dusty followed a few minutes later and found Charles pouring coffee into a beautiful urn. She sat down at the table and watched silently as he prepared a tray of baked goods—muffins, scones, and fresh hot bread with all the fixings. It looked scrumptious, and Dusty could hardly resist the urge to grab one and stuff it in her mouth.

Lizzy walked in holding a medium-sized Chihuahua in her arms.

"This is Poncho, the head dog of the house," she said.

At her feet, five more dogs of various sizes and breeds came scurrying in. They were all wagging their tails and panting, but not one of them barked.

It was so adorable that Dusty couldn't help but ask, "How sweet! Any cats?"

"Just one," Lizzy replied. "His name is Dante—because he's wise and watchful. He'll show himself when he's ready. The dogs were left here at some point while I was gone, and we've become very close. They're family now. You've met Poncho, and this one is Chico, then Cholla, Biscuit, Lulu, and Eva. They're the keepers of the house."

She paused, then added with a grin, "I need to get a name for the house. I like naming things."

Dusty smiled. "I have a name for your house—Lady."

Lizzy gasped. "My mother always referred to the house as the Painted Lady. Back then, it was colorful and beautifully painted. I love that name. We shall call her Lady. Thank you, Dusty. That feels right."

Dusty smiled again and felt at home. They sat down together to enjoy the coffee and the delicious assortment of baked goods Lizzy had spent all morning preparing.

Across the room, Lizzy gave Charles a stern, sorrowful look. Dusty didn't notice. Charles shook his head slightly, then made an imaginary slicing motion across his neck with his finger.

Lizzy looked like she might cry. She turned away from Dusty to compose herself.

The morning had begun so calmly, so full of promise, that no one could have foreseen the turn it would take later that same day.

After breakfast, Lizzy took Dusty for a walk around the premises. She spent most of the time asking questions about Dusty and her family.

At first, Dusty found it a little odd, but she remained polite and answered as best she could. However, when the questions began to feel a bit too personal, she stopped at the entrance to a narrow garden path and turned to Lizzy.

"Why are you so interested in my life?" she asked. "What does any of this have to do with the investigation?"

Lizzy took several moments before answering. When she did, her tone was stern.

"Just curious. You're an odd little urchin, and I'm feeling you out before I divulge anything. I'm very serious about the secrecy of this estate, and I need to know who I'm dealing with. Honestly, I haven't quite decided what I want or need to tell you yet."

Dusty crossed her arms. "Maybe you should just tell me what you need done. You might not need to divulge anything more. Is it legal, illegal, or just a monumental decision you need help making?"

She paused, then added, "Whatever it is, you must have felt I could find some answers—or someone in my line of work could—before you called the agency. Maybe you just need someone to represent you, and I'm not the right presence. Either way, let's get on with it. We're burning daylight."

As she said this, Dusty felt that strange feeling again.

"Let's keep walking," Lizzy said reluctantly. "We'll go to the ground entrance of the basement and pick up the story there."

As they approached the back of the house, Dusty saw an old cellar door made of thick wooden slats—larger than any she'd seen before. The extra-wide boards made it difficult to lift and secure.

Underneath the door was a short flight of ten stone steps leading to a large green door with a small window on the top half. It looked foreboding, and Dusty felt one of her internal warning bells go off. Something told her they were entering a different phase of the investigation.

Lizzy reached into her pocket and pulled out a ring of old keys. She located one that resembled a skeleton key, slipped it into the lock, and with a firm twist, opened the door.

A musty odor of dirt and dampness greeted them. Dusty wrinkled her nose at the smell, but there was another scent—something unfamiliar and out of place for a basement. She couldn't name it, but it made her uneasy.

They stepped inside a large room filled with old furniture, paintings, carriage wheels, and crates of all sizes. Dusty would have loved to explore it all, but she reminded herself that wasn't why she was here.

As she moved deeper into the basement, Lizzy startled her by speaking.

"We need to go to the far end of this room and turn right. There are no lights, so we'll need flashlights."

She stepped to the side and picked up two heavy-duty flashlights, handing one to Dusty.

Dusty switched hers on. The beam illuminated a basement full of treasures.

"Wow," she breathed.

"Take a deep breath," Lizzy said with a smirk. "You haven't seen anything yet."

As they walked, it became clear that the basement was much larger than the house's footprint. Hallways—or what looked like them—had been dug out, leading to the north side of the property and looping back toward the carriage house.

But Dusty realized they weren't hallways. They were tunnels—connected to the main house and the hillside behind it.

She turned to comment to Lizzy, but before she could speak, a sound echoed behind them. It sounded like a muffled voice saying Lizzy's name.

Lizzy froze, her face pale. She turned toward the basement entrance, but before she could move, a loud boom echoed through the space.

It was distorted by the cave acoustics but still loud enough to send a jolt of fear through both women.

Lizzy screamed and bolted for the entrance.

"Move slowly!" Dusty hissed, grabbing Lizzy's arm.

But Lizzy shoved her in front and switched off her flashlight.

Dusty wasn't sure why Lizzy had done that, but she wasn't about to turn hers off. They reached the entrance, but there was no light coming from above. The door had been shut, and the exterior cellar doors had been dropped back into place.

The darkness was heavy and pressing. Dusty tried the inner door, but it wouldn't budge.

Lizzy inserted her key, but it wouldn't turn.

"Someone locked it from the outside," Dusty said grimly. "We're trapped."

Lizzy looked uncertain. "I think I mentioned to Charles where we were going... but I'm not sure."

"Is there another way out?" Dusty asked.

"Yes," Lizzy replied with a sigh. "It's a long walk. There's an exit at the base of Cleopatra. But I've only been halfway—I'm not sure if the rest of the tunnel is still passable."

"Wait—who's Cleopatra?" Dusty asked.

"It's the hill. The town is built on it." Lizzy sighed.

"Oh," Dusty said sheepishly. "Right. I knew that. Just... wasn't thinking straight."

She was uncomfortable. Confined spaces and darkness weren't her favorite combination.

Lizzy shook her head. "Maybe Charles thought we left the doors open and just shut them. It doesn't make sense."

They began walking again, and Dusty asked, "How long have you known Charles? Does he know everything about this estate?"

Lizzy was silent for a long time. Then, like a dam breaking, her words spilled out.

"Charles is my husband. Yes, he knows everything I know. But I don't think he's the one who shut those doors on us. Honestly, I don't know who did."

She took a deep breath.

"I know it sounds strange, and I'm not trying to scare you. But since I rediscovered these tunnels, strange things have been happening. That's why I brought you here. I needed help putting all the pieces together... and someone to watch my back."

Lizzy's voice trembled. "I didn't mean to deceive you. I just don't trust easily. Things don't add up. I've found family heirlooms, antiques, and a massive amount of gold bullion—possibly from the train robbery my father was accused of."

Dusty raised her eyebrows, but Lizzy kept talking.

"I don't know what to do with it. Should I give it to the bank it was headed for? The mine that sent it? The insurance company that paid out the claim? It's too complicated, and I didn't know how to research it all."

Her voice dropped to a whisper. "Then things started moving down here—on their own. I kept thinking someone else was down here. I got spooked. Then I saw that article about your agency. I thought I was being guided to call."

Lizzy looked at Dusty. "I didn't expect to like you. I thought you'd be older. When I saw how young and full of life you were in your western outfit... I second-guessed myself."

She paused.

"I believe someone knows about the gold. I need help. I need to know who to call. Are you experienced enough to handle this?"

Dusty never got the chance to answer.

As they rounded the next turn in the tunnel, her flashlight started to flicker. A sound—like someone stumbling ahead—echoed through the darkness.

Lizzy turned her flashlight back on and aimed it down the tunnel. Dusty lowered hers. Her shoulder was throbbing, and she needed her gun.

She slipped her arm out of the sling and retrieved her boot pistol. The pain made her wince, but she didn't hesitate. She grabbed Lizzy's hand and pulled her to the ground, pressing her back against the wall.

Lizzy turned off the flashlight. They sat huddled in the dark, listening as footsteps scuffled closer. Suddenly, a beam of light flashed in their direction, blinding them.

Dusty waited for a voice, a signal—something. But the light just kept coming.

She whispered, "Stay here. When I say 'now,' turn on the flashlight. Okay?"

Lizzy squeezed her hand in agreement.

Dusty crept forward, staying low. She'd gone about fifteen feet when she realized the light had been set against the wall—but the person who placed it was gone.

She froze, listening.

A low grunt came from the next chamber.

Dusty stood slowly and peeked around the corner. There, she saw the golden hue of stacked bullion... and a tall, burly man in a flannel shirt with suspenders loading bars onto a large cart.

Dusty gripped her gun.

"Put your hands in the air and turn around slowly!" she commanded. "No funny business."

She stepped away from the wall, watching as the man turned toward her.

"Now!" she shouted.

A beam of light hit the man's eyes. He blinked, shielding his face with one hand—while the other pulled a handgun from his belt.

As he fired, Dusty dove to her left, rolled, and came up firing. Her shot hit him in the chest. He gasped and dropped.

She rushed over, kicked his gun away, and checked for a pulse. He was still alive.

"Lizzy!" she called. "Do you know him?"

Lizzy ran over and stared. She shook her head. "No."

"Are we close to the tunnel's end?" Dusty asked.

"I'm not sure," Lizzy said. "But we're closer to the exit than to go back."

Dusty nodded. "One of us should go for help. Or maybe we load him on the cart and go together?"

Lizzy looked doubtful. "How are we going to explain this?"

"One thing at a time," Dusty replied, already unloading the cart. "Let's get him out. I'll handle the rest."

They moved the gold and managed to lift the wounded man onto the cart. Together, they pushed it down the rough, rocky tunnel. It took almost an hour to wind their way through and clear enough brush to exit the cave opening.

The man was still breathing and had begun to moan softly. Within minutes of reaching daylight, they flagged down an old jeep coming up the dirt road on the side of Cleopatra Hill. With help from the driver, they loaded the man into the vehicle and headed toward the nearest medical facility.

Dusty had the driver drop them off near the bottom of the hill where her car was parked, so she could follow behind. It was a gamble, but Dusty needed time alone with Lizzy to talk.

"I think our story should go like this," Dusty said. "We were walking the tunnels and the grounds so you could educate me on the history of the Bask House. That's when we came upon this man, loading what appeared to be gold. When we confronted him to find out why he was on your property, he shot at me—and I fired back, hitting him in the chest. We don't know who he is, but we're very interested in finding out. We'd like to notify the police and the FBI about the gold and request a formal investigation into how it got there. How does that sound?"

Lizzy nodded slowly. "Well, that's pretty much the way it went down, isn't it?"

"Yes. It's just about how we word it," Dusty said. "If you're questioned about the gold, you can say there were always rumors about the train robbery—but you only recently discovered it. You hired me to help notify the authorities. What do you think? Does that sit right with you? We're telling the truth—we're just not giving them more than they need."

Lizzy nodded again and remained silent for the rest of the ride.

3

SHADOWS OF THE BASK HOUSE

They had caught up to the jeep within a few minutes and followed it to the town of Clarkdale, where there was a local doctor's office. Together, they helped carry the wounded man inside.

Dr. Whitman met them in the entryway and directed them to bring him into an exam room. Once the man was settled, the doctor turned to Dusty and Lizzy.

"You two wait out front while I work on him," he said.

Lizzy stepped outside to call Charles and give him an update. Dusty watched her closely, noticing that Lizzy seemed to be saying more than what had actually happened.

They overheard the nurse calling for an ambulance to transfer the man to Flagstaff Hospital. A few moments later, the nurse approached them and said, "He's stable for now."

A Yavapai County patrol car pulled up outside. An officer stepped out and entered the building. His name tag read Officer Merrill. He approached the front desk and asked, "Where's the man who was shot? And who brought him in?"

The nurse pointed at Dusty and Lizzy. "They did. He's still with the doctor."

As the officer approached, Dusty noted how he was sizing them up—making mental notes, trying to read the situation.

He introduced himself. "I'm Officer Merrill. One of you want to tell me what happened? Were you there when he was shot, or did you find him after the fact?"

Lizzy glanced at Dusty. "You go ahead and give him the rundown. I need to sit for a while."

Dusty nodded and began explaining. "We were going over the estate grounds. Lizzy was bringing me up to speed on the history of the Bask House. We went down to the basement to look through some stored items and decided to walk the tunnel to see where it led. Lizzy remembered it from her childhood, growing up in the house."

She paused, then continued. "When we saw lights in the tunnel, we approached. That's when we saw the man loading what looked like gold onto a cart. The scene didn't feel right, so I raised my .25 caliber and told him to put his hands up and turn around. Instead, he pulled a weapon from his waistband and fired at me. I returned fire, hitting him in the chest."

She reached into her jacket pocket. "I have my gun and his. I didn't want to leave them behind."

The officer gestured. "Let's go ahead and secure those."

Dusty nodded. She asked the nurse for a couple of tissues, wrapped both weapons carefully, and laid them on the counter. The officer bagged them and took them out to his vehicle.

She saw him on the radio, likely calling in a report. A knot tightened in her stomach as she wondered how long it would take before her dad found out.

She winced, lifted her arm, and slipped it back into her sling—it was pounding.

When Officer Merrill returned, he apologized. He walked over to the nurse, asked a few questions, and examined what looked to be a wallet—probably the victim's. After bagging it, he returned to his patrol car again.

Dr. Whitman came out a few minutes later.

"I think he's going to live," he said. "The bullet missed his heart but punctured his left lung. He'll need surgery."

In the distance, they could hear the approaching siren of the ambulance.

Dusty turned to Lizzy. "We'll probably head back up to the house soon. You might want to call Charles again and let him know." Then she walked outside and approached Officer Merrill just as he was stepping out of his car.

"You need help?" he asked.

"How long until we can leave?" Dusty asked.

He hesitated. "Technically, I should take you in for questioning."

"What?" she said, shocked. "The man was trespassing and he shot at me first!"

"I still need to see the place where it happened. As soon as the ambulance gets here, I'll follow you up."

They walked back inside, and Dusty informed Lizzy that the officer would be following them.

Then she turned to Officer Merrill. "Do you have a name on the man who was shot?"

The officer nodded. "Yeah. It's Nate Helm. Address on his license says San Francisco, California. Do you know him?"

Dusty's mind raced. She needed a moment to think. She didn't want to reveal too much, but she also couldn't afford to be evasive.

"Sir," she began, "I think you or I should call the FBI. That gold has a history, and this needs to be handled legally. I'm just getting involved with this client, and I need to protect her and the family's information."

She paused. "So... should you contact them or should I?"

The officer narrowed his eyes. "What do you mean, client?"

"I'm a private investigator," Dusty said firmly. "I work for Abrams Investigations. Mrs. Sherwood hired me to help with research and provide protection as she navigates the legal issues tied to the estate."

Officer Merrill blinked. "You're a P.I.? You're joking, right? Why would a P.I. want the FBI involved? Don't you think that's a little dramatic, girlie?"

Dusty gave him a sharp look and pulled a small notepad from her jean pocket, along with a pencil tucked in her shirt collar.

"What's your badge number again?" she asked coolly. "You might want to take a step back and think about the bigger picture here. And nothing goes to the press until the FBI clears it. Comprehend, Officer Merrill?"

He gave her a theatrical look of disbelief, then got into his patrol car just as the ambulance rolled up.

Dusty walked back into the office to retrieve Lizzy.

On her way out, she handed the nurse a business card. "Name's Dusty. Call me if you need anything."

They got into the Mustang and drove back up the hill in silence.

Lizzy sat quietly the entire ride, and so did Dusty.

When they reached the "Lady," they pulled into the circular drive and parked.

As they started up the porch steps, Lizzy turned to her.

"Well, now the cat's out of the bag," she said. "What do we do next?"

"First thing—I call my office and update Abrams," Dusty replied. "Then I'm heading back into the tunnel with my camera to document everything. We should be hearing from the FBI soon, and that'll tie us up for a bit. Is there anything else you haven't told me?"

Lizzy shrugged. "Like what? Isn't there enough going on without adding to it?"

Dusty gave her a look. "You must have thought about how this would play out. I don't mean the shooting—but the money. That was always going to be the issue. Now we've got more complications."

She took a breath. "The simpler and more straightforward we are, the better. I want to check out a few things behind the house before I make the call. Want to come with me, or wait here?"

"I think I'll wait and have some tea with Charles," Lizzy said. "Try to fill him in. That okay with you? Oh, and by the way—why didn't you tell me you were carrying a gun?"

Her tone was sarcastic.

Dusty didn't respond. She was too focused on why Lizzy was suddenly acting so strange. Something about the tunnel encounter still didn't sit right.

She headed to her room to put ointment on her shoulder. As she neared the back of the house, she saw Charles coming out of the carriage house.

When he spotted her, his expression shifted—he looked caught.

"What's up? Did you need me?" she asked.

"No, not at all," he said, fumbling. "I didn't know you were back. I was just putting a phone in your room. There's a jack, I just hadn't installed a phone yet. Figured you'd want one to call your office."

He avoided eye contact, quickly heading to the back entrance. As he pulled the screen door open, he glanced back—startled to find Dusty still staring at him. Without a word, he ducked inside and slammed the door.

The hairs on the back of Dusty's neck stood up.

She shivered and entered her room. Reaching for the phone, she dialed Iola's private number. As the line rang, she heard a distinct click on the other end.

She was being listened to.

Deciding to use the opportunity, Dusty mentally shifted gears. This would become a test call—one she might be able to use later to trip up whoever was listening.

Iola picked up, and Dusty began her summary of the day—sprinkling in a few ad libs, just in case someone was listening on the other end.

When Dusty mentioned she had shot someone, Iola actually let out a yelp.

Dusty tried to make it sound as non-dramatic as possible, though she couldn't help catching her breath a couple of times for effect. She assured Iola she would call her back once she finished dealing with the authorities in the tunnels.

"I wish I was there," Iola said. "But I know you can handle yourself."

There was a pause, then Iola added more seriously, "Dusty, I know you pretty well. I can tell when you're not telling me everything. Just... be careful, okay? And be in the office the day after tomorrow. I've got several other cases waiting. See you then."

She hung up.

Dusty slowly pressed the button on the phone cradle and released it—just in time to hear Charles's voice from the other end of the line.

"I think she knows something she's not telling us."

A second later, she heard the click as he hung up.

Dusty did the same. Then, with a smirk, she muttered in a sing-song voice, *"Wampachaw."*

She walked to the door and made sure it was locked. Then she rubbed some eucalyptus oil into her aching shoulder and stretched out on the bed.

She only meant to rest her eyes for a moment... but within seconds, she drifted off to sleep.

4

THE SETUP

When she awoke, twenty-five minutes had passed. Dusty stared at the ceiling, trying to keep her vision clear. She had seen something—herself in the tunnel, hidden from sight, watching Lizzy talk to the man she had shot. They seemed to know each other, and they were arguing.

All she could make out was the man telling Lizzy, "You better turn in the gold—and turn it in pronto."

Now she was completely confused and unsure how to use the information. Dusty lay there in shock, questions bouncing through her mind, frustration simmering beneath the surface. She'd have to think it through later.

This was turning into a horse of a different color, and she knew now that Wampacha's warning had been exactly on point.

She sat on the edge of the bed, contemplating her next move, when someone knocked at the door. It was Charles.

"The police have arrived," he said.

Dusty took a deep breath, ran her fingers through her hair, and pulled on her boots.

Time for Act II, she thought. Her stomach growled loudly. She realized how hungry she was—maybe she'd find a snack on her way through the kitchen.

As she opened the door, she ran right into Charles and Lizzy. They pushed her gently back into the room, shut the door behind them, and Lizzy asked sharply, "What are you going to tell them?"

Dusty replied, "The truth. What else would I tell? I'll answer their questions to the best of my ability. I think we should keep anything from before today close to the chest—at least until we know who the man in the tunnel is. What are your thoughts?"

Lizzy looked at Charles, then said, "I think that's a good idea. But I'm extremely stressed about the FBI."

"Don't worry," Dusty said. "They might actually take some weight off our shoulders. Hopefully, they'll fill in a few of the gaps."

Lizzy's expression hardened slightly, just enough for Dusty to notice.

"What is it?" Dusty asked.

"My money," Lizzy replied flatly.

Dusty opened her mouth to dig into that comment, but a knock came at the door.

"The FBI," she said quietly. "You'd better rethink that. We'll talk later—privately."

Dusty stepped outside. With a quick laugh and her thumbs in her belt, she said, "Let's get started. We're burning daylight."

She nearly faked a limp to do her best Chester imitation—*Gunsmoke* was one of her favorites. She was nervous. It was a foreign feeling, and humor helped.

Turning to Charles, she added, "I sure am looking forward to some good vittles when I get back."

Then she smiled and introduced herself to the agents.

The first to shake her hand was an older gentleman.

"I'm Wiley Newton," he said.

The second smiled. "Stan Roth."

The third had a toothpick in his mouth. He looked her over a moment before speaking. "I'm the lead on this investigation. Name's Clint Walker. We'd appreciate you taking us through the events of the day."

She grinned. "Mind if I call you Cheyenne? It would do my heart good—and you're very handsome."

What the hell am I saying? she thought. *I must be giddy. My love for westerns is going to get me in trouble someday.*

Clint snorted, but smiled. "You can call me Mr. Walker, little lady."

She caught the "little lady" remark and thought, *Wow, maybe he's part John Wayne.*

Oh well, enough fun, she thought, *better get down to business.*

They entered the basement through the same door she and Lizzy had used earlier. Dusty grabbed a flashlight and led the way down the first tunnel.

"Wait," she said, stopping. "Let me bring you up to speed on the history of the house and why this money is probably here."

She looked around—no Lizzy, no Charles.

"It all began with Nathaniel Bask in the late 1800s..."

As she recounted the tangled story, she watched the agents' faces shift in the eerie glow of their flashlights. It reminded her of campfire ghost stories. With that thought, she continued deeper into the tunnel.

Soon, she realized she was having trouble retracing her steps. She stopped, looked around—and sure enough, Wampacha was in her head.

Left, then right, right—and you will be there. Open your eyes and see, he whispered.

The investigators stared at her.

She smiled. "Just talking with my inner guide."

Clint raised an eyebrow. "What'd he say?"

"He wants me to get on with it. I'm trying to remember the tunnel turns. Today was my first time down here, and I thought Lizzy and Charles were coming with us."

"They said they'd stay and talk to the other agent," Clint replied. "Didn't realize this was a maze. What were you looking for down here? Something in particular? Did Sherwood know the man was taking the gold? Did she know it was even here? Is that where she was taking you—to the gold? Is the gold the reason she hired you?"

Wow, Dusty thought. *Someone who asks more questions than I do.*

"Let's take this a step at a time, shall we?" she said.

They rounded a corner, and Dusty realized they were back at the scene of the shooting. But something was off.

"Have you already been here?" she asked.

"No," Clint replied. "Why?"

"It looks different."

She scanned the area. "There were 21 gold bars on the cart. We took them off to move the man out. They were scattered all over this side. Now they're stacked—and there are only 18."

She pointed around the other side. "That's where the man was working. I didn't have time to check the area before—we were in a rush. I just grabbed his gun, threw it in my pocket, and we started the long haul to the tunnel exit. We cleared heavy brush to push the cart through and flagged a car down."

Clint asked, "Where exactly were you when you fired your weapon?"

She walked them through everything. The approach. The confrontation. Her commands. The light. The gunfire.

The roll and return shot. The pulse check. The decision to get him help.

"That's a very interesting story," Clint said. "But it doesn't add up, now does it?"

"I'm just telling you how it happened," Dusty replied. "I remember it pretty clearly."

Clint stepped closer. "What caliber gun were you carrying?"

"A .25-caliber boot gun. Normally I carry a .38, but I left it in my room."

"You turned the guns over to the deputy, right?"

"Yes. Both—his and mine."

Clint locked eyes with her. "Your .25 didn't wound Nate Helms."

Dusty's heart skipped.

"So where's the .38 you own?" he asked.

"In my room—but I didn't have it with me. I can check it when we get back. I fired the .25. I'm sure of it."

"Did Mrs. Sherwood have a gun?" he asked.

"No—not that I saw. What are you getting at?"

"If you fired a .25, you weren't the one who shot Nate. So unless there was someone else down here, she had a gun. Are you sure you didn't see another muzzle flash? Maybe that's the 'echo' you thought you heard?"

Dusty stood there in complete disbelief. *Had she been fooled throughout this scenario with Lizzy?*

She tried to steady her voice.

"I've told you exactly how I remember it. But maybe my view isn't the whole picture. You've raised good questions—and I can't answer them right now. The first thing I need to do is check my .38. I'm telling you, I only fired the .25."

She looked around the tunnel. "We should do a full sweep. The tunnels are deep—it might take days."

She suddenly shuddered and slowly sat herself down against the hard rock wall, her head was spinning and she could not get anything to line up

Agent Walker looked concerned and gave orders for Roth and Wiley to continue down the tunnel. He offered to walk Dusty back and meet them at the other end.

As they reached the basement entrance, Walker asked, "Any other scenarios come to mind?"

"I'll think on it. But right now, I haven't eaten, and it's been a very long day."

"I'll be back at 9:00 a.m.," he said. "But I need to check the .38 to see if it's been fired."

As they entered her room she felt uneasy and told agent Walker that she had a very bad feeling about all of this.

He asked her where she had put the .38? She pointed to her travel bag and told him he could look in it. He carefully opened it and stared at the contents for a few seconds before taking anything out.

He removed her jacket, her toiletry bag, and her lipstick, laying the items on the chair. Then he brought out the gun belt holding the .38 in a leather holster. He lifted it with his handkerchief and laid it on the bed where she sat. He used the handkerchief to lift the gun by its grip and put it to his nose. He looked her straight in the eye and said, "It's been fired recently."

A knot twisted in Dusty's stomach. She leaned forward, reviewing the day in her mind. Then—click. It hit her. The plan. The setup. She was the scapegoat.

Well, she thought, *I'm not going down that easy.*

She walked outside and watched the sun set. She needed to call Iola, but couldn't risk using the house phone. Walker had taken the .38 but decided not to arrest her—for now. He said he'd get it to ballistics and return in the morning.

As she walked toward the back of the house, Charles stepped out with a tray.

"I was just bringing you dinner," he said. "Would you prefer to eat inside with us?"

"I'd like that," Dusty said.

They sat at the kitchen table. Dining room dinners would likely never happen again.

She asked where to sit.

"Same place as breakfast," Charles said.

Dusty looked at Lizzy. "Are you okay?"

Lizzy offered a weak smile. "Let's eat. Maybe it'll help us feel better."

Dusty looked at her plate: meatloaf, mashed potatoes, green beans. Lizzy had meatloaf and green beans—no potatoes.

Why no potatoes for Lizzy? she wondered. *Were they drugged?*

Still, she was starving. She took a sip of water and stabbed a green bean.

"I'm so tired," she said.

"You've had a busy day full of surprises," Lizzy replied. "What did the FBI say?"

Dusty started talking fast, spinning a vague version of the truth—leaving out the .38 and third-gun theory.

She made it sound like the cops were looking at her as a suspect, "It seemed like they didn't believe anything I was saying."

"I am not really thinking clearly about any of it and I think that they aren't telling us something important" Dusty tried to sound worried.

"Like what? Lizzy asked, "Do you think they are going to arrest us?"

"Not us, but maybe me, I think the guy from the tunnel died and they are not telling us." Dusty said this with as much conviction as she could put into it.

She took a bite of meatloaf, watching Lizzy closely. *Why didn't Lizzy have potatoes? Were they up to something?* She could not be sure, so she decided a little drama might be the trick.

"I've made such a mess." Dusty stood up abruptly. "If I lose my license, I'll deserve it. I think I'll turn in for the night and be ready when they come back in the morning."

She rushed out the back door and into the carriage house, locking it behind her.

She picked up the phone, dialed Iola, and heard the click—someone else was listening.

She left a message, careful with her words, hoping Iola could read between the lines.

She lay down, checked her pager—nothing.

She stayed dressed and prayed she hadn't eaten anything dangerous.

Next time, she thought, *I'm packing crackers and peanut butter. Hunger messes with my head.*

Back in the main house, Charles walked into the kitchen.

"She left a message for her boss," he told Lizzy. "Sounded convincing. But I don't think she ate the potatoes. So she probably didn't get the sedative."

He frowned.

"I need to know if the cops took her .38 or still think it was the .25. One way or another, they will know tomorrow and then we better have our stories straight. I can't read her. One minute she's a cunning detective, the next—just a sniveling kid."

He leaned in. "If she's right and Nate's dead, this gets easier. I can't believe you messed this up so bad."

Lizzy looked away.

"We need a plan," Charles continued. "We can't leave any doubt with the FBI. She's our biggest problem."

Lizzy said nothing. She agreed—but something inside her had shifted. She had liked Dusty. The plan had seemed foolproof, but Dusty wasn't who the paper made her out to be. She remembered how the article in the newspaper made Dusty seem cocky and a bit callous.

Lizzy had thought she was just a brash, trigger-happy rookie. Now she saw a young woman with a sharp mind—and heart. But she couldn't tell Charles that. He'd eliminate them both without hesitation. She had made her bed. Now she'd have to lie in it.

When would it all end? Lizzy thought to herself. She was weary and over it all. She had grown to love this old house in Jerome, but that would be coming to an end soon.

5

ALL THAT GLITTERS

It was after visiting hours at the Flagstaff Hospital when Nate Helms was moved from ICU to a regular room. He hadn't spoken to anyone. He wasn't even sure what exactly had happened—but he knew one thing for sure.

That bitch Sherwood was behind it all.

He was about to call the nurse when a man with a badge walked into the room.

"I hope you're ready to get some of this off your chest," the man said. "I'm Agent Walker. I'm here to listen to your story before I take the next step in my investigation... of a lot of gold."

He pulled up a chair and leveled his gaze. "Why don't you start at the beginning. How do you know Elizabeth

Sherwood? When did you cook up the plan to relieve her of the gold on her property?"

Nate Helms looked fragile in the hospital bed, and truthfully—he was scared.

"Take your time," Walker said, his voice dropping to a low hiss. "I've got all night. Think it through and get every i dotted and t crossed before you start talking, because if you lie to me, I will have no mercy on any of you."

Nate sat up slowly. "I don't know what you're talking about. My stepsister hired me to help remove the gold. She said she was turning it over to the proper authorities. I've been working on it for months—clearing the road, reinforcing the tunnel, getting it ready to load onto a semi. She promised me half the finder's fee."

Walker said nothing.

Nate continued. "I was down to the last hundred bars. Then this little woman sneaks up on me and pulls a gun. I pulled mine, a light blinds me, and I fire. That's the last thing I remember—until this afternoon when it all started coming back. I don't know who held the light. But I don't think that's who shot me. My shot probably went high. Then it was just a blur." He stated the last sentence with a shudder.

Walker leaned forward. "Let me get this straight— your stepsister is Elizabeth Sherwood?"

Nate nodded.

"Where was she turning the gold into? Where have you been staying? Did you see anyone else in the tunnels these past months? And where's the gold you already removed?"

"It's a long story," Nate said, leaning back as a nurse entered the room.

"Could I get some water, please?" he asked.

Once the nurse left, Nate started again.

"My father, Homer Helm, left my mother and me around 1946. He came to Jerome to work in the mines. My mom died from pneumonia shortly after. My aunt wrote to my father, and he promised to send for me as soon as he got settled. She didn't hear from him again until 1948, when he said he'd struck gold and was coming to get me. He had a new wife—Anika—and said I'd have a sister, Matilda. I was ten. I was excited... but he never came."

He paused. "I joined the Army in '58, served until I was 29, ended up in a military hospital in Hawaii for six months. After I got out, I went back to my aunt's. She gave me a box of letters and photos. That's when I learned everything—or thought I did."

He took a breath. "I wasn't even sure my dad was alive, but I had Matilda's name and an old address. I came to Jerome. She brought me into her strange little world. I've been helping her move that gold for two years. She said she was going to report it—get her 10% finder's fee and split it with me."

He looked down. "A few days ago, she got weird. Stopped bringing me lunch. Even that creepy butler stopped showing up. I've got a gas generator to run my conveyor belt down there—I just hope they shut it off and secured everything. I've been working alone. Was I shot? Who shot me? What the hell is going on?"

Walker gave him a long look. "What made you think she had all that gold in the first place? What history did she give you?"

"She said it came from a train robbery connected to the mine," Nate replied. "Said it had been hidden for decades."

Walker nodded. "The woman who confronted you— do you know who she is?"

Nate took a sip of water. "No. Just that she surprised me. I don't think she shot me though. I heard a shot... but I didn't see who pulled the trigger."

Walker sighed. "Well, you were shot with a different caliber than her gun. And Matilda—Elizabeth—she's your step-sister, right?"

Nate nodded again.

Walker continued. "Did she ever say what happened to your dad?"

"No." Nate looked down at his bandages.

Back at the guest house, the light of dawn crept through Dusty's window. She had been awake for hours before finally drifting off.

She woke up to the sound of someone turning the knob on the door. She had a chair under the doorknob and quietly reached for a lamp to use as a weapon.

Her guns were in the hands of law enforcement, and she had nothing to protect herself against Lizzy and

Charles. She was a sitting duck if they wanted to try anything.

She decided to stay put in her room until Walker showed up.

She thought that she had figured out most of what was going on, but only time would tell. I need coffee, she thought. But she wasn't about to leave the room.

She was getting a little fidgety and hoped that Walker would show up soon; she needed some answers.

After getting dressed and jotting down some notes, she reached a breaking point. Against her better judgment, she removed the chair from the door, ready to go find caffeine.

Just then, someone knocked.

When she opened the door, Agent Walker was standing there.

"Glad you came early," she said. "I need coffee. Immediately."

Walker looked rumpled. She noticed it right away.

"Where did you sleep?" she asked. "Or did you?"

"I didn't," he replied. "I've been sitting out front since midnight. Couldn't shake the feeling something was going to happen to you. You didn't have your gun, and your phone is tapped."

He paused. "I think we've got the answers now—and that makes you a target."

He looked around. "Grab your things. Let's take your car into town. Quietly. Let's leave without alerting anyone."

As they stepped outside, the back door of the main house opened. Charles appeared.

"Is something wrong?" he asked. "Has something happened?"

"No," Dusty replied casually. "We were just heading to the house for coffee before getting started."

She tossed her bag back into the guest house and followed Walker.

"There's a group from the FBI coming to search the tunnels," she explained. "And I've just been informed that I'm in informal custody until my gun and travel bag are tested. Seems they found a match on my .38. Which is strange, because I never brought it with me."

She turned to Charles. "Anyone else who might've had access to my room?"

Charles shrugged. "I thought Elizabeth said you were carrying a gun?"

"I was—my boot gun. She didn't know about it, and she didn't have anything in her hands that day. So how did the .38 get into play? Think about it, Charles, because I'm just sick of trying to figure it out, think on it, please, and see if you can come up with a scenario that fits."

Charles narrowed his eyes. "You're the detective."

"Yeah, and I've admitted from the start that I fired a weapon. The problem is, I didn't fire the one that shot Nate."

At that moment, two FBI trucks rolled into the driveway.

Dusty turned to Walker and whispered, "Why are they here?"

"Just like you said," he replied. "To go through the tunnels."

Walker looked at Charles. "Mr. Sherwood—sorry, Mr. Durant—let's go find your wife, shall we?"

Dusty was reeling. As they entered the kitchen, all five dogs went wild, barking and racing up the stairs. Elizabeth was nowhere in sight.

"I'll go find her," Charles offered.

"No need," Walker said. "Let's just have some coffee and wait."

Charles looked pale but went through the motions. He poured two cups.

Dusty took a big swig from her cup and it was like the lights came on. She looked at Walker with a wild look on her face.

Walker nodded slowly, watching her.

Moments later, the front door opened and slammed shut.

Dusty jumped up and ran to the porch, Walker and Charles following closely behind her.

When they got to the porch, Elizabeth was being put into handcuffs by one of the agents.

"You little snipe," Elizabeth spat at Dusty. "You think you're so smart—got it all figured out? You shot him and tried to con us out of our money. I'll sue you and your agency!"

Walker stepped forward. "Is that right? Then why were you running? What are you afraid we'll find?"

"It's her word against mine," Elizabeth snapped. "The thief is dead. He can't back up whatever lies she's made up."

"Well," Walker said, smiling. "Good news—he's not dead. He's alive. And talking."

Elizabeth's face fell. "I can't leave. Who will take care of my dogs?"

Walker said, "We will get them taken care of for today and figure the rest out as we go. How many are there?

Elizabeth relented, "There are five dogs and one cat. Can Charles stay and take care of things til we get this ironed out?"

"No," Walker replied firmly. "Because I believe he's your accomplice in all this."

"Are you arresting me or just questioning me? I don't think that you have the right to do either." She said with much disdain.

Dusty stepped forward from the back of the group and locked eyes with Elizabeth.

"I believe you meant to kill Nate Helm—and me—and make it look like a shootout," she said evenly. "You thought I was unarmed. You had Charles get my .38 after you and I started into the tunnel."

She took a breath, voice steady but firm. "When we heard that loud bang and came back to find the door locked, he must have left my gun for you to find. That way, when we went into the tunnel to find the exit, you could stage the shootout. That's why you turned your flashlight off—so I wouldn't see the gun."

Dusty took a step closer. "But when I fired at the same time you did, you realized I was armed. You pitched the gun aside and didn't know what to do."

She narrowed her eyes. "When we were at the clinic, waiting on the police, you called Charles and had him retrieve the weapon from the tunnel and return it to my bag. He also moved more of the gold—the count was different when Walker and I went to the scene."

Dusty's tone sharpened. "Was that the plan the whole time? To hire me so you could get rid of Nate? How were you planning to move all the gold that was still there? What was the next step? Where's the rest of the gold?"

She gave a wry, bitter laugh. "Let me guess—the gold in the tunnel is the amount you were willing to sacrifice to the feds, because you already moved the majority of it over the last year. By killing Nate, you would've painted him as a thief and gotten a finder's fee on the tunnel gold while hiding the rest. Or have you already fenced that part?"

Dusty's voice dropped, cold and cutting. "I was just your patsy—to be used to cover the theft. Is that where Charles comes in? Is he really your husband... or just your partner in crime?"

She glanced around the area, her final question hanging in the air like a challenge. "By the way—where is Charles?"

Walker nodded to two agents: "Find Charles."

Walker placed Elizabeth in his car.

She glared at Dusty. "You think you're so smart? This isn't over. You haven't heard the last of me."

Dusty smirked. "I hope not. I'll be reading about you in the paper soon."

From around the side of the house Charles emerged in handcuffs with an agent at his side. Walker walked over and spoke with the two of them and told the agent to put Charles in the back with Elizabeth.

They exchanged car keys and the agent got in Walker's car and drove down the hill.

As the FBI searched the house and tunnels, Dusty asked, "What now?"

Walker replied, "Well, this isn't how I planned this to go down, but we got the same outcome."

"What are we going to do with the animals?" She asked.

Walker gave her a smile, "We can have the county hold them for a while, in case she makes bail. I'll have to look into it."

Dusty rested her hands on her hips. "Do you think the charges will stick?"

He gave a short nod. "Yeah, I do. With what we've got so far—and what they're likely to confess once the pressure's on—it's solid. Especially if we can trace any of the gold."

She studied his face for a moment, then added, "And how did you figure out Charles' last name?"

"That's why I came by last night—to keep an eye on things," he said. "I'd started digging into both of them, and something didn't add up. Why wasn't she using his last name? Turns out, he's got a long rap sheet. They've been planning this for a while.

"When they first moved here, I think they intended to sell the property, but then they found the antiques... and eventually the gold," Walker continued. "Charles is a known thief and gambler—been arrested plenty of times.

"I hadn't connected all the dots yet, so thanks for helping us with that," he added. "Let's see if it holds. I've got a feeling they'll both sing like canaries once we get them downtown."

"What did Nate say? Did he know what they were up to? Is he in on it?" Dusty asked.

Walker shook his head slightly. "She's his stepsister. He thought she was turning everything in, and that they were splitting the finder's fee. He seems legit—but we'll have to dig deeper. It's a complicated mess," he added.

Dusty gasped. "I should've caught that last name. Sherwood told me her mother had married a man named Helm."

Just then, Walker's radio crackled to life. The voice on the other end announced, "Tunnel posse reports all clear."

"All clear? What do they mean?" Dusty asked, glancing at him.

"They didn't find anything else," Walker replied.

"What happened to the rest of the gold?" she pressed.

"Oh, we've got it secured," he said calmly.

"What?" she exclaimed.

"We had it in custody this morning," Walker explained. "Nate told us where he'd moved it—a storage warehouse in Prescott. He's been hauling small loads almost daily, driving his truck into the unit and stacking it all on pallets by hand, getting it ready for the authorities to pick up. He's been doing this for months."

Walker exhaled and shook his head. "He's not the sharpest tool in the shed, but he seems like a fairly moral man. He was pretty shaken up that she wanted him dead. Poor guy's got no family left, and... he really seems to like Sherwood. Seems he really thought they were doing the right thing."

"Do you think he'll testify against her?" Dusty asked.

Walker shrugged slightly. "Well, she did try to kill him, so he's mostly broken-hearted about that. I think he's a bit confused by everything. We're going to have him evaluated—he may have been easily manipulated. He seems a little slow, but we're not sure yet. Either way, it'll all work out."

He glanced toward the hillside and continued, "With that said, I'm heading back down. They'll lock up and secure the house after the dogs and the cat are relocated. I'll give you a call in a day or so and fill you in on whatever I can."

"Okay," Dusty said. "I'll be waiting to hear from you. Just call the number on the card I gave you—they'll find me. I'll be gone for a few days to spend time with my brother before he leaves for boot camp."

She turned, walked back to retrieve her bag, then headed for her car.

On the windshield, there was a note.

"When I return your weapons, maybe we could have dinner? —Cheyenne"

Dusty laughed until she was sick.

6

COLLATERAL DAMAGE

She stopped in Jerome and used the pay phone to call the office. When Abrams picked up, she sounded a little frazzled. Dusty figured she had already heard the news about the arrests and quickly began explaining what had happened.

"Slow down—what are you talking about?" Abrams asked.

"They arrested Lizzy Sherwood and Charles—the butler. Well, actually, his name is Durant, but I'll fill you in on everything when I get there. I should be at the office in about three hours. I'm going to stop and get something to eat in Cordes Junction, and then I'll be there. I'm also going to call my folks, just in case Dad's gotten wind of all this. See you soon," Dusty said.

After she got off the phone with her mom, she felt better. Her dad was at work and probably already knew what was going down, but she told her mom she'd stop by around dinnertime and take them out to the Chinese place they loved.

Arminida had insisted on cooking dinner instead. She said there was no need to go out after such a long day.

That was her momma—always thinking of others.

Dusty stopped at the restaurant in Cordes Junction and had pancakes and bacon, along with three cups of coffee. She wrote down some notes about everything that had happened over the past three days.

As she sat there, she contemplated the tangled mess she'd been pulled into and shuddered at how many different outcomes could've played out. Wampacha's warning had certainly helped her reevaluate things.

She mentally scolded herself for how easily these deviants had fooled her in the beginning—and how notoriety came at a steep cost. Still, she knew she'd been lucky. She'd learned some hard, valuable lessons. And she'd need to spend some time reflecting on it all.

She knew Wampacha would help her.

That afternoon, she spent time typing and filing her notes and catching up with Abrams.

Iola's only comment? "I wonder who's going to pay the bill Sherwood owes the agency."

When she arrived for dinner that night, Dusty was greeted with hugs and smiles from her mom, dad, sister, and brothers.

Her mom had made meatloaf, mashed potatoes with gravy, and green beans—one of Dusty's favorite meals. Even though the last time she'd had that menu she was paranoid about being poisoned, her mom's meatloaf now made her feel safe and loved. And being surrounded by her family made everything feel extra special.

She was so glad to be there.

Rocky only had a few days left before heading to boot camp, so they all agreed to have dinner together every night until he left. The plan was for Dusty to bring dinner over the next night, and then take everyone out the following night—Rocky would get to choose the place.

She felt warm and fuzzy as she headed home that evening, silently thanking God for blessing her with such a wonderful family.

Before going up to her apartment, Dusty stopped by the manager's office. Rick was just locking up. He felt like extended family now, and Dusty was always glad to see him.

"Come out with us to dinner tomorrow," Dusty offered. "It'll be good. Just family and food. You're always welcome."

Rick shook his head. "Nah, that's your time. Not mine. Besides, celebrating someone heading into the military... not really my thing."

"I get it," she said gently. "But the offer still stands."

"Appreciate it. Goodnight, Dusty."

"Night," she replied.

Inside her apartment, everything looked just the way she'd left it. She exhaled and smiled—she was glad to be home.

After a long shower and washing her hair, she felt like a new person. She rummaged through her refrigerator, but it was mostly empty—just a lonely can of Pepsi and a mildewed loaf of bread.

Definitely time for a grocery list. She thought.

She jotted a few things down and sat on the sofa, then got up to turn on the television. But before she reached it, the phone rang.

She picked it up. "Hello?"

"You need to be in the office first thing in the morning," came Iola Abrams' voice—blunt and to the point. "That means 7:00 a.m. Don't be late."

The phone clicked and went dead.

Dusty stood there, baffled by the curtness in Iola's voice.

What had she done now? She wondered.

Looked like it was going to be a long night, thinking about all the possible scenarios that might be coming back to bite her in the butt.

Dusty got up early and took a long, leisurely shower. She sipped a Pepsi and finished scribbled out a grocery list before heading to the agency. She arrived at 6:45 a.m. and went straight for the coffee pot. As she poured a cup, she heard Iola call her name.

She took a deep breath and walked down the hall.

"Good morning!" Dusty said brightly.

"Is it?" Iola replied, dry as ever.

Dusty raised an eyebrow. "Well, you don't look very happy this morning. What's going on?"

Iola frowned, clearly irritated. "This Jerome client is a pain in the ass. She's making all kinds of false statements about the agency—and about you. Why don't you sit down and start from the beginning. Don't leave anything out."

Dusty exhaled loudly, then sat across from her. "Okay."

As she began recounting the events of the last three days, she realized just how much had happened. She'd made it through relatively calm at the time, but now, retelling it all, she felt her hands start to tremble.

The reality of Lizzy's plan began to sink in. This hadn't just been about fraud or deception—it had been a setup. A near miss.

Dusty realized the full extent of Lizzy's plan. This client had spent time planning her murder, and the only thing that saved her was one small detail—her boot gun. Without it, she might not have made it out alive.

By the time she finished explaining everything—and how she and Agent Walker had managed to piece it all together—Dusty leaned back in her chair, visibly shaken.

"I truly believe they are still planning to take me out," she said quietly. "One way or another."

Iola stood up suddenly, launching into a rant. She cussed, paced, and vented about how underhanded and dangerous the whole thing had been—and how awful she felt for being the one who'd sent Dusty into it.

When she finally sat down, Iola picked up the phone. "Get me a dozen donuts and a full pot of coffee. ASAP."

Moments later, the two women sat across from each other, drinking coffee and devouring donuts. Between bites and bursts of laughter, Iola finally calmed down.

Then her tone sobered again.

"I need to fill you in on the accusations Lizzy Sherwood Durant made—about you, and about the agency."

Dusty nodded. "Go ahead."

The list was long. Fabricated nonsense. Wild accusations that painted Dusty and the agency as corrupt, careless, and incompetent.

"They're lies," Iola said, frustrated. "But they're detailed lies. And they could cause damage if we don't shut it down fast."

Dusty leaned forward. "I think we'll be okay. Between my notes, the FBI's documentation, and our records on her file, we're covered. Lizzy and Durant are already getting twisted up in their own story. It's only a matter of time before it all falls apart."

Iola gave her a long look, then nodded slowly.

Dusty hesitated. "I am worried about one thing, though."

"What's that?" Iola asked.

"Lizzy has five little dogs and a cat. They were supposed to be taken to the county shelter, but I don't know what's happening to them. They didn't do anything wrong. I'd feel terrible if they were put down instead of being put up for adoption."

Iola softened. "I'll check on them when I call the FBI this afternoon. For now, take a few days off. Be with your family. We'll start fresh on Monday."

They stood and hugged. Dusty gave a tired smile, then walked back to her office.

She sorted through her mail and paused when she found an envelope from the Davis family. Inside was an invitation to the ribbon cutting for the new trauma center they were opening in New Mexico—dedicated to their daughter, a victim of the serial murder case Dusty had helped solve.

They wanted her to attend... and speak.

Dusty shuddered at the thought of standing in front of a crowd to talk about murder. She knew she needed to give it serious thought—what to say, how to say it, and how to keep her emotions in check.

Just thinking about the innocent lives lost, and the monster who had taken them, made her stand up and take a deep breath. Anger bubbled beneath her surface. She wasn't done—not by a long shot. She'd spend her life hunting people like that. Evil didn't get to win.

As she walked back to refill her coffee, her thoughts drifted to what might come next. She'd feel better once she saw her next case.

The thought of dinner with her family brought a smile to her face. She headed toward Iola's office.

7

THE WOMAN IN THE BLUE DRESS

Iola and Dusty had spent most of the day figuring out how to handle the situation. They had lunch brought in from the deli downstairs and, by the afternoon, had both calmed their nerves.

There was still a lot to get through in the coming days, and several new cases were already waiting.

"Never a dull moment," Iola said as she closed her briefcase. "Go home, Dusty. We'll hit it again tomorrow."

Dusty left the office around 5:00 p.m., another gun borrowed from the agency tucked into her bag until her confiscated ones were returned. Lately, she was accumulating and losing firearms faster than she could count. The thought weighed on her—how often she'd gotten out of tight spots with a gun in hand.

She stopped at Kentucky Fried Chicken and picked up dinner for the family. The smell of two buckets of chicken and sides filled the car, making the ride to her parents' house feel even longer. She was ready to eat again.

When she arrived, she brought everything into the kitchen and set it on the table.

"Looks like you brought enough for an army," her mom said, smiling.

"We can only hope there are leftovers—but I doubt it," Dusty laughed.

Dinner was perfect: laughter, good food, and the comfort of being surrounded by family.

Until little Milo walked over to her chair and asked, "Sissy, tell us about who you shot this time!"

Dusty had just taken a bite of biscuit smothered in butter and jam—and promptly spit it out in surprise. The sticky mess landed smack-dab on her sister Layne's white blouse.

Layne groaned. "Great. Somehow, you manage to ruin my clothes even when you're not wearing them."

Everyone burst into laughter—except Milo, who stood waiting, eyes wide, still expecting an answer.

Dusty glanced around the table. "Okay, who else wants to hear the story—besides Milo?"

Slowly, every hand went up.

"Alright," she said, settling back in her chair. "It's a pretty elaborate scheme that was waiting for me in Jerome..."

She launched into the story of the Sherwoods—of Lizzy, Durant, the near setup, the tunnel, the gunfire. When she finished, the table fell into stunned silence for a few seconds—before everyone started talking at once.

Dusty turned to Milo. "You get the first question."

Milo tapped his finger to his lips, deep in thought. "So... you didn't actually shoot the man? You missed him?"

Laughter erupted again—even her dad, who had scowled his way through the whole story, let out a quiet chuckle.

"That's right," Dusty said. "I missed."

Her father looked at her seriously. "You think if you hadn't had your gun, she would've shot you too?"

Dusty swallowed hard. "Yes. That's exactly what would've happened. Thank you for giving me the boot gun—it saved my life."

Her dad stood up and walked out of the room without another word. It made her want to break down and cry. Instead, she forced a smile and looked back at the others.

"Any other questions?" she asked.

Rocky raised his hand. "Yeah. How much do you get paid to put yourself in the line of fire like that? Is it worth it?"

Dusty thought for a moment. "It pays well enough," she said. "But it's not about the money anymore. It's about the mission. I want to help people—families who are desperate for answers. Some of it is heartbreaking, but I'm driven to do what I can to stop what's causing their pain."

She looked around the table, her voice steady and full of conviction.

"I know it sounds crazy, but there's satisfaction in doing the right thing for others. I'm sure there will be all kinds of different cases—each one its own kind of adventure—but I love it. I really do. And I hope I'm good at it."

She smiled. "I always admired how Dad handled his job. How he helped people. I think that's what life's about— but we all have different ways of doing it. Layne will save lives in the medical field. You," she nodded at Rocky, "will serve in the military. And Milo—who knows? He might end up being president."

They all laughed, but she kept going. "We owe our callings to the greatest people we've ever met—Mom and Dad. They set the bar high for us. We've had the best mentors God could give us."

Dusty was adamant now, "I say go forward and lead with the expectation of the universe that we will succeed in our lives as testimonies to our kids and the next generation, or maybe just be a positive ripple in the pond of life. Whatever, give it your all."

"Damn," Rocky said, grinning. "Get off your soapbox, will ya? Sorry I asked."

Dusty laughed and pulled him into a hug. "I love you guys. I'm so proud of all of you. Always."

She left that night with a heavy heart. Her dad never came out of the bedroom—not even to say goodnight.

Dusty considered calling him once she got back to her place, but first, she needed to pick up a few groceries.

Something about grocery shopping always made Dusty anxious. She wasn't a careful shopper—never checked prices, just tossed things in the cart. And every time, she was shocked at the total when she got to the register.

She didn't have much patience for shopping of any kind. In high school, her friends had spent entire weekends at the mall. Her sister Layne was a bargain-hunting queen and had tried to drag Dusty into it more than once. But Dusty was strictly a grab-and-go kind of shopper.

She liked nice things, sure—but didn't care enough to spend hours chasing discounts.

Still, she had a soft spot for A.J. Bayless grocery stores. Something about them felt like the Old West. The location on Indian School Road even had a small museum showing what early grocery stores looked like. She loved visiting it—like stepping back in time.

This Bayless was right by her parents' house, so she pulled in to pick up her short list of essentials.

As she walked in, she noticed an older woman in a dark blue dress with oversized horn-rimmed glasses staring at her intensely. Dusty offered a polite smile and kept walking toward the soda aisle.

She grabbed a six-pack of Pepsi and dropped it into her basket—then felt someone walk up behind her.

Turning slowly, she found the woman in the blue dress standing uncomfortably close, practically breathing down her neck.

Dusty stayed calm. "Is there something I can help you with?"

The woman leaned in. Her voice was quiet, shaky.

"Someone is trying to kill me."

Dusty took a step back and studied her. She looked well put together—clean dress, pearl necklace, a nice watch, and a leather purse. But her shoes told a different story. Worn and scuffed, they looked like they'd walked a thousand miles.

"Have you called the police?" Dusty asked gently.

The woman took a deep breath. Fighting back tears she said, "Yes. They think I'm senile. They won't listen to me. But I know who you are... and I want to hire you. I need to know who's trying to hurt me—and why. What have I done to make someone want to harm me?"

Dusty's posture straightened. "I'd have to talk to my boss and see how we'd handle a direct contract like that. But I'm sure we can figure something out."

She paused, then asked, "What's your name?"

Without answering, the woman turned and began walking slowly toward the front of the store. She never looked back.

Dusty hesitated, debating whether to follow and press for more information—but decided against it. She didn't even know what she was stepping into. For all she knew, the woman could be a kook. God knows, there were plenty of those around.

Instead, she pulled out her shopping list and finished grabbing the rest of her items.

By the time she reached the checkout line, her cart was full—with everything on her list... and a whole lot of snacks that weren't.

After paying, she started toward the exit—and spotted the woman again, standing just outside the entrance with a single shopping bag in hand.

Dusty turned back to the cashier. "Do you know that woman?"

The young woman glanced up, then nodded. "Yeah, she's a regular."

"She seems to be in trouble. Does she have someone with her?" Dusty asked.

The cashier craned her neck to look outside. "No, she usually calls a cab or walks. I think she lives nearby. Used to come in every day around noon, but lately she's been showing up later—after dark. I haven't noticed anything unusual, though. Why? What did she say to you?"

"Oh, nothing," Dusty replied casually. "She just seemed a little... afraid."

She glanced at the cashier's name tag. "Thanks for the info, Judy."

Dusty had just started her car when the woman approached again.

"Would you mind giving me a ride home?" she asked. "I live pretty close. My feet are hurting something terrible."

Dusty started to say no, but just then she heard Wampacha whisper in her ear:

"Your help is needed, little one. Listen carefully."

Oh boy... where was this going? She thought to herself.

"Yes, come on. I'll give you a lift," Dusty said. "Where to?"

"2611 Devonshire, Unit 101," the woman replied.

As Dusty backed out of the parking space, she glanced in the rearview mirror and noticed Judy, the cashier, standing at the front window, watching them.

Interesting, Dusty thought.

Suddenly, in a loud voice, the woman announced, "My name is Eunice."

She clutched her bag tighter and continued, "I haven't been home in two days because someone's in my house."

Her voice shook as she looked at Dusty, eyes wide with fear. "If I hadn't gotten out the back door when they came in, I know they would've killed me."

Eunice's shoulders slumped. "I didn't know what to do, so I hid in my neighbor's garage that night."

She paused, visibly struggling to keep her composure. "I waited until dark yesterday to come to the store—to use the bathroom and buy something to eat. I went back to the garage afterward and did the same thing today."

Her eyes welled up with tears as she whispered, "But I need to go home. I'm so tired."

Then, more urgently, she pleaded, "Will you just check my house and help me call the police if there's any sign of a break-in? Please?"

Dusty took a deep breath. "Okay, I will. But you need to give me your full name and hand me the keys so I can check the house before you go inside. I'll just do a quick walk-through and then come get you. Sound good?"

Eunice began to cry. She rambled on, scared and exhausted, pleading for help. "I just need some sleep. Why won't they leave me alone?"

"Who needs to leave you alone?" Dusty asked. "Do you know who they are? Or what this is even about? Because none of this makes sense yet."

Eunice fell silent.

Dusty drove straight to her house—it was only two blocks from her parents'. Coincidence? She thought. Maybe. Eunice claimed to know her mom and dad, but Dusty didn't remember ever hearing her name.

When Dusty turned off the ignition and opened her door, she noticed Eunice was fast asleep. Gently, she woke her.

"I'm going in. I need your key. You stay here with the doors locked, and I'll check it out."

Eunice looked frantic. Dusty didn't know if it was because she was not fully awake or if she was just that scared, but Eunice refused to be left in the car alone. She got out and went to Dusty putting the key in her hand.

She said, very solemnly, "Lock your car. My purse and all my info are in there in case something happens.

Please find out who's doing this to me. I've never hurt anyone on purpose. I try to be a good person. Why is this happening?"

Dusty locked the car.

"Eunice, how long have you felt like someone's been watching you? It has to be longer than just a few days for you to be this scared. Do you have any idea who it might be?"

Eunice simply shook her head and started walking toward the complex. When she reached the sidewalk beside the driveway, she paused and waited for Dusty to catch up.

Then, quietly, she said, "I think I saw something a while back... in the Bayless parking lot. There were some men roughing up this guy who was trying to get into his truck. He finally got the door open, but one of the men hit him in the back of the head with a club. Then they threw him in the bed of the truck and drove off."

Dusty listened carefully, eyebrows raised.

"As they were pulling out, one of the guys in the back saw me," Eunice continued. "He pounded on the window and told the driver I was there. The brake lights lit up. I ran back into the store. The cashier—Judy—was right there at the entrance. She had to have seen it too."

Eunice's voice trembled.

"But when I yelled for help and told the cashier what I saw, she said she didn't see anything," Eunice explained. "I asked her to call the police, but nothing happened. I waited and waited."

She swallowed hard. "Finally, another customer came into the store. I ran to them crying and begged them to call the police again. They went and told the manager. He came up front, and I explained everything all over again. He didn't seem to believe me, but he eventually called the police."

Dusty nodded, listening closely. "And what did the police say?"

"They talked to the cashier first," Eunice said. "She told them she hadn't seen anything—and rolled her eyes, like she thought I was making it up. The officers came over to me, I told them what I saw. They looked around outside but didn't find anything."

Her voice lowered. "As they were about to leave, I asked if one of them could give me a ride home. One of the officers looked at me and said, 'What is this really about? You just want a ride home? Did you make all this up?'"

Eunice shook her head. "I told him no—that it really happened. But they didn't believe me."

Eunice took a deep breath.

"They drove me home," Eunice said softly. "One of the officers walked me to the door and looked around inside. He asked if I lived alone, how long I'd lived there, and if anyone checked on me."

She paused, then added, "I told him I didn't know many people—just a few from my church."

Eunice took a breath before continuing. "He asked if I could describe the truck. If I'd gotten a license plate or remembered what any of the men looked like. I couldn't remember anything right away."

Her voice dropped even lower. "But a couple of days later, I saw the same men driving through this complex. I knew they were looking for me, so I ducked back into my house."

She rubbed her hands together, clearly still shaken.

"Over a week later, I heard them breaking in. I've been hiding ever since. I just... I can't get it all straight in my head, but I think it's them. When I saw them in the complex, I got a better look at the vehicle they were in."

"What did the truck look like?" Dusty asked.

"It was a blue Ford pickup. Said F-150 on the side. Looked new-ish, but I'm no expert. There were three of them. One was bald, with a snake tattoo on his left arm—he was driving. The guy in the middle had dark hair. The one in the passenger seat had long, beautiful blonde hair. I almost thought it was a woman."

Dusty exhaled. "Alright. Let's get in the house and talk."

They rounded the corner of the first building— labeled Bldg. A. The first door on the left read #101.

Dusty slid the key into the lock, opened the door, and flipped on the light.

The place was a mess. Clothes, books, and knickknacks were scattered everywhere.

"What do you think they were looking for—besides you?" Dusty asked.

"What makes you say that?" Eunice replied cautiously.

"Well, they trashed the place like they were searching for something. Do you keep money in the house?"

"No. It always looks like this," Eunice admitted, a little sheepishly. "I'm not very organized, and I'm constantly looking for things I misplace. I don't have much patience for tidying."

"Oh. Sorry," Dusty said. "I just assumed they were looking for something."

She moved through the kitchen—it was surprisingly neat. The two bedrooms looked fine, but the bathroom was a disaster. She returned to the living room and cleared a spot on the couch.

Eunice sat across from her in a worn recliner.

"Would you mind if I used your phone to call my boss?" Dusty asked. "I'll check if we can take on your case—if that's still what you want."

Eunice nodded.

Dusty continued, "There's no sign of forced entry. No marks on the locks or door, so I doubt the police will take this too seriously. I can't tell if anything's missing, but once you're rested, take a look around and let me know."

She leaned forward slightly. "I'll install deadbolts on both your front and back doors. If they picked the lock once, they won't get in that easily again. Sound good?"

Eunice took a deep breath, then began to ramble.

She kept thanking Dusty—over and over—for believing her, for listening. Her words tumbled out in a rush, tangled with emotion. She apologized repeatedly for being all over the place with her story, insisting she was just scared and tired.

"I really hope you'll take my case," she said, her voice wavering. "But... then what? If you figure out who it is, what happens to me? Will I have to go to court? Will they go to jail?"

Then, almost as an afterthought, she added, "Oh— and my phone's under the couch. No one ever calls me, so I just put it there. It was in the way."

Dusty stood up and reached under the couch, pulling out a large, black rotary phone. It was heavy—solid enough to be used as a weapon in the right hands. She lifted the receiver and started to dial Iola's number.

Then she frowned.

The line was dead.

Dusty followed the cord behind the couch and knelt by the wall where the phone jack was located. The line had been cut.

Clean.

She stared at it for a moment, a chill running up her spine. For the first time, she fully believed Eunice's story.

Whoever had broken into this home had intended for her to be stranded—completely cut off if she dared come back.

Dusty stood slowly, the weight of it all settling in.

She returned to the living room and sat down, trying to come up with a new plan. Across from her, Eunice had dozed off in the big recliner. Her head tilted back, and soft snores filled the quiet room.

Dusty leaned back into the couch, her eyes fixed on the cut phone line and thought to herself:

This just got very real.

8

QUIET DESPERATION

Dusty let Eunice nap for a while as she tried to piece everything together in her mind. None of it made sense yet. She needed to contact the police, review the report from that night, and try to track down both trucks. The black truck must have belonged to the man being assaulted—but the blue Ford? That one might have just been in the parking lot. Dusty needed more information to work with.

When Eunice finally woke, Dusty told her, "I'm going out to my car to grab the groceries that need refrigeration. I'll knock twice when I come back. It'll only take a few minutes."

Eunice didn't like the idea but reluctantly agreed. She locked the door after Dusty left, then waited for the two-knock signal before opening it again.

Dusty only had four items to put in the fridge, but when she opened it, she was struck by how empty it was. There were no signs of food at all. She glanced around the kitchen—no bread or fruit on the counter, no visible nutrition anywhere.

"You don't have any food in here," Dusty said, concerned.

Eunice looked surprised. "I always have cheese and mayo in the fridge," she insisted. "Mostly I eat just once a day, and that's from whatever I pick up at the store. On Sundays, I bring home a sandwich or cookies from the church table."

"Well, there's no cheese or mayo in there now," Dusty replied. "We'll get you stocked up tomorrow. I'll go to the grocery store and the hardware store to get some new locks. First thing in the morning, we'll go to my office and talk to my boss. We need her on board with all this. Do you have any money to work with?"

Without saying a word, Eunice got up and walked into the bathroom. She closed the door behind her and stayed in there for a little while. When Dusty heard the toilet flush, she assumed Eunice had just needed to go to the restroom.

But when Eunice came out, she was holding a large plastic bag, partially wrapped with tape. She handed it to Dusty and asked, "Will this get us started?"

Dusty gasped. The bag appeared to be stuffed full of money.

She opened it a little farther and quickly estimated that there was over $10,000 inside.

"Where did this come from?" she asked.

Eunice replied, "The attic opening in the bathroom. It's been there a long time—there are several more bags up there. My late husband started putting money up there when we moved in, back in 1960, and he kept doing it until he died. He said it was our nest egg."

"How long has he been gone? Does anyone else know you have this money?"

"He died in February of 1968," Eunice said. "I don't think anyone else knows."

Dusty walked over and placed a hand gently on Eunice's shoulder. Looking her in the eye, she said, "We need to put this in the bank. Do you have a bank account? Where do you cash your Social Security checks?"

Eunice nodded. "I have an account at Valley National Bank, right next to the A.J. Bayless store. But my husband always told me not to deposit the money—we'd have to pay taxes on it every year. I don't even know how to write a check."

She paused, then added, "I deposit the Social Security check and take most of it out to live on."

Dusty tilted her head. "How do you pay your bills?"

"I pay with cash," Eunice replied. "For the electric and water bills, I go to the utility center at the grocery store. We paid cash for the house, so no mortgage. When the property tax bill comes, I go to the bank, get a cashier's check, and mail it in. I take money out of the bag for taxes, health insurance, and medical bills. I get money orders for those—and for the phone, too. I don't even know how much is in the bank. I get statements, but I never open them."

Dusty exhaled slowly. "Eunice, we need to get you some help. Try to get some sleep. I'll stay the night, and tomorrow morning we'll go to my office, talk to my boss, and get this all straightened out. Okay?"

Eunice looked uneasy. "Where will you sleep? I sleep on the couch."

"Well, not tonight, Eunice. You go to your bedroom and relax. I'll stay out here and keep watch."

Dusty could tell Eunice wanted to argue, but she let it go. She walked down the short hallway to the room at the end and closed the door behind her.

Dusty had brought her gun in from the car, just in case. She'd carried it inside along with the groceries and hidden it—of all places—in the refrigerator.

She walked into the kitchen to retrieve it, but as she passed the window, she caught a glimpse of movement outside. Something—or someone—had just passed by.

She stepped over to the sink and lowered the blind. Then she grabbed her gun from the fridge and tucked it into the waistband of her Levi's. Moving back into the living room, she began securing the other windows. She remembered seeing the blinds already closed in the bedrooms, and the bathroom had frosted glass, so that was covered.

She turned off all the lights except the one in the bathroom, then laid her gun on the coffee table and stretched out on the couch.

Damn. This isn't how I thought the evening would go. She thought to herself. She hoped Eunice would get up early. Something about all of this still didn't sit right.

As she drifted off to sleep, she thought she could hear Wampacha's voice, chanting softly to the beat of a native drum.

She slept like a baby.

She woke to the sound of water running in the bathroom—and someone knocking on the front door.

Damn. She thought. *What time is it?* She needed coffee.

The clock on the wall read 6:00 a.m. *Who in the world was knocking this early?*

She slipped the gun into the back waistband of her jeans and walked to the door. Peeking through the peephole, she saw a Phoenix police officer holding his badge up.

She recognized him immediately and wasn't in a hurry to open the door.

Slowly, she cracked it open. "How can I help you, Officer Ryan?"

Ryan blinked in surprise. "What are you doing here? Is somebody dead?"

Then he coughed and tried to suppress a laugh. He thought he was being funny.

She didn't.

"All is fine here. What can I help you with?"

"I stopped by to check on the lady who lives here. I saw a car in her parking spot and figured I'd do a welfare check. I was out here a while back on a call—she thought someone was after her. Why are you here? Do you know Ms. Thorman?"

Dusty held up a finger. "Give me a minute to check with her, and I'll be right back."

She knocked on the bathroom door, and Eunice quickly opened it.

"I didn't mean to wake you," Eunice whispered, looking embarrassed. "I'm so sorry."

Dusty quickly filled her in about Patrolman Ryan at the door. They both returned to the living room and invited him in.

While Eunice explained the situation to the officer, Dusty excused herself to search the cupboards for coffee. She spotted a pot on the stove and hoped that meant there was some tucked away. She also wanted to return her gun to its hiding spot in the fridge—no need to give Officer Ryan any more reason to raise an eyebrow.

But after scouring every shelf, no coffee was found.

She sighed and returned to the living room.

Eunice wrapped up her account and turned to Dusty. "Okay, you take it from here."

Dusty smiled proudly at her. Eunice was letting her decide how much to share—especially about the money—and trusted her to guide the next steps.

Dusty turned to Ryan. "At this point, we don't know whether someone is trying to rob her or if they're trying to silence her for witnessing a crime—or both. Since she already filed a report with the info she had, I assume there's something on record. We've got some new details to add."

Ryan squinted at her. "What new info? If nothing was stolen and there were no signs of a break-in, I don't see the point in reopening this."

Dusty stood. "Eunice saw the same men again—driving through this complex in a newer blue Ford F-150. She got a clear look at all three. Then a week later, she heard them breaking in—that's when she hid in her neighbor's garage."

She looked at him with feigned confusion. "I'm sorry—I thought she told you all of this already. I haven't had my coffee yet, so I might've missed something."

"No, we didn't get to any of that," Officer Ryan said. He turned to Eunice and asked, "So, after you talked with me and I brought you home, you saw them in the parking lot—right here?"

Eunice nodded.

"How long was it until the possible break-in?" he said.

"One week to the day," she replied. "I was so scared, I hid in the neighbor's garage. I finally needed food, water, and a bathroom, so I walked to the store after dark. The next night, I did the same thing—and that's when I recognized Dusty. I knew she could help me."

Dusty added, "There was a cut phone cord and missing food. I believe they either picked the lock—or it wasn't locked in the first place. Eunice had her key with her when we got here and gave it to me, but the door was already unlocked. When I put the key in, it didn't click, so I'm guessing either scenario is possible."

She continued, "I tried to use the phone to call my office, and that's when I saw the cord had been cut. I think they might've been here more than once. Maybe they ate the food she had or took it with them. There wasn't much to begin with, but whatever was there is gone now."

Dusty exhaled. "So that brings us to today. We're taking her cash to the bank, possibly any jewelry too, and getting a safety deposit box. Then we're going to my office to speak with my boss. I stayed the night because I knew how frightened she was, and I couldn't think of any other way to calm her down."

She paused and waited for him to say something.

Officer Ryan nodded. "Alright, Eunice. Let's get a description of these hoodlums, and then I'll let you get on with your day. I'll run down what info I have, and Miss Roads here can keep me updated if anything new happens. Sound good?"

Eunice reached for his hand and gave it a grateful squeeze. "Thank you for listening—and for believing me."

Dusty smiled. "You give him the descriptions," she said, standing up. "I'm going to go throw some water on my face."

9

WE ARE ALL FAMILY

Dusty and Eunice drove to the agency. Once inside, they headed upstairs, and Dusty ushered Eunice into her office.

"Wait here while I talk with my boss," Dusty said. "Do you want anything?"

"Coffee would be nice," Eunice replied. "Cream and sugar, please."

Dusty smiled. "Be right back."

As she shut the door behind her, she stopped at the receptionist's desk. "Could you get coffee and any pastries we have for the client in my office?"

Iola stepped out of her nearby office just in time to overhear.

"Client?" she asked, raising an eyebrow. "What's going on? I already have something lined up for you to take on. Come in and fill me in—and Missy, please bring us some coffee too, thanks."

Dusty followed her into the office.

"When did we get a Missy?" she asked. "What happened to Jen?"

"Jen decided after the shooting that this wasn't the right place for her," Iola said. "So I hired Missy yesterday."

Dusty shook her head. "Nothing stays the same, does it?"

"Nope," Iola said, settling behind her desk. "Now tell me about this *client* in your office."

Dusty sat down with a sigh. The shooting—especially the death of an agent who had gone rogue—was still a fresh wound. But she pressed on, recounting the events with Eunice from the beginning, doing her best not to leave anything out.

Iola stayed quiet until Dusty got to the part about the bags of money.

"You're telling me there's cash in your trunk?" Iola asked.

"Yes," Dusty replied.

Iola asked, "How much money are we talking about?"

Dusty shook her head. "I don't know for sure, but I think there might be close to $100,000—give or take a little."

"You mean it's all in your trunk?" Iola said, eyes widening.

"Yes," Dusty replied. "It's wrapped in three bags, and she also brought her jewelry to put in a safety deposit box. I didn't know what else to do."

She looked at Iola earnestly. "Will you talk with her?"

Just then, there was a knock on the door. Dusty opened it to find Missy standing there with the coffee tray.

"Take it to Dusty's office, please," Iola instructed.

Missy got an indignant look on her face. "I already took the old woman her coffee."

Iola narrowed her eyes. "Then you'll take *our* coffee too, please. And refer to our clients with respect—it's *client*, not *old woman*."

Missy turned quickly and headed down the hall and entered Dusty's office without knocking.

Suddenly, there was a loud shriek.

Dusty immediately knew Missy had startled Eunice, so she headed down the hallway.

When she entered the office, she saw that Eunice had spilled coffee all over the desk—and herself—and was beginning to cry.

"Missy, go get a towel. Now," Dusty said firmly.

She turned to Eunice and knelt beside her. "It's okay. Are you hurt—or just startled?"

No answer.

Dusty glanced up and saw Eunice staring—not at her, but at Iola, who had just entered the room.

Dusty stood, confused. "What is going on?"

Iola gently took the towel from Missy, then shut the door behind her.

She knelt beside Eunice.

"Hello, Mother," Iola said softly.

Dusty blinked. *What the hell?*

Dusty could not believe what she heard. *How in the world did this go down? Did Eunice know Iola was her boss? Was this some kind of wild story?*

"Okay," Dusty said slowly. "I'm game. What's going on?"

Eunice finally found her voice. "Hello, Iola. Why are you here? Who called you? I thought you might be dead—you disappeared from my life. I tried to contact you, but you don't live in Tucson anymore. Are you glad to see me?"

"Of course I'm glad to see you," Iola replied. "But you sent me out of your life. And I'm still not interested in seeing your deviant husband again. So in that respect, I haven't changed my mind. Now—what's all this about someone trying to kill you? We'll catch up later. But don't bring that man near me or I won't help you at all."

Eunice blinked. "I haven't seen you in 20 years, and *that's* what you're thinking about? Fred? Fred died in '58. I remarried in 1960—to George Thorman. We bought the townhouse here in Phoenix that same year. George was a kind man. He took care of me."

She paused. "He died of a heart attack in '68. I've been living alone ever since. No man in my life—just like you told me. Remember? You said I could do it on my own."

Iola's voice softened. "That was 20 years ago. I've been in Phoenix since 1960—right here. I didn't even know where to look for you. I tried. I searched for marriage records, death certificates, anything. What happened to Fred? How did he die? Where's he buried?"

Eunice took a deep breath. "Fred was killed in a bar fight in El Paso. But the weird thing is... they didn't report him as Fredrick Daniels. Turns out, that name was fake. His real name was Robert Fredrick Lansing. He wasn't from New Mexico like he told me—he was from Texas."

She looked away. "I was married to him for almost 15 years under a fictitious name. So when I married George, I used Lansing—Fred's real name. He's buried in pauper's field in El Paso. I had no money, and he didn't deserve more than he got."

Eunice shook her head. "I made a lot of mistakes. I went to Tucson to find you, but I came up empty. I waited tables at a Mexican restaurant, and that's where I met George. He got offered a job in Phoenix, and we moved here. The incident at Bayless really happened—everything I told Dusty is true."

She paused again. "I saw Dusty and remembered the article about her solving a big case. So I approached her. You know the rest."

Iola nodded slowly. "Well, one thing doesn't work for me. How did you recognize Dusty? There's never been a picture of her in the paper."

"I go to church with her mother—Armindia Roads. I've seen Dusty before. And with the sling on her arm... I assumed it was her. The article said she took a bullet in the right shoulder."

"Well, I'll be damned," Iola muttered. "Alright. We need to get moving. Dusty—go get the file off my desk and review it. I'll take Eunice to the bank and call the PD to get the police report. Meet me back here at one. I'll bring lunch."

She turned to Eunice. "Come on Eunice. Let's head out."

Eunice hesitated. "Aren't you ever going to call me 'Mom' again?"

"Of course," Iola said gently. "But right now, you're my client."

She turned toward Dusty and gave a small smile. "Thanks, Dusty. See you afterwhile."

Dusty had to sit down for a minute and try to sort out what had just happened.

Eunice was Iola's mother.

It was just too far out there for Dusty to fully comprehend. She was happy for them both, but it felt like the universe at either its weirdest—or its best. She wasn't sure which.

She wandered into Iola's office, grabbed the file that was waiting for her, and returned to her own office. She didn't even open the file. Instead, she set it aside and pulled a 3x5 card from her desk drawer, jotting down a list of all the outstanding tasks she needed to attend to.

First on her list: return a message from Pam Davis's mother about the trauma center opening. She wasn't looking forward to the call, but she knew they were working hard to set a date for the ribbon-cutting, and they wanted her to be there.

The call went more smoothly than she'd expected. Dusty told them she could attend if the ceremony could happen on a weekend, and that she needed a month's notice to get time off. They agreed and sounded grateful—and she could tell staying busy with the center had helped them begin to heal.

Next, she called Detective Garcia with the Albuquerque P.D. to check if there had been any update on Melinda Whitton's funeral. Dusty had made herself a promise: she would be there—come hell or high water.

When Garcia picked up, he told her Melinda's body had been taken to California by her father. He'd lost track of the specifics.

Dusty felt something collapse inside her. Overwhelmed, she burst into tears—and then unleashed a barrage of unprofessional words at the officer before slamming the phone down.

Still sobbing, she picked it back up and dialed Melinda's father.

He explained gently that Melinda had been cremated. He hadn't decided yet whether to inter her remains or scatter her ashes.

He sounded broken. Dusty softened.

She asked him to please let her know when he made a decision—if he would allow her the honor of attending.

"I'd be grateful to have you there," he said.

Dusty told him about the trauma center, and how she planned to speak and donate something in Melinda's name. He said he'd like to attend as well and make a donation of his own. Together, they made a plan to make it happen.

Needing a break, Dusty stood up and stretched. She walked down the hall to Iola's office, but the receptionist stopped her.

"She hasn't returned yet," she said.

"Any messages for me?"

"Nope. It's been a quiet morning."

Back in her office, Dusty pulled out the number for Agent Walker and left a message asking about the Sherwood pets and when she might be getting her weapons back.

Just as she hung up the receiver, the phone rang. It was her mother.

"Thank goodness you're there! We were getting worried. We called your apartment last night and again this morning, and when we couldn't reach you, we started to think something had happened."

"I'm sorry," Dusty said. "It was an eventful evening. I'll fill you in over dinner."

"By the way, where did Rocky decide he wants to eat?" she asked.

"China Doll on Osborn," her mom replied.

"Sounds great. I'll meet you there at six if that works for everyone."

Her mother said it did—and added that she was anxious to see her.

When Dusty hung up, she paused and let herself feel the weight of everything that had happened.

Her family was going in 90 different directions. Rocky heading to the military. Layne starting medical school. Milo growing up too fast. Her parents aging even faster.

She needed to slow down. Recenter. Reprioritize.

Just then, she heard Wampacha's voice in her mind:

"At different times, different priorities. And so mote it be."

A tremble ran through her body.

She whispered aloud, "Family first."

Wampacha replied: *"We are all family."*

The words hit her like a wave. She broke down, her sobs echoing through the office.

Her door burst open. Iola stood in the doorway, her face stricken. "What's wrong? Are you okay?"

Dusty looked up, wiping tears from her face. "I just now got what the universe wants from me. I don't know if I can do it. I'm frightened—for the first time in my life. *Really* frightened. It's all been laid out before me. Before *me*! Do you understand what I'm saying?"

"I think I do," Iola said gently.

"I was just told I don't have a choice," Dusty said, her voice shaking. "And that my family can't be my priority. What the hell? How can I commit to that?"

She dropped her head onto the desk.

Iola stepped inside, shut the door, and pulled up a chair beside her.

"There will always be choices to make, Dusty. And sacrifices. It's never going to be easy," she said quietly. "Family is a priority—but there are a lot of families out there that need you."

She paused. "It'll almost be like living two lives. You'll have to make quick decisions for both. But you're not an ordinary investigator. You have special talents—gifts—that can help in ways others can't. I believe it's part of your destiny. And I think, deep down, *you* know that too."

She placed a hand on Dusty's shoulder.

"Take your time. It'll become a natural part of your life. You'll grow into it—and you'll grow stronger with the responsibility. I promise."

Her voice was solemn, full of the kind of truth Dusty couldn't ignore.

Iola leaned down and wrapped her arms around her in a hug.

Dusty let her head drop to the desk again—and fell fast asleep.

In the stillness she put her head down again and received healing from Wampacha. His flute played softly in her mind. *His flute playing was getting better and better*, she thought, just before sleep took her.

When she woke, she realized an hour had passed. She felt... lighter somehow. The weight of the world had eased a bit.

She walked down to Iola's office and knocked on the door, but there was no answer. At the receptionist's desk, she asked where Ms. Abrams was.

"Iola took the afternoon off to move her mother," the receptionist said. "She left word that she'll call you at 10:00 p.m. tonight to catch you up. She also left this number for the animal shelter in Prescott—Sherwood's dogs and cat were taken there."

Back at her desk, Dusty made the call.

The shelter confirmed that Agent Walker had left strict instructions: the animals were to be kept until further notice, the FBI would pay boarding fees, they were to be kept safe, and he was the contact person.

Dusty hung up with a smile, picturing Walker with five little dogs climbing all over him at the end of this nightmare. Then, unbidden, she pictured herself with Dante the cat.

Oh, no, she thought. *That can't be. I have way too much imagination.*

Shaking her head, she dug out Agent Walker's card and called him. He picked up on the first ring.

"Hello, Agent Walker here," he said in a deep, controlled voice.

Dusty laughed and, in her best cowgirl drawl, said, "Hello there, stranger. What's new in your corral?"

There was a beat of silence before he replied, "This must be Annie of the Oakley family. Good to hear from you. Is there something I can help you with?"

"Did you get the message I left you this morning?" she asked.

He sighed. "Just got back into the office—hold on. Here it is."

A moment later, his voice was all business. "Okay, so the animals are fine for now. They're at the Prescott Animal Shelter. Your guns may be held for some time—they'll probably be needed for court. Better get a new weapon, and get that shoulder out of the sling. You should be in physical therapy. And go to the firing range—things feel different after you've taken a bullet."

He paused, his tone softening. "By the way, I read up on how you took that bullet. Impressive. You're old for your age. I'd like to hear the story of your young life—over dinner."

"Well," Dusty said with a smirk, "if you're linking that with getting my guns back, I might be waiting a while to break bread—unless you need more information on the Sherwood case sooner. I'd certainly be open to it."

She laughed as she heard him stammer, clearly caught off guard, searching for the right words.

"I'll call you as soon as I know when I'll be back in Phoenix," he finally said. "I'll try to make it sooner rather than later."

When she hung up, Dusty took a deep breath and exhaled with purpose. She was exhausted and wanted nothing more than a peaceful nap.

But before she could make that happen, her phone rang again. The front desk was on the line.

"We have a call from the FBI for Iola," the receptionist said. "Since she's not in, they'd like to speak with you."

"Okay, send it through."

The phone rang again, and Dusty picked up quickly. She listened carefully as the caller explained the reason for the call. When she finally had the chance to speak, she said she'd call them back after speaking with Iola Abrams.

She hung up slowly and stared at her hands—shaking. She was in total shock.

The FBI was sending them a check for approximately $160,000 as a finder's fee for recovering the gold and getting it to the authorities. They just needed the agency's tax information for the federal ID number.

Boy, will I have something to tell Iola tonight, she thought.

The day had been full of surprises.

10

A TIME TO GIVE THANKS

Dusty arrived at the China Doll a little before six and asked for a table for six. They seated her in a round booth tucked into a corner—private, comfortable, and with plenty of space for everyone to spread out.

She decided to order for the whole group and told the waitress to bring their largest family meal: six entrées, all the sides, egg rolls, cream cheese wontons, and hot tea for everyone. "And give the bill to me," she added. "No one else."

Right at six o'clock, her family came bustling through the door, voices overlapping in a cheerful racket. The party began instantly—good food, plenty of laughs, and the comfort of familiar faces.

Midway through the meal, Rocky admitted he was starting to feel nervous about leaving. The table went quiet.

Myron's voice wavered as he said, "That's normal. You'll do fine. Before you know it, you'll be home on leave."

"You still want us to come to your boot camp graduation, don't you?" Dusty asked.

"Of course," Rocky said with a smile. "I just hope I graduate and don't mess up."

"It's not going to be easy," Myron said, looking him in the eye. "But you'll take to it like a duck to water."

In just two days, Rocky would be gone, and things would change for everyone. What lay ahead was anyone's guess, and none of them could imagine the strange and unexpected events that were coming.

Dusty suggested, "Tomorrow, let's go to Mary Coyle's for ice cream—and get the Mountain." A Roads family favorite which had a heaping mound of ten different ice cream flavors topped with different sauces and sprinkles.

Everyone agreed. They drifted out to the parking lot, still talking, reluctant to say goodnight.

"Let's call it a night," Rocky finally said. "See you tomorrow, Dusty."

She hugged him, then knelt to give Milo a squeeze. After she hugged him, he looked at her with serious eyes.

"I wish I could go with him. What the hell am I gonna do now?" Milo said.

Dusty nearly laughed and cried at the same time. That Milo—he never ceased to surprise her. *Oh, how I love this tribe of mine*, she thought. Maybe Wampacha was wrong.

Back at her apartment, Dusty turned on the TV, jumped in the shower, and washed her hair; *I might need to color it again*, she thought. As she towel-dried, she realized something: her shoulder didn't hurt. Not even a little.

A weight she hadn't realized she'd been carrying seemed to lift. The arm was still weak, but the stiffness and soreness were gone.

Tomorrow, she decided, she'd ask her dad if she could borrow a set of dumbbells for rehab—and she needed to get back to the shooting range. First, though, she'd have to buy a gun. Maybe two.

She combed out her hair, sat down on the couch, and the phone rang.

It was Iola.

"I'm moving my mother in with me," Iola said without preamble.

"Wow. That's a big change," Dusty replied. "What made you decide that?"

"I went over the police report again," Iola said, leaning back in her chair, "and then I had a little chat with Judy—the cashier at the grocery store."

Dusty raised an eyebrow. "And?"

"I don't like it. Something about her doesn't sit right with me. I think she might be involved somehow."

"Involved in the break-in?"

"Exactly. Which is why I'm not putting the townhouse on the market just yet."

"So what's the plan?" Dusty asked.

"I'm going to set up surveillance. If they try to break in again, maybe we'll get at least one of them—and one is all it takes to start pulling the rest in." Iola said. "My mom will be safe with me, and her money and jewelry are already in the bank."

"Good plan," Dusty agreed. "Do you want me to do the surveillance?"

"No. We need you on the new case. Did you look it over?"

Dusty admitted she hadn't, then filled Iola in on everything else that had happened.

Dusty told her about Melinda's funeral details, the Pam Davis Trauma Center opening, checking on the Sherwood animals, her call from Walker, and dinner with the family. When she got to the part about the FBI's call, Iola was stunned.

"Well," Iola said slowly, "we'll have to think this through. Wonders never cease."

"I swear you've been busy," Iola said. "See you in the morning. And don't buy a gun—the agency has one for you. Also another boot gun. Don't go spending your hard-earned money on that."

Great! Dusty thought. Now she could spend the money on a new TV console for her parents, just like hers. She'd have it delivered and set up as a surprise.

She drifted off to sleep thinking about ice cream, the gift for her parents, and all the changes swirling around her.

Somewhere in the quiet, Wampacha's flute accompanied her dreams.

Dusty woke at 6:00 a.m., quickly dressed, and tried to do something with her hair. After a few failed attempts, she pulled it into a ponytail, slipped on her Yankees baseball cap, a western shirt, her riders, and a pair of comfy boots.

Sliding into the Mustang, she headed for the office, practically drooling at the thought of coffee and donuts that were sure to be waiting for her.

She knew she'd be loading up on sugar today and told herself she needed to be careful before she started looking like Porky Pig. She was eating way too much unhealthy food, but she also knew she wasn't going to stop anytime soon—so she might as well enjoy it while she could.

Upstairs, the rich scent of coffee wrapped around her like an embrace. She poured a cup, grabbed a day-old bismarck, and headed toward her office. Glancing back at the front desk, she didn't see anyone else in yet. She assumed Iola was in since the door was unlocked, though she hadn't noticed her car in the lot.

She knocked on Iola's door—and was surprised when Eunice opened it.

"Oh, hi," Dusty said. "I thought Iola would be here."

"She went down to the drugstore on Central to refill my prescriptions," Eunice said cheerfully. "She'll be right back. I'm just straightening up and trying to be helpful. Did she tell you she moved me in with her? I couldn't believe it—she actually wants me to live with her! I had to pinch myself. If I hadn't seen you at Bayless, I might be dead by now."

Eunice's expression softened. "You know, Officer Ryan was asking about you. Wanted to know just how old you were. Iola told him it was none of his business—and that you were way out of his league. She's so quick."

She shook her head, still smiling. "I can't believe how all of this happened. Thank you for stopping to help me—you put everything in motion. It's like God sent you."

With that, Eunice hugged her tightly and kissed her cheek.

Dusty closed the door and hurried back to her office, hoping her coffee hadn't gone cold.

Fifteen minutes later Iola was sitting in front of her with a carafe full of hot love and a tray of donuts. Their day had begun.

Iola said, "So, what do you think about the money from the Sherwoods? I know it's protocol to give a ten-percent finder's fee, but that amount would mean the $400,000 is now worth over a million and a half. I don't know that we should take it. But on the other hand, what else would they do with it? They can't give it to the guy who got shot, given the circumstances he's in—so I don't feel so bad taking it. How about you?"

"Well, if they clear Helms," Dusty said, "you could give him ten percent. That would certainly help him out. Just think of what that could do for the agency. I think you should accept it. It's clear the universe wants you to have it—I think it's great."

"Okay then, that's settled. We'll accept it," Iola replied. "What else is on the agenda?"

Dusty told her she was going to get into the new file and catch up on some reading, and then she was off to Mary Coyle's for ice cream with the family. Rocky's bus was leaving the next morning, and they were all freaking out a little.

Dusty started to tear up and looked away. Iola hugged her. "It's a hard day for all of you. Take all the time you need.

"By the way," Iola continued, "I need to say thank you for helping my mom. I can't tell you how much it means to me. I knew I missed her, but when I saw her in your office, I just about had a heart attack. It's beyond any hope I had that I'd see her again. Having her back is a dream come true. Thank you. I thank God every day for bringing you into my life. God bless you, Dusty Roads."

They both started blubbering and had to sit down with a box of Kleenex for a while.

Dusty finally said, "I'm so happy for you and Eunice. Life is pretty darn good."

After Iola left her office, Dusty picked up the new client folder and began reading about a strange incident in Overgaard, Arizona, involving a missing man and wife who had vanished two years earlier. Their son and daughter, after exhausting all efforts with the police, wanted to hire Iola and Dusty to find out what happened to their parents.

The story was almost unbelievable. The couple came from an Amish background. Though they were in their seventies, they were in good health, seemed happy, and had built up a small business in Overgaard selling baked goods and jams from their son's farm.

He wrote that they seemed very content. On a Saturday afternoon in April 1968, he had driven to Heber to pick up feed for his chickens. When he returned, his parents were gone. Since neither of them had ever driven a car—and the buggy they used to get around in was still there—he became immediately concerned.

The police, however, didn't seem worried. It was two days before they sent out a search party to check the fields. The son had started looking immediately but found nothing. Posters and ads were sent out and the search had been ongoing for the last two years, but no one had ever called or reported any sightings.

It was bizarre. They were good people, had no enemies, and bothered no one. But they did possess a large amount of cash, which was also missing. The son did not think anyone else knew about the money, and he was baffled by the whole scene. None of it made any sense at all. He was hoping Dusty could solve the puzzle—and he was willing to pay whatever it took.

As she read the summary the son had written, Dusty was fine until she hit that last sentence: willing to pay whatever it took. It stuck out like a sore thumb. She felt compelled to help; the thought of something like this happening to her own parents was unthinkable.

Still... something smelled a little fishy.

Of course it does, she told herself. *There you go, jumping ahead—assuming something with no basis.*

She closed the file and called the phone number listed on the front.

A male voice answered on the second ring.

"Hello?"

"Hi, this is Dusty Roads. May I speak to Michael Yoder?"

"This is he. When are you coming up?"

"I just looked over the file," she said. "I'll be up on Monday. I'll call when I get settled at a motel in the area."

"There's a bunkhouse empty until late September. You're welcome to stay there," he offered.

As tempting as it was to stay in a bunkhouse and play cowboy, Dusty remembered the guest house and phone situation at the Sherwoods and declined. "I'll get a room as close to your location as possible and meet with you Monday," she said.

He sounded put out but agreed. "The Pine Lodge in Overgaard is about the only close one. Maybe a cabin in Heber—or go to Payson and drive in every day."

Then he hung up.

Well, before I make any calls to a local motel, Dusty thought, I need to run this by Iola.

It was almost noon, and she needed to get to Mary Coyle's. She left word at the desk, and on her way to the car she spotted Iola and her mom coming in, laughing and holding hands. The sight filled Dusty with happiness—she was so glad things had worked out so well for her boss.

She stopped to share her plans, telling Iola where she was headed and about the phone call to the Yoders. Dusty added that she'd find a motel and be ready to go on Monday.

"There's no need for that," Iola said with a smile. "I've already arranged a place for you. I'll fill you in later."

They exchanged goodbyes, and Dusty set off toward a mountain of delicious ice cream.

On the way, she made a detour to Levitz, even though it was out of the way. She needed to take care of something first. Inside, she ordered the console for her folks and arranged for delivery later that afternoon. With that done, she headed back toward Mary Coyle's, where a cluster of familiar faces greeted her with open joy.

Dusty always felt a little like a celebrity when she saw her parents—the way they looked at her, so captivated and proud, filled her with a warmth that nothing else could match. She ordered coffee for Rocky, Layne, Mom, Dad, and herself. Little Milo piped up, "Hey, what about me?"

"You can have some of mine," Armindia teased, sliding her cup toward him.

It didn't make Milo particularly happy, but at least it kept him quiet for a while.

When their orders finally arrived, and everyone was ready to dig in, her dad lifted a hand. "Let's say a blessing, shall we?"

They all bowed their heads, voices falling into gentle harmony as they gave thanks for everything they had been given.

11

THREADS OF DESTINY

By the time they left Mary Coyle's, Dusty felt a little sick. Way too much ice cream had been eaten, and half the toppings seemed to be smeared on clothes instead of cones. They laughed at every spill and dribble, each mess only adding to the fun.

"This will be our first stop when you're home on leave," Dusty promised.

Rocky grinned. "I'd better change out of my uniform first."

That set everyone laughing again. As they got up to leave, Mom asked, "So, are you heading back to work?"

"No," Dusty said. "I'm going home with you. I have a little surprise for you."

Before she could explain further, Milo wailed, "You didn't shoot someone else, did you?"

The entire ice cream parlor went silent, all eyes turning toward Dusty. Armindia flushed, then quickly said, "Such an imagination." She scooped Milo into her arms and hurried him out. The tension broke, and everyone burst into laughter again.

When they rolled up to the house, Milo spotted the truck parked in front and cried, "There's a big truck here to pick up Rocky!" He began to sob.

Armindia held him tight. "It's not for Rocky, sweetheart. Settle down." She glanced toward Dusty. "That looks like a Levitz delivery truck."

"It is!" Dusty beamed. "Surprise!"

Dusty took charge of moving furniture and sweeping the floor where the new console would go. By the time the deliverymen brought the set in, she had everything ready. It was beautiful—just like Dusty's own. Once it was adjusted and tuned in, they all settled to watch High Chaparral.

Later, they ordered pizza and root beer, and Rocky and Myron broke out the guitars. They sang and laughed long into the night, savoring every moment of this perfect evening before their son and brother left for his new adventure.

No one wanted to admit it, but the goodbye was already pressing at their hearts. Rocky had insisted only Mom, Dad, and little Milo come to the bus stop. That left Layne and Dusty to say their tearful farewells at the house.

Dusty hugged him hard, blinking back tears. Then, around midnight, she finally drove home. She cried the whole way and long into the night.

Early the next morning, Iola called and asked Dusty to come to her house right away. She gave Dusty the address, and within minutes Dusty was dressed and on the road.

Iola's home was in the Encanto district, an upscale neighborhood in Phoenix where elegant bungalows mingled with sprawling estates. Dusty had always admired the area, but she had never pictured Iola living here.

At the gated entrance, Dusty pressed the call button. Iola's cheerful "Good morning" came through the speaker as the iron gate began its slow swing open. Driving in, Dusty felt a flicker of intimidation at the sheer size of the house and the perfectly kept grounds. This wasn't the image she had of her boss. Who exactly was this woman?

When she reached the front steps, Iola threw open the door and wrapped her in a big hug. Dusty, still overwhelmed, followed her inside. They passed through a beautiful living room, glimpsing a library and an office beyond double doors, before reaching a massive kitchen that seemed plucked from a European country estate. A primitive wooden table stretched across the space, surrounded by heavy chairs, and warm light poured in through tall windows.

Despite its grandeur, the kitchen radiated comfort. Dusty's wide eyes softened; she felt instantly at home.

"Sit down, and I'll get you some coffee," Iola said with a grin.

Dusty sank into a chair, still absorbing the space. Through the glass-paneled French doors she saw a cobblestone path leading to what looked like a miniature twin of the main house. Roses climbed every wall, spilling color across the garden. For a moment, Dusty could have sworn she was in England—or France.

Taking a long breath, she finally said, "You've been holding out on me, partner."

"How so?" Iola asked, pouring steaming coffee into a flowered mug.

"I guess I pictured you in a townhouse or a condo. Maybe a ranch house, or even an old farmhouse. But this?" Dusty shook her head with a smile. "This never entered my imagination. Don't get me wrong—it's beautiful. Big, but welcoming. It gives me a good feeling... just surprised me, that's all. Who are you really?"

Iola only slid the mug across the table and, without answering, walked down the hallway and disappeared.

Dusty sipped the rich, fragrant coffee, letting it warm her hands. The place begged for a story to match its walls, and Dusty realized she didn't know much about Iola's past beyond what she had learned since Eunice entered the picture. None of it fit with this. She was eager to hear the tale and knew Iola wouldn't disappoint.

When her cup was empty, she stood to wander, her curiosity tugging her toward the garden doors, wondering where her boss had gotten off to. Just as she reached them,

Iola returned—with Eunice at her side, giggling like a schoolgirl.

"Hey, Eunice," Dusty greeted warmly. "How are you?"

"I'm doing great," Eunice said with a glow. "I feel like I'm living in a dream. Everything is wonderful." She smiled up at Iola and wrapped her arms around her.

"I'm glad you're safe and happy," Dusty said. "Have you found any info on the parking lot drama?"

Iola's expression shifted. In a whisper, she replied, "We'll talk about that later."

Dusty moved back to the table as Iola refilled the cups, setting the carafe down between them.

"So," Dusty said, steadying her gaze on her boss. "What's the urgent matter you needed me for?"

"It's more of an exciting matter than urgent," Iola said with a playful western drawl. "But I wanted to talk to you before you left for Overgaard—and give you a set of keys to my cabin up there. Thought it might take your mind off the family drama with your brother leaving this morning. I figured we could have breakfast together, partner."

Dusty smiled faintly. "Well, breakfast is always a great idea. I'm starving. And thanks for trying to ease the pain. What do you want me to make—pancakes, eggs, waffles? What sounds good?"

Instead of answering, Iola slipped her arm through Dusty's. "Let's take a walk in the garden first. There are a few things I need to tell you."

Dusty blinked. *Iola has a cabin in Overgaard? Eunice moving around in the kitchen? What exactly was going on?* She overheard Iola telling Eunice, "Make things ready. We'll be right back." Eunice smiled and headed toward the kitchen. *Was she fixing breakfast? Setting something up?*

Outside, the garden glistened in the morning light. Iola paused to bend toward a rose in full bloom, inhaling deeply before turning with a soft smile. "Life is pretty good, isn't it? First God brings you into my life. Then you bring my mom back into my life. And now... all of this means something again. For years, this house and these grounds were beautiful but empty. A very lonely place. Now it's full of love and laughter."

Her voice softened as she continued. "I was married once, in the early sixties, to a prominent attorney. Peter. He died unexpectedly after just four years together. Before him, I'd been doing research and investigative work, and I kept working for his firm after we married. We were a great team. But when he died... everything shattered. I didn't know what to do, and for a while, I didn't care."

She sighed, brushing her fingertips over the rose petals. "A few days after Peter's funeral, his partner approached me about buying me out. I had no idea what he was talking about. It turns out that Peter left everything to me, this house and property and his share of the firm. There were stocks and bonds and all kinds of investments, and I was overwhelmed with it all."

Iola's eyes grew distant, recalling. "One day, I was sitting right here in the garden when a man trimming the roses came over. He spoke kind words, wishing me a safe journey helping others. I asked him what he meant—who were these 'others'? He said he saw me as a warrior, easing pain and answering questions for those in need. I smiled, asked his name, and he said, 'I am a son of Wampacha.'"

"At first, I thought he was a kook. I even called the yard service to ask about him, but they swore no one had been scheduled here that day. I went back out to send him on his way, but he was gone. Only when I returned to the house did I see him again—on the patio, but dressed differently this time, in a tribal tunic. He told me not to worry, that he would be with me to guide my journey. And when the time was right, he'd bring a kindred spirit to complete the circle and bring light to many."

Her gaze met Dusty's, steady and burning. "When you told me about Wampacha, I thought my heart would stop. I've never spoken of this to anyone. He's been with me over the years, pulling me through some sketchy situations, but I never thought about the rest of his promise. And then you walked in. This is why I've trusted your gut from the start. And why I know we're destined to do this together."

Dusty stood silent, her mouth open in awe. Finally, she whispered, "I'm amazed... but not surprised. Lord, it takes your breath away when it all comes together. My heart is so full I think I'm going to cry. It's a big assignment for us both, but I can feel it—they're here with us, rejoicing in the story, in the journey finally taking shape."

For a moment, they both turned toward the far edge of the estate, as if expecting to see Wampacha and his son standing there, celebrating with them. The moment lingered, thick with presence.

The moment passed and they turned back toward the house but as they walked away they heard a very distant drumming and a high-pitched, almost ceremonial yell and they knew that they would never be alone.

They opened the door, and the rich smell of bacon and coffee hit them square in the face. In the kitchen, Dusty noticed a new figure working alongside Eunice—or perhaps Eunice was the one keeping her company.

A lovely woman in a flowered apron looked up with a smile. "My name is Heidi. I'm the housekeeper and cook for Miss Abrams. I hope you're hungry—I made plenty."

"No problem there," Iola teased. "Dusty is always hungry."

Laughter filled the room as they gathered around the old, welcoming table. A platter of pancakes, eggs, bacon, and fried potatoes waited in the center, steaming and golden.

Dusty let out a loud "Yippee!" that sent everyone laughing again. She dug in with enthusiasm, hardly coming up for air until two pancakes, two eggs, two strips of bacon, and a generous heap of fried potatoes had disappeared from her plate.

"See? Told you," Iola said with a grin. "When you've finished devouring your breakfast, we've got a few more things to talk about."

Leaning back in her chair, Dusty patted her stomach with satisfaction. "Them's good vittles. Heidi, you've outdone yourself. I look forward to our next meal together."

Heidi laughed, wiping her hands on her apron. "I can hardly wait."

12

BURDEN OF THE NEXT VISION

Iola and Dusty carried their coffee into the office, closing the doors behind them. They settled into two overstuffed chairs, the kind that seemed to invite long conversations.

"Well," Iola asked, leaning back, "what do you think of all this?"

"Very impressive," Dusty admitted. "You've got everything a person could want—and a career as exciting as they come. What more could you ask for?"

Iola's smile softened. "Nothing. Not now that you and Mom are here. She's safe, Heidi's here to keep her company, and I can focus on work and traveling again."

Her tone shifted, more serious now. "As for the parking lot situation—it has some credence. I spoke with cashier Judy, and she knew a lot more than she let on. Her brother is the bald one of the trio. His name is Archie Brent. The blonde is Eddie Graham, and the tattooed guy calls himself Billy 'Bad Ass' Bond. They're very real—and very bad news. Judy seemed terrified that Billy would find out she'd talked. She said the man in the parking lot that night was a security guard where they all once worked. His name was Eric Pratt. He'd caught Billy stealing on the job and was trying to extort him for hush money. Judy thinks Billy killed him."

"What's more," Iola continued, "She said the black truck was hidden at her brother's house and she knew he would go to jail for what Billy did. They were hunting down my Mom and if you had not shown up the night you did, she would have been run down on her walk back home.

Dusty straightened in her chair. "Killed?"

"Possibly," Iola said grimly. "Judy didn't know for sure, but she suspected Pratt was dead. If Eunice had passed on anything about them, you were a target too."

Dusty frowned. "Me?"

"Judy swears she tried to talk them out of it, but she had given them all a good description of you, so you were in their sights for elimination if Eunice had given you information or descriptions of them." said Iola.

"I notified the PD." She continued, "Judy's in a hotel for now, until we can pick the men up. Odd thing, though— no one has reported Pratt missing. His employer, Govway, claims he's on vacation until the end of the month. I found no family, no one to vouch for him. The police checked his place—neighbors said he drove a '62 black Chevy pickup with a spotlight on the front. That convinced me moving Mom here was the right call. I considered putting her in the guest house, but she likes being close."

Iola took a sip of her coffee, her eyes steady. "I've given everything I know to the police. With you gone to Overgaard for a while, I think it will all shake out. What do you think?"

Dusty studied her cup before answering. "I think Judy's still holding back. Did they find the truck?"

"Not yet," Iola said. "I'll check with PD Monday."

Dusty nodded slowly. "Then we wait and see. Now tell me—how do you have a house in Overgaard of all places? Do you know the Yoders? The area?"

"The place in Overgaard is more of a cabin," Iola said with a fond smile. "Rustic, but comfortable. Running water, two bathrooms—shower in one, tub in the other. Peter updated it in the fifties. We loved it there. Got away every summer to escape the heat. When I sold my half of the firm, they wanted to buy it for a retreat, but I couldn't part with it. It's sat mostly unused since then. You'll love it."

She reached into a drawer and handed Dusty a ring with two keys. "One's for the cabin. The other's for the Ford pickup I keep in a shed behind it. Full tank, jumper cables in the back. My neighbors, the Leathermans, are wonderful people—I'll let them know you're coming and have them get things ready."

128

Dusty weighed the keys in her hand, feeling their promise.

"As for the Yoders," Iola continued, "I only know what I've read. Missing parents. Rumors of missing money. There's a sister, but she's stayed out of it. A sad case if it's just a disappearance. Sadder if it's murder."

"What makes you think murder?" Dusty asked.

Iola's eyes sharpened. "Where there's money and someone vanishes, murder is always my first thought. We'll see soon enough." She set her cup down, her tone shifting again. "By the way—I have something to give you."

Iola rose from her chair, crossed to the desk, and pulled open a drawer. From it she produced three things: a blue box with silver trim, an abalone box that shimmered in the light, and a purple velvet Royal whiskey bag.

The bag rattled when she set it down. Inside were two boxes of shells—.357 rounds and .25 caliber cartridges. The blue box held a heavy .357 Magnum, its blued steel gleaming. The abalone box revealed a delicate derringer-style boot gun, beautiful and lethal all at once. From a cabinet, Iola fetched a holster for the Magnum and laid it across the desk.

"These are loaners until the FBI releases your own," she said. "Your ankle holster should fit this little .25 just fine. But I suggest you get to the range with the .357 before you leave town. Maybe take your dad with you. Get comfortable. Please."

Dusty ran her fingers over the Magnum, feeling its heft. "I'll do it," she promised.

"Good." Iola's eyes softened. "Now, there's something else I'd like your opinion on."

She opened the office doors, and Dusty followed with her empty cup, still wondering what her boss had up her sleeve. They walked through the French doors into the backyard, heading toward the guest house at the end of the cobblestone path. Iola unlocked the door, and the scent of sage and earth met them.

The curtains flung back to reveal a charming space: overstuffed furniture, a tidy kitchen, a door leading off to bedroom and bath. At the far wall, another door opened into a one-car garage. Iola pressed a button, and the garage door lifted, revealing an alley two blocks long.

"It's a dead end on the west, but it opens onto 15th Avenue on the east," Iola explained. "Quite a handy place to stash a car." She hit the button again and the door rumbled shut.

Back inside, she showed Dusty the bedroom. It was cozy, well-appointed—everything a woman could want.

Dusty laughed lightly. "I think Eunice would love this."

Iola's eyes softened. "What about you? Do you love it?"

"What's not to love?" Dusty said. "It's got everything."

"Then it's yours—if you want it. You'd be safe here. You could stay forever." Iola's voice caught, a tear glimmering as she held out the keys.

Dusty hesitated, her heart full. "Iola, I'm honored. Truly. But I've got a big family, and I'd want them over all the time. I know you'd say that's fine, but after a while it might wear on you. Maybe down the road it'll make sense. But not right now. Thank you—for this, for everything. I won't forget it."

Iola only looked deep into her eyes. "Not nearly what you've given me, partner."

They closed up the guest house and returned to the main house. Dusty gathered up the weapons Iola had loaned her, but before she could leave, Iola grinned. "Why don't you load those first? The bag will be lighter—and you'll be ready for the O.K. Corral." She laughed. "Listen to me. I'm starting to talk like you."

Dusty set the bundle on the kitchen table and opened the box with the .357. She lifted the revolver, surprised by its weight compared to her old .38.

"It packs a wallop," Iola said, "but those .38 special rounds in the box will ease the recoil. Cheaper to practice with, too. You need to get comfortable—between the weight, your shoulder, it'll be different."

Dusty nodded, loading the derringer and sliding it into her boot. It felt smoother, lighter than her old .25.

"That one's from Peter's collection," Iola explained softly. "Rounder design. More delicate. But it'll serve until you get yours back. Don't forget, you still have a .38 in New Mexico too—it should be returned soon."

When Dusty finally made it to her car, she slid the Magnum under the seat, tucked the ammo and abalone box into the glove compartment, and decided to wear the boot gun as she drove. Its weight tugged unfamiliar at her ankle, but she figured she'd better get used to it.

She leaned her head back against the seat and sighed, the last few hours crashing over her. She had simply accepted everything Iola had said about Wampacha's son and the connection between them. Of all the things the universe had brought her way, this was the biggest yet.

She longed to tell her Dad, but wasn't sure he was ready for it. His own burdens were heavy enough—why add to them? For now, she decided, it was better to wait.

When she got back to her apartment, she stopped at the office and told Rick she'd be gone most of the next week. She asked if he would keep an eye on things.

Inside, she went straight to the shower. She stayed in far too long, and by the time she got out, her skin was wrinkled. She combed her hair, slipped into her housecoat, and laid down in bed. She had left it open that morning when she'd rushed out, and now, seeing it again, she couldn't resist. Within minutes, she was fast asleep.

Her dreams opened another portal to what awaited her in Overgaard. When she woke, her cheeks were damp— she had been crying in her sleep. Another gut-wrenching vision had been shown to her. God help her, she hoped she was strong enough to face it.

13

WHAT THE PICTURE REVEALED

Dusty woke up a little disoriented. She took a few minutes to replay the events of the day: Rocky leaving, Iola knowing Wampacha, Iola's wealth, and now the trip to Overgaard. Just thinking about it all left her exhausted. And hungry. That was reason enough to get up.

She combed out her hair—tangled after sitting in a towel for hours—then pulled on a T-shirt and jeans that looked clean enough. Her socks didn't match, but they'd do. She strapped on her ankle holster, slipped the .25 into her boot to test the fit, and decided to wear it, determined to get used to the rub.

From the fridge she grabbed a Pepsi and two slices of cheese, then tried calling her parents. The phone rang and rang. She hung up, figuring they weren't far and she could just stop by. Dusty grabbed her keys and headed out.

At the gas station on Camelback and the 17, she pulled into the Mobil, filling her tank and debating a car wash. Her Mustang deserved it. She also wished she'd remembered to change the oil before heading out of town again. Inside the station, she asked the attendant if anyone worked on Sundays. He shook his head but offered to take care of it right then if she had time. Oil change over a wash—it was an easy choice.

Dusty went inside to wait, picked up a dog-eared newspaper from a chair, and scanned the pages. She never kept up with the news; old headlines might as well be new to her. She forced her mind away from Iola and the morning's surprises—it was too much.

Then the hair on her neck prickled. She lowered the paper slowly. Parked outside the station window was a primered '62 Chevy pickup with a floodlight mounted on the front. Even under the primer, she knew it—Eric Pratt's truck. Beside it stood a man with striking blond hair, talking to the station attendant.

Dusty slipped away from the window, her pulse pounding. Coincidence? She didn't believe in those. Moving toward the garage, she caught fragments of their conversation. Nothing about her, but that meant nothing. Back in the office, her eyes landed on a Silent Witness poster. The Phoenix PD number was taped right to it. She picked up the phone and dialed.

"This is Dusty Roads with Abrams Investigations," she whispered. "I'm at the Mobil on 27th and Camelback. Eddie Graham is here—there's a report on him by Officer Ryan. I need backup. He hasn't seen me yet, and it won't be pretty when he does. Please hurry—"

She froze. A rifle barrel stared her down from the garage entrance. The blond's voice was sharp: "Hang up the phone."

Dusty obeyed, hanging up slowly, then drew in a deep breath. She stepped from behind the counter, her voice pitched soft and girlish. "What do you want? Are you robbing the place? I won't say anything. I'm just here for an oil change—I can come back." She said in her girliest voice trying to sound scared and helpless.

He didn't buy it. With the rifle barrel, he motioned her toward the garage, shoving the barrel into the back of her shoulder to hurry her along. Outside, he ordered her into the driver's seat of the truck, hands in front of her.

As she stepped up, Dusty led with her right leg. The .25 slid free. She spun, slamming the rifle with her forearm and shouting for him to put the weapon down. He staggered, grinned straight at her. Dusty squeezed the trigger, rolling left to dodge the inevitable return fire.

The crack of the rifle was deafening, like a jet breaking the sound barrier. Glass shattered as the round blew through the truck window. She fired—the derringer's pop pathetic in comparison, like a pinball hitting a flipper—but it worked. The blond dropped, chest hit.

Dusty kicked the rifle away, pistol trained on him. He coughed, looked up with a grim smile. "I ain't going nowhere. Put the gun down."

She laughed. "I may be small, but I'm not stupid."

He stood straight up and lunged at her, grabbing her arm and twisting it til he had her in his grip. She struggled and tried to get her gun out of his reach, but he was just too strong.

She wanted to throw the gun, but he was choking her and she could not get her arm up. If she dropped it, he could easily pick it up. She felt the life leaving her body, and just as she began to lose consciousness, air came flooding back into her lungs. As his arm released the choke hold, she fell away from the assailant and saw Officer Ryan bring the blonde down.

Ryan cuffed him and turned him over, checked his pulse, then stood, looking straight at Dusty. "You okay? Are you hit? What the hell went down here? Were you tracking this guy?"

"Yes, I'm okay. No, I'm not shot. And no, I wasn't tracking him. I just stopped here for gas and an oil change." Dusty's eyes went wide. "Oh my gosh—where's the attendant?"

She bolted toward the garage. The attendant was sprawled on the floor. For a moment, she thought he was dead. But a pulse beat faintly beneath her fingers and blood matted the hair on the back of his head. He was knocked out. Maybe left for dead.

Ryan radioed for an ambulance, updating dispatch. Before he was done, two additional squad cars rolled in. He briefed them quickly while Dusty knelt beside the unconscious attendant. A tire iron lay nearby, streaked with blood. Not the rifle, then. The blond must have blindsided him with that. She wasn't sure the man would make it.

The ambulance crew rushed in, loading the attendant and giving Dusty a quick once-over. Moments later, the blond was loaded into the same vehicle as his victim. Odd. But maybe standard procedure. Dusty drifted into the garage, needing space from the chaos.

On the bulletin board, she scanned business cards for the attendant's name. Nothing. She started to turn away, then froze. A photo she'd skimmed past caught her eye. The attendant, grinning with his "good buddies"—Archie Brent, Eddie Graham, and Billy Bond.

She ripped the picture off the board and ran outside, waving it at Ryan.

"I don't like this," she snapped. "Those ambulance drivers may be in danger. Someone should follow them. Did you check for other weapons?"

Ryan's face hardened. He sprinted for his car, radio crackling as he pulled onto Camelback toward Baptist Hospital.

Dusty's hands shook. She ran to her Mustang, but one of the officers grabbed her door.

"Stop. Where do you think you're going?"

"I'm backing up Ryan," she shot back. "Those two in the ambulance? They know each other. They could try something—hurt the EMTs." She yanked at the door handle, but his grip didn't budge.

"Stay right here," the officer ordered. "Don't move."

Dusty slammed the door shut, muttering under her breath. She was ready to leave anyway—until she noticed her keys weren't in the ignition. Or on the seat. Or the floorboard. Panic rippled through her.

Back inside, she spotted them on the garage floor. Relief hit. Thank God—her house key was on that ring. These guys were capable of anything. Were they faking unconsciousness? Were they really that hurt? Damn, she needed to act.

Marching back outside, she confronted the officer. She read his badge aloud, voice sharp: "Mason. Did you send backup? Is Ryan okay? What's going on? Answer me!" She grabbed his arm. "Standing here yappin' isn't saving anyone's life."

Mason sneered. "Not that you need to know, but Ryan boarded the ambulance. Got a gun on them. Attendant even took a potshot at him—missed. Ryan coldcocked him. He's got it under control. No need to worry about your savior. He's fine."

The two uniforms laughed. Dusty glared. "No thanks to you. You're both lame. A little brush-up on what your job actually is might be in order. We'll see who gets the last laugh."

Mason's smirk vanished. He turned his back.

"Who's going to take my statement?" Dusty shouted after him. "Anyone? Or is that too much work?"

It was going to be a long afternoon.

She pulled out her phone and called her dad. He answered on the first ring.

"Hey, Dad. You busy?"

Fifteen minutes later, Dusty was still waiting on Mason when her dad pulled up in the lot at Yates next door. He started toward her, only to be stopped at the tape.

"This is a crime scene," Mason barked. "No admittance. Police only."

Her father flipped open his badge and kept walking without a word.

"Who called the county?" Mason demanded. "What are you here for?"

Myron stopped, fixing him with a look of disgust. "I'm here for my daughter. Got a problem with that?"

Dusty stood from the curb where she'd been sitting and hugged her Daddy. "I swear, Dad, I was just getting my oil changed."

After Dusty told her dad everything that had happened, he said, "Let's get out of here. Momma's got the coffee on and supper's in the works."

"I can't go yet. They still haven't taken my statement," she said in exasperation.

"What? That was almost three hours ago." He frowned. "Let's go see a man about a plan here."

An hour later, the officers finally finished with her, and once again Dusty had to turn over her new boot gun for evidence. She'd need to call Iola as soon as she got to her parents' house. Before leaving, they stopped to talk with Ryan about the ambulance scene.

He asked, "How did you figure out the connection between the station attendant and Eddie Graham?"

"The picture from the business card board," Dusty reminded him. "I brought it out and showed you, and you jumped in your patrol car and took off. I remember asking if you had searched either of them for weapons, but you were already driving away."

"I must have heard you," he admitted, "because that's all I kept thinking about—that I hadn't searched the attendant. Where's the photograph? I'll put it into evidence."

Dusty patted her back pocket. "Where did I put it?"

She walked back to her car. On the driver's seat sat the photo—and beside it, a gray feather. Picking it up, she handed both to Ryan.

"Where did the feather come from? Birds in your car?" he asked.

Dusty ignored the question and passed the feather to her father. Then she met Ryan's eyes. "Thank you. You saved my life. God bless you, Officer Ryan. And by the way, I'm filing a grievance against those two lazy guys in uniform over there, just so you know. Come on, Dad—dinner's waiting."

Ryan stood watching her go, utterly captivated by the wanna-be cowgirl who, with every encounter, managed to capture a little more of his heart. Her boss had told him she was out of his league, but he'd already made up his mind to prove otherwise. When he'd driven up and seen how compromised she was, his heart nearly stopped. Sneaking up on the blonde had felt like it took forever, and it scared him how badly he hadn't wanted to let go once he had him by the throat.

He was falling fast for this caricature of Annie Oakley. He only hoped she might give him a chance. He even liked her dad, and he admired the bond they shared. Ryan knew he had his work cut out for him, but he laughed softly at the thought—it would all be worth it someday.

14

THE PATH AHEAD

The first thing Dusty did was call Iola and fill her in on everything. She thought Iola took it rather well, and Iola promised she would call again when Dusty got home later that evening.

As the Roads family sat around the dinner table enjoying goulash and garlic bread, Dusty couldn't help but feel the void Rocky had left for them to carry the next four years. Milo was unusually quiet and withdrawn. Armindia tried to cheer him up with a description of dessert.

"It's your favorite, Milo—cheer up. It's not every day I make chocolate pie."

"No," he muttered, "you usually make it for Rocky's or my birthday. Why now?"

"I'm just trying to put a smile on your face," she said gently.

Dusty asked Milo if he wanted to hear what had happened at the gas station that day. Her dad's eyebrow shot up, and he shook his head slightly, but it was too late. Milo sat up straighter in his chair.

"Did you shoot someone?" he asked.

"Yes," Dusty admitted. "I actually did shoot someone today. Do you want to hear what happened?"

"Yes! Are you okay—did you get shot?"

"I'm fine. My neck's a little sore because the bad guy got me in a chokehold, but Officer Ryan from the PD saved me. He snuck up behind him, got him in a chokehold, and I was set free. It was a bit of a chaotic mess for a while, but all turned out well. Do you want the whole story?"

"Of course! I need all the details so I can write Rocky and keep him updated on all the messes you get into. He'll love it. So tell it slowly so I can remember as I write." Milo leaned in, eyes wide with focus.

Dusty laughed. "I didn't know you could write yet. Are you sure you won't need some help?"

Armindia chimed in. "Not only does Milo print very well, he's also working on his cursive."

Dusty smiled. "You know, I used to win handwriting awards all the time for my penmanship."

"I know," Milo said. "Dad reminds me all the time how perfect you were before you went rogue."

Dusty looked at her father, a sudden heaviness in her chest. She hated that she caused him worry. "Sorry, Dad, that my life is such a hardship on the family. I probably shouldn't share so much, but I don't think I could go without your input. I'll try to do better."

Her father coughed, cleared his throat, then said, "I just don't want Milo thinking it's okay to shoot people. He needs to hear all of it—to understand you had no choice. And as for my input, it'll always be there. Your mother and I are completely on board with who you are and where your life is leading you. It's not easy to watch, but this is the journey you're on, and it seems universally organized in a strange way. Just be safe. And let's talk about your weapons after you finish telling Milo the story."

Dusty told her parents she wanted to go to the firing range the next morning and hoped they would come with her. Her father looked at her mother and said it sounded like a plan—and Milo would enjoy it. Milo smiled eagerly. "Okay, let's hear it, sis. The whole story. Don't leave anything out."

When she finished recounting it, she looked at Milo. "Is there anything I should have done differently that you noticed?"

He spent the next half hour peppering her with questions. Where had she gotten the gun? Why not carry a bigger one so the guy wouldn't have gotten up?

"That's true," she admitted, "but I wouldn't have gotten the drop on him. A bigger gun couldn't have been concealed, and he would have taken it from me right away. The outcome could have been entirely different. But it all aligned, and now they'll get the other two who were involved. Maybe there are more—I can't say. The case will be handled by my office from here on, since I'm leaving for Overgaard Monday morning."

"What's in Overgaard?" Milo asked.

Dusty quickly filled the family in on the missing people case. She wasn't sure where it would lead, but promised to keep them updated.

Later, Dusty stayed to watch *The Lawrence Welk Show* with the family. They loved the new television, and she noticed a few record albums left out after listening to them on the stereo. She was glad they were enjoying it. Milo announced that Saturday morning cartoons were better on the new set, and added that he thought Mr. Rogers had the same television. Dusty had no idea how he would know that, but Milo was like a walking encyclopedia. They all listened when he spoke. It was a little spooky, but you just knew he knew.

When Dusty got back to her apartment, the phone was already ringing. She rushed inside to answer it.

"Hey, I just walked in—what's happening?" Dusty said.

It was Iola. She said all was well, but she was concerned about the day's events. She wanted an update on the blonde and mentioned she had a call in to the PD to get a copy of the report.

Dusty filled her in on the parts she'd left out around her parents so they wouldn't worry. She also told Abrams she thought once the blonde was interrogated, everything would come together for the cops and unravel for the bad guys—or at least that was her hope.

After a quiet moment, Dusty added, "I forgot to tell you about the feather I found with the picture. What do you think that meant?"

Iola didn't hesitate. "I think it was Wampacha's way of letting you know he's with you."

Dusty's voice softened. "I thought so too."

They spent an hour talking about the morning and all that had happened. Dusty said she hoped things might slow down a little.

"Don't count on it," Iola warned. "I think we're in for some bumpy roads in the days ahead."

Dusty told her about going to the range the next day and taking the family with her. Iola said she hoped Dusty got in some good practice and that she would try to hunt up another boot gun. Dusty explained that she had already made the officers write down the make and model of the antique gun, and had even insisted Officer Mason initial both paragraphs about it. She didn't trust him—he had it in for her—and she didn't want the weapon to "go missing" by accident.

Iola found that interesting, then asked if Dusty thought her parents might want to stay in the cabin while she was in Overgaard—or even longer, if they wanted to escape the heat. The unexpected offer touched Dusty so deeply she almost began to cry. She promised she would ask them in the morning and let Iola know.

After she hung up the phone, Dusty sat quietly, trying to meditate. She needed to connect with Wampacha.

That night, she drifted into a peaceful sleep—and there he was, the spirit she felt so connected to. The depth of her love and gratitude for him nearly overwhelmed her. She tried to tell him how much his guidance meant to her. He smiled, lifted his hand for a moment, and then spoke.

"Oh, little one, we have been together many times. We are all connected, but you and I share a family pod. Your father knows me, Iola knows me, and many others will come and go— companions we have traveled with in many journeys past. Let this connection tie us together, and know that an army of help is here for you.

"Our maker is fighting a war like no other, and all the travels you will be sent on are to eliminate very bad people. In some ways, it will never end. But not only will you help remove evil— you will also send out positive waves of encouragement and testimony. You are walking the path of a warrior, clearing the way so that more souls can see the defined path between good and evil."

"Don't be afraid. Don't grow overly cocky. And don't ever lose that fire in your gut to protect and help those in need. This journey will grow heavier as the years go on, so treasure every chance you get. Love, laugh, and rejoice in the beauty that has been given to all who will receive it."

When Dusty awoke, she was filled with love and hope—for the planet, for the land she lived in, and for all the innocent children who did not deserve the horrors waiting in the world. She felt armored, wrapped in a faith

147

she hadn't known she carried. And in that moment, she was certain she saw a path ahead, lit just for her, to accomplish her mission.

15

BULL'S EYES AND BURDENS

Early the next morning Dusty went over to her folks' house. They all headed out to her mustang which had the smallest, most uncomfortable back seat. Being a two-door, it was a pain to get in and out of. It was a wonderful two-person car, but as a family car it didn't quite fit the bill.

They drove out to the range on Lake Pleasant Road, deciding they'd stop for breakfast after their practice. Mom brought her .270 Winchester—a gun she said she'd used since she was a young girl. Dad brought his Smith & Wesson, and Dusty brought the .357. It would be interesting firing that big ole gun.

When they arrived, the range was nearly empty, which suited them fine. They set up their targets and took turns firing. Her dad had fired a .357 revolver before and gave Dusty good pointers on her stance and two-handed hold. At her first shot, Dusty lost her balance and stepped back nearly a foot, but even so, she hit just left of the bullseye.

Her dad was impressed. "Good shooting," he told her, surprised at her knowledge of using .38 shells in the .357.

Dusty explained, "Iola schooled me on it. She's got plenty of .38 rounds from my other weapons that are being detained. Why let them go to waste?"

Dusty stepped aside as Armindia moved into position. The .270 was a bolt-action, and Dusty had never seen one fired. The rifle held seven rounds. Dusty figured her mom would shoot a few, then adjust her stance—but to her and Dad's surprise, Armindia fired all seven, as smooth and agile as a ballerina.

They stood there, mouths hanging open, as Armindia pulled the target back. A quarter-sized hole marked the bullseye.

"Looks like a few of them hit the bullseye, Mom," Dusty stuttered. "Dang—you didn't even need the practice."

Her dad shook his head. "All of them hit the same spot. She didn't miss one."

Armindia smiled. "I think I'll do another round. It's been awhile."

Dusty laughed, hugging them both. "You two are amazing—and you wonder why I wanted to be Annie Oakley."

Her mom reloaded and went at a new target with the same energy and the same results.

"Amazing," Myron said. "I never knew you could handle a gun so well. How are you with a handgun?"

"Well, I used to be pretty good," Armindia replied. "Want me to shoot with Smitty and see how I do?"

At first Dusty thought her dad would say no, but he finally smiled and handed her his gun. Armindia fired like she'd been shooting it every day of her life. She looked completely at home with it in her hand. When she stepped back, her head seemed a little higher, her shoulders straighter, and a smile as big as Texas spread across her face.

Myron reloaded the Smith & Wesson and took his stance. He hesitated at first, but when four rounds hit the bullseye, his body seemed to relax.

Dusty stepped up with the .357, loaded six, and fired in succession. All bullseyes.

She turned to her parents. "I think we've had enough practice—it doesn't get much better than this."

They all laughed, emptied their chambers, and put their guns away.

When they got in the car, Milo said, "How old do I have to be to get a gun?"

His dad turned and looked at him sternly. "Not for a while. When you're twelve, we'll join a junior gun club so you can learn about weapons."

Milo shook his head. "I think it'll be before then. See if there's one that'll let me sign up earlier."

Dusty and her parents exchanged looks of disbelief—then cracked up.

"We'll talk about this later, Milo," his dad warned. "Don't get any ideas about carrying a weapon. You're only five years old. Wise beyond your years or not, you have to wait."

Milo shrugged. "We'll see."

They all knew they had their work cut out for them raising Milo. If their oldest could take them on such a journey, only the Lord knew what lay ahead with this boy.

As they drove away from the range, they smiled, while Milo sat deep in thought—probably already plotting how to secure a weapon before twelve. If anyone could figure it out, it would be him.

They decided on IHOP for breakfast. As they drove back into Phoenix, Dusty brought up Iola's offer for her parents to join her in Overgaard.

"I'd love the company," Dusty said, "and it'd get you out of the heat."

Her dad said, "We'll talk it over and let you know later today."

Milo smirked at Dusty and gave her a thumbs-up. Oh boy, this would be interesting.

At IHOP, after placing their orders and getting coffee poured, her dad spoke. "Just in case you hear any scuttlebutt around the Sheriff's Office, I want to give you a heads-up." He glanced at Milo. "I'm letting you in on this because I know you and your sister will keep it under your hat and not go blabbing it before we know the outcome. Okay?"

Dusty felt herself begin to sweat. She looked at her mom. "Okay, what's going on?"

Her mother lowered her voice. "Your dad's developed a bit of a heart irregularity. He's going in for a checkup with the S.O. doctors to determine if he can stay in the field. It's just protocol—we'll see what they say."

Dusty's heart dropped. "Have you been sick? How did you discover it? How long has this been going on? And why don't you want Layne to know?"

"She already knows," Armindia explained. "She's the one who discovered it. She's been practicing on us during school—vitamin injections, listening to our hearts, taking our blood pressure. She noticed how tired your dad's been, so she started tracking things. His blood pressure was a little elevated, but one day he came in tired and sat down without even taking off his gun and uniform. She was right on it."

"She heard the irregular heartbeat, got him in the car, and we went straight to St. Joseph's ER. I knew it wasn't good when he didn't fight going. At first they thought atrial fibrillation or a valve, but now they're not sure. Layne thinks it's a drug interaction. She's had several discussions with the doctors, but they don't like being corrected by a student—it's been touchy."

"Because of his line of work, he had to tell the S.O. Now we're waiting for their doctors to check him tomorrow. We didn't tell Rocky before he left—no sense worrying him more."

She sighed. "We'll let you know as soon as we do. If he has to take time off, we might take you up on the Overgaard invitation."

Dusty stayed quiet on the ride back to her folks' house and declined going in.

"I need to do laundry and get groceries for Overgaard," she told them.

Her mom promised to call as soon as they knew anything. Dusty told her that once she was settled up there, she'd call and give them the number. She hugged them tightly.

"I love you all so much," she said. "I hope you can come up."

When she got in the car, she made a mental note to call Layne later about Dad. Until then, there wasn't much she could do. She headed home to get ready for the next adventure.

16

BURNING DAYLIGHT

Dusty stopped at the grocery store and picked up two jars of peanut butter, two boxes of crackers, beef jerky, cans of Vienna sausages, four six-packs of Pepsi, a loaf of bread, a bag of apples, a pound of sugar, some butter, and celery. That should hold her in case of emergencies—or late-night worry.

Back at the apartment, she gathered her laundry and got it started so she could finish up and make a few phone calls.

While she waited in the laundry room, she sat down and thought about all the events of the weekend. She couldn't believe she had shot someone again. It was starting to worry her, and she was sure it would become a reputation she didn't want following her around forever. She decided that when she got back from this job, she would enroll in a self-defense class—learn another way to protect herself without a firearm. She knew this would be an important step in surviving the path Wampacha was leading her down.

After folding the laundry and putting it away, she dug out a backpack and a canvas bag to carry her clothes and personal items. The canvas was too big, so she packed food in it instead and moved her clothes to the backpack. She tucked in a pair of tennis shoes and several pairs of socks. Something told her she might be hiking—her visions with Wampacha had shown rocky terrain and climbing. She prayed she'd stay strong and out of pain, ready to handle whatever came her way. If only she had a horse, she thought, and decided to call Iola.

When she hung up, Dusty felt better. Iola had given her good insight on what lay ahead and said she might even be able to get a horse if needed. She also passed along the phone number for the Overgaard property and promised to make sure the line was working.

Now Dusty needed to call her sister and figure out what lay ahead for her Daddy. She started to choke up just thinking about it. Her Daddy, big strong and invincible in her eyes, was having a major health problem. She just could not imagine him being ill. Why hadn't she noticed the signs? How many times had he said, I'm just tired?

As the phone rang she hoped her sister would pick up but it was her Mom who said hello. Dusty asked, "How are things going?"

Armindia said, "We're all fine. I hope we can come up to Overgaard. What's the number there?"

Dusty gave her the cabin's number and explained that there was some kind of answering machine. "Just leave a message if I don't pick up," she said.

When Armindia handed the phone to Layne, Dusty overheard her say, *Be quick*.

"Hello," Layne said. "What's up? I hear you're going north tomorrow."

Dusty gave her a quick update before asking, "Can you tell me what your thoughts are about Dad? I'm so glad you caught this. Do they have him on meds? How bad is it?"

Layne answered vaguely. "I'll call when I know something significant." She hung up so quickly Dusty barely got a goodbye out.

Dusty felt hollow. Was it because Layne couldn't speak freely? Or because she thought Dusty couldn't handle the truth? Either way, it left her in a turmoil of emotions. She had to stay focused on her job and pray all would turn out well for her family.

She decided she needed to eat something, so she got in her car and drove to a little hole in the wall called Ma and Pa Clark's on McDowell and ordered a steak sandwich— cooked to perfection on an old electric skillet. Whatever they did with the garlic and steak, it was the comfort food that she needed to get her through the night. She thought about ordering one to take with her, but did not want to take a cooler.

Hopefully, Overgaard had a good café. If not, she would be eating peanut butter sandwiches. That reminded her—she'd forgotten jelly. She laughed at herself. She needed to slow down the food thoughts and start exercising.

That night she tossed and turned, her mind circling around her dad, Wampacha, Rocky, the Yoders, and Iola. When she finally dozed off, it was to the hauntingly sweet sound of the native flute she had grown to love. Its song lulled her into a safe, peaceful sleep.

At 6:00 a.m. she awoke with a jolt. It felt like someone had been shaking her, urging her to come back.

Come back? From where? She thought.

What had she been dreaming? Where had her dreams taken her?

Shaking it off, she grabbed a Pepsi from the fridge and laid out the rest on the table, along with the butter and celery, ready to load into the car. She was going to need a small cooler after all. The dry goods had been packed the night before.

After a hot shower, she washed her hair and let the water run over her tense shoulders. She needed to relax, to quiet her racing mind. She'd been in overdrive for days, and she hoped the trip to Northern Arizona would be the diversion she needed.

Part of her was excited about the new location; part of her was afraid of the rugged terrain she'd seen in her visions. Only time would tell and she knew she was burning daylight and needed to hit the road.

She pulled her hair into a ponytail and buttoned up a crisp white western-cut shirt with pearl snaps—a small splurge from her first big check a year ago. Hard to believe she was still rotating the same few shirts and tees she'd bought back then. Fashion wasn't her priority, but the shirt, paired with her hopsack riders, fancy belt, and buckle made her feel special. She put on her polished Justins and though they were showing some wear, still looked good.

Her ankle holster felt better today; in time she'd hardly notice it. Iola had told her to swing by the office—there'd be a new derringer waiting.

Dusty double-checked everything, sliding her boot box into the back seat with her ammo. The box had taken on a strange life of its own—ever since it had held a suicide weapon, then been stolen during another deadly incident. Now she used it for ammo. Somehow it had become a piece of her equipment she felt compelled to carry.

At the office, she picked up the derringer, snagged a large coffee and two donuts from the break room, and grabbed the Overgaard file. Missy had just started the coffee; Iola wasn't in yet. Dusty ate one donut on the spot and tucked the other away. She was in and out in fifteen minutes.

She headed north through Cottonwood, then turned onto State Route 260. By the time she reached Payson, she was overwhelmed by the beauty of Arizona's high country. She'd driven through before by way of 87A, which was pretty in its own way—but nothing compared to coming in on 260. This, she thought, must be what they called God's country.

Her radio was tuned to KHAT, and Waylon Jennings was singing *Brown Eyed Handsome Man*. She sang along until the signal cut out climbing the hill. She slid in a cassette—Tammy Wynette's *Stand by Your Man*—and let her voice keep her company as she drove. By the time she'd finished her office coffee, she needed a bathroom break.

As she dropped down into Payson, a western scene unfolded before her eyes. It made her smile wide—it was like stepping back in time. She pulled over, taking it all in. *I miss this way of life,* she thought. *And I've never even lived it. Or have I?*

At a gas station, she asked the attendant to fill her tank, then ducked into the restroom. She couldn't help but think about how different this stop was from her last one.

When she came out, a scruffy-looking kid was leaning into her car, boot box in hand.

"Hey!" she yelled.

The attendant turned from the pump to stare. Bullets lay scattered across the ground. Dusty rushed around to the driver's side.

"What the hell is this? You let anyone into a customer's car?" she shouted, bending down to gather the bullets.

"I thought he was with you," the attendant said. "Did he take anything? That'll be six dollars."

Dusty handed him a five and a one. "You gonna get my windshield?"

He grinned. "Next time."

So much for the chivalry of the Old West.

She climbed back in the car and suddenly heard Wampacha's voice.

Just a little reminder—it has never been a peaceful environment. Don't get wrapped up in the romance you think existed. It has always been, in one way or another, a dog-eat-dog world. Pay attention, little one. Listen to your warning signals. Say my name.

Dusty gripped the wheel, heart pounding. She drove northeast, now worried about what lay ahead—and wondering if she could get through it without shooting anyone.

17

RED DIRT ROADS

As she passed Kohl's Ranch, Dusty smiled at a memory—coming up here with her church group one year. It had been her first time on a horse, and she laughed at how she'd acted like he was a real bronc, when in truth he never broke into more than a trot. Boy, I did have quite an imagination, she thought.

The winding roads were beginning to wear on her. She had chosen this route because she needed to clear her head and just drive, but she hadn't realized how long and exhausting the way around would be. Nearly five hours later, with the day half gone, she was more than ready to reach Overgaard.

Driving into the small town, she noticed that street signs were scarce. Thankfully, Iola had given her clear directions: turn left off 260 onto Green Mountain Road, then watch for a small yellow sign with a black "A" about two miles in, turn right, and drive a quarter mile. All of it was dirt—not just any dirt, but a deep reddish color. Thank goodness Green Mountain had a sign, or she would have missed it.

When she pulled up to the cabin, Dusty took a deep breath. It was beautiful—solid log and chinking, the old pioneer method of building, strong and lasting when well maintained. Dusty had always loved reading about the settlers who built homes that still stood today. She could hardly wait to go inside, but first she wanted to walk the land, get her bearings, and mark the directions. This place was remote, and she needed to know how to find it in the dark.

North of her, about five hundred yards away, stood another cabin. Probably the neighbors Abrams had mentioned. In the outbuilding she found the truck Iola had told her about. She decided she would use the truck and park the mustang in there after giving it a good wash tomorrow to get the red dirt off.

As she headed back toward the cabin, the sound of a vehicle caught her attention. She realized she hadn't heard it until it turned off Green Mountain on to Abram Road. She wanted to keep her location private if she could but in a small area, news traveled fast.

The vehicle turned out to be a really pretty tan-colored F150 long bed with a man and a woman in the cab. They yelled "hello" and with big smiles as they got out and came toward her.

"We're your neighbors up the hill," the woman called. "We take care of the place for Iola. Just wanted to check in." She handed Dusty an envelope. "This has our number, plus local businesses and a couple of eating spots you might like."

"I suppose you already have this number and Iola's," Dusty said with a polite smile. "Those are the only ones you'll need to touch base with me."

She asked, "Is there anything I should know about the cabin? The water, electricity—have you checked the truck? Is it good to drive?"

The man stuck out his hand. "John Leatherman. This is my wife Jill. Everything's working. We started the truck this morning and left the keys inside. Jill straightened the place up, but the dust never quits around here. She also fixed some dinner for you—well, it was supposed to be lunch, but there's a salad with it now so you've got dinner. There's iced tea and lemonade in the fridge too.

"Just call if you need anything or want us to show you around. Oh, I forgot, I drew you a map." He handed her a folded piece of paper. "Signs are scarce out here."

"I noticed," Dusty said with a grin. "Thank you so much. You've gone to a lot of trouble. I'll be back each night, and I may have visitors later in the week—my mom and dad might drive up to escape the heat. I hope I'm not too much trouble."

"Not at all," Jill said, handed her a box.

Then Dusty hesitated. "May I ask—you heard anything about the Yoders? The elderly couple who disappeared a couple years ago?"

John shook his head. "Only that they vanished. Nothing ever came up in the search, and folks stopped talking about it. I knew the son a little. Quiet guy. We set up next to each other once at the farmers' market."

"Thanks," Dusty said. "If you hear anything—after word gets out I'm here snooping around—please let me know. I can get on people's nerves, be a little pushy, but any little thing might help. For now, I'd better unload and check out the cabin. Thanks again for everything—you've been very thoughtful."

She shook their hands and headed inside with an envelope, a bowl of salad, and a head full of questions.

The cabin took her breath away. A massive stone fireplace dominated the room, its rocks gathered from all across Arizona—veins of turquoise, amethyst, copper, and black onyx running through them. Every piece of furniture felt purposeful: a worn leather couch and chairs edged with brass brads and copper trim. The kitchen gleamed with slate counters and a hand-hammered copper sink. The bedrooms were dressed with Navajo and Hopi blankets, and paintings of Sedona's red rocks hung on the log walls. Even the baths boasted copper tubs and showers.

Dusty stood in awe. *This is what a home should be.* It was moving, emotional—almost as though she had built it herself, poured her own soul into its walls.

Then she felt Wampacha.

Little one, this is your space to expand your senses. Your dreams and learning will be powerful here. Breathe, and explore your gifts.

His words came like a whisper in the wind. Dusty's heart swelled. She paused to count her blessings, grateful for her connection to the universe.

In the fridge, she found a container of stew. Tempting, but she settled for an apple, saving the stew for later. She needed to make calls, then head into town and out to the Yoders' place.

She searched for the phone—there were two, one in the living room corner and one in the first bedroom. Sitting on a pine straight-backed chair, she dialed Iola. As it rang, she noticed something odd about the window glass.

When Iola answered, she said, "I was starting to worry. What took you so long to call?"

Dusty explained about the long drive, meeting the neighbors, and her deep emotional connection to the cabin.

"I thought you'd like it," Iola said. "It has quite a history. What did you think of John and Jill? Did they set everything up for you?"

"They did," Dusty said. "I'm good to go. I'll head to the Yoders' now and call you later. One thing, though—the windows. What's different about them? Only the bathroom windows open, and the screens and doors are heavy, almost like iron."

"They are iron," Iola said. "The kind used for horse shoes. Fireproof. The glass is bulletproof, custom-made for this cabin. It's quite a story, but I'll tell you later. For now, get on the road. How are your senses? Do you feel the place?"

"So far, so good. Talk later." Dusty said.

Dusty hung up and switched vehicles. She parked the mustang in the shed and climbed into a 1962 Chevy long bed with the biggest tires she'd ever seen. It rode like a bobtail semi—nothing comfortable about it—but it sat high and looked ready to climb mountains. With two gas tanks and four-wheel drive, she felt ready for anything these dirt roads could throw her way.

18

THE YODER ENCOUNTER

The Yoder farm was off 260, north of Overgaard, on a semi-paved road. The turn onto the property was dirt, marked with a large, professionally made sign that read: *"Largest truck farm on this side of the Mogollon Rim."*

The farmhouse looked majestic in the late afternoon sun, like something out of a Robert Wood painting. Once again, Dusty was awestruck. As she drove toward the house, she noticed a man in a red shirt walking out of the barn, so she steered in that direction instead of stopping at the porch.

As she got closer, she saw the man was carrying a shotgun. Dusty stopped where she was, leaned her head out the window, and called, "No need for a gun—it's just Dusty

Roads from the Abrams office." She instantly wished she had worn her .357 and made it part of her dress code.

The man laughed, set the gun on a flat wagon nearby, and walked toward her truck. Dusty doubted her derringer would even break the skin on this hulk of a man. She had never seen such massive muscles before. Her daddy had a great build from weightlifting, but this guy looked like Paul Bunyan. She half expected to see his sidekick, Babe the Blue Ox.

"Mr. Yoder, I'm glad to meet you," she said, extending her hand and trembling at the thought he could crush it.

He let out a booming belly laugh. "I'm not Yoder. I'm Sven Johanson. I work for Mr. Yoder." He laughed again, long and hard, for nearly a minute.

"What's so funny?" she asked. "Why are you laughing?"

With a straight face he replied, "I thought the truck was empty. I could barely see your head over the steering wheel. I figured someone was hiding on the passenger side with a gun."

"Do things like that happen around here? Someone hiding with a gun, sneaking up on you?"

"It has. Wouldn't surprise me," he said. "But I'll let Yoder fill you in on the kinds of personalities we deal with."

"How long have you worked for Yoder?" she asked.

"A long time, kid. How long have you been out of diapers?" He chuckled again and headed back into the barn.

Dusty backed up to the house, where a man in suspenders and a blue flannel shirt sat rocking on the porch. His beard and long hair were the color of wheat. He puffed on a pipe, and she caught the sweet smell of tobacco as she climbed down from the truck.

"Mr. Yoder? Dusty Roads. May I come up on the porch?"

"Please do. If the pipe bothers you, I'll put it away," he said.

"I don't mind. It smells like the cherry blend my daddy used to smoke. I love the aroma of a good pipe tobacco. I even tried smoking a pipe once, but I had a problem with drooling."

Yoder looked straight at her and burst into laughter.

Oh boy, she thought. *What am I, the sideshow?*

"I'm sorry," he said between laughs. "That caught me off guard. Just picturing you with a pipe and drool was too much." He studied her. "You're a funny gal. How old are you anyway?"

"Old enough to smoke a pipe and old enough to try to find your folks," Dusty shot back. "Let's get serious for a moment, shall we? Why an investigation now, after all this time? You must have suspicions, or you wouldn't put this kind of money into an outside investigator. Is there insurance involved? Or are you simply a son needing answers for his broken heart? I don't have time to fool around, so tell me all you know—all the scenarios you've thought of. And I need to talk with your sister. Where is she?"

Yoder set his pipe in the ashtray and rose from the rocker. His whole demeanor shifted.

"Let's get something straight," he said slowly. "I run the show here, and I don't take orders well. Don't think your cute little antics change that. I need to find them because it's the right thing to do. They could be alive, they could be dead—but either way, it's my duty to keep searching until I know what happened. If you think you can help, I'll give you a shot, though I'm inclined to hire someone else. I don't think we'll work well together, and that could be a problem. I'll sleep on it, and we'll talk in the morning. In the meantime, you'd better work on your manners."

With that, he disappeared into the farmhouse.

Dusty walked back to her truck and saw Sven standing by the barn, shotgun in hand. *This is going to be a bumpy ride*, she thought, *truck or no truck*. She didn't like it one bit.

The sun was setting, casting a golden glow over the land as she headed back toward the cabin. On 260, she noticed a yellow flatbed hay truck behind her, keeping its distance. The feeling of being followed prickled her skin. She considered pulling into town to let it pass, but with nightfall coming fast, she decided to push on.

She pulled over to the side of the road and waited. The yellow truck roared past, and she recognized Sven behind the wheel. Dusty drove on, shot through the small town of Overgaard, and didn't see the truck again—but she was sure he had noticed her turn onto Green Mountain Road.

At the cabin, she pulled around back and went in through the rear door. With the lights off, she sat at the window, watching for dust or headlights on the road. Seeing nothing, she finally flicked on the kitchen light and warmed up the stew. She set out two bowls—one for salad, one for the steaming stew. Jill had even packed a bottle of Green Goddess dressing, and the salad had everything but the kitchen sink: lettuce, tomatoes, onions, olives, even sliced hard-boiled eggs.

"Dang," Dusty murmured. Dinner was a reward all its own, along with the beauty of the cabin, the sunset, and the sweep of the land.

After cleaning up the kitchen, she called home and then Iola. Exhaustion tugged at her, but she needed to check in with those who cared before finally heading to bed.

When she spoke with her mom, she learned that the testing confirmed Layne had been correct: it was a drug interaction. Seldane and erythromycin had put his heart into arrhythmia, and now he would have to take medication for the rest of his life to manage the condition. It was still uncertain how this would affect his work at the S.O.

Her mom said she wasn't sure if they would be able to come up to the cabin. Dusty promised to call the next evening to check in again. She told her to give Daddy her love—and added that she loved her more than she could say.

When she called Iola, Dusty was still fighting back tears. Between exhaustion and being an emotional wreck, she was barely holding it together. She filled Iola in on the encounter with the Yoders and asked for her thoughts.

"Weird. That just sounds weird," Iola said. "Are they rednecks or Neanderthals? What's their problem? Do you feel uncomfortable? If you do, let's send someone else up there."

Dusty replied, "Well, I can't go putting my tail between my legs whenever someone barks at me. I'll see what he says in the morning and evaluate from there. I'm going out early, and I'll call you before noon from in town. Don't worry. Yes, they're weird personalities, but they could still be alright. Let's see tomorrow."

With that, she hung up and went to bed.

19

SHADOWS ON THE BACK FORTY

The morning sunrise streaming through the crackled, thick glass was beautiful. Dusty lay in bed for a few minutes, enjoying the light bouncing off the logs. To her amazement, the fireplace stones seemed to come alive, their many minerals catching and shifting the light. What a show—it was as if the moment had been planned just for her.

As she got ready to leave, she heard the sound of a familiar flute. *"Good morning, Wampacha,"* she said. *"Blessings for you and me on this glorious day."*

Wampacha's soft, sweet voice rose in her mind, and she listened closely.

The men you met yesterday are good men—a little backwards, perhaps, but with good hearts. Your journey will unfold with their help.

She hesitated before asking about her daddy.

The universe is in control of that situation. It will work out for him—not what he thinks he wants, but what he is needed for. Assure him he is moving into higher work for the future. You will watch a transformation of his higher self into a visible nurturer of your cause. There is a plan unfolding. Believe, and keep the good fight going. I am here for you and your followers. Water the flowers with hope and strength in your belief of what you are doing. So mote it be.

And with that, he was gone. Dusty shook her head, trying to sort it all out. Locking the cabin, she reassured herself that she believed in her guide and that he would always give her the truth. If Wampacha said to trust Michael Yoder and Sven Johanson, then that was exactly what she would do.

She tossed a large pillow onto the driver's seat, climbed up, and perched on it so at least she could be seen over the steering wheel. Sitting tall, she steered the truck toward the day ahead.

She munched on an apple and sipped from her thermos of coffee. Grimacing at each swallow, she muttered that it tasted like dirt. She figured it must have been the water she used to make it. She'd have to start boiling or buying distilled water—she couldn't last long drinking coffee that bad.

At the Yoder farm, Dusty parked at the house. No one was on the porch, though she could see movement at the barn. She had her gun holstered at her side, with her boot derringer snug under her pant leg. As she neared the barn, she noticed two saddled horses tied to the hitching post on the east side.

Who's going riding today? she wondered aloud. She called for Michael Yoder, and Sven emerged, looking gruff.

"Good morning, Sven—it's a beautiful day. How are you this fine morning?" she said cheerfully.

His jaw dropped slightly, and he stammered that he was fine before adding that Michael was in the barn feeding. Dusty asked if she should wait outside or if she could go in. He motioned her inside, then walked toward the tethered horses.

She stepped into the big barn and once again marveled at the structure and the smells. She closed her eyes, inhaled deeply, and smiled. She loved the scent of hay and manure—it was raw, earthy beauty, the smell of life itself.

When she opened her eyes, Michael Yoder was watching her, smiling. She admitted sheepishly, "I love that smell. It's like the rawest beauty of the earth on a farm or a ranch. It never ceases to get me. Life is so rich and full of ordinary things that tell stories from so many lifetimes."

Michael coughed lightly before replying. "So there's an old soul behind that young girlish face. Who would've guessed? I love that smell too. Not many of us in that club, but I know what you mean. It tells us a lot about the earth. I'd like to take you out to the back forty and show you the rest of the farm. Do you ride? I saddled a couple of horses for us. And I'd also like to apologize for the altercation yesterday. I hope we can start fresh. What do you say—new day?"

Dusty smiled. That sounded good to her. She'd love to ride, see the place, and talk more about the disappearance of his parents.

She excused herself to fetch her hat from the truck. Outside, Sven met her with a large mug of steaming hot coffee. She took it gratefully—thank goodness it was good coffee—and thanked him. Things were looking up, just as Wampacha had said.

She grabbed her hat, drank deeply of the dark liquid, and counted her blessings. Then she noticed Michael emerging from the barn with two rifles, which he slid into the saddle scabbards.

"Are we going hunting?" she asked.

"Not planning on it," he said. "But I never ride without my rifle. I brought one for you, too—it's always good to be prepared. I noticed you carry a .357. Is that your choice of handgun?"

"I usually carry a .38," Dusty explained. "But I've got three of them being held by different police agencies from shootings I've been involved in. So the .357 is on loan from the company."

"Have you ever fired it? I only ask because I fired one once, and it knocked me down."

"Yes, I've fired it. You definitely have to figure out your stance. I'm also loaded with .38 bullets, and they take some of the recoil out. I've got so many .38s and no guns at the moment. They're interchangeable in this model—so why not?" She flashed a big Dusty grin at this unusual cowboy.

"Okay, let's saddle up and get on with the day. There's lots to see and tell. Feel free to ask me anything that comes into that head of yours, and maybe between the two of us we can figure this out."

With a quick spur to his beautiful buckskin, he was off.

Dusty mounted the dark bay mare he had saddled for her and let out a loud, "Yee-haw!" Her hat blew back—thank goodness for the chin tie—so it just dangled against her shoulders. She urged the bay into a gallop to catch up, then pulled back on the reins to trot alongside him.

"What's her name?" she asked.

"Whinnie. I've had her since she was born. She used to whinny constantly, telling me stories, so the name just kind of stuck."

"What's your buckskin's name?"

"His name is Buster. He's twenty years old and the best horse in the world. Have you ever seen the movie *Smoky the Cow Pony?*"

Dusty stopped Whinnie short. "That's one of my favorites! I've cried a million tears watching that movie."

"Well, Buster is Smoky's alter ego. He's saved my hide more times than I can count, and I owe him the fact that I'm still on this old mud ball."

She laughed. "You're the only other person I've heard use that phrase—besides my Daddy."

Michael smiled and tapped his horse, trotting ahead.

It was a strange feeling, riding with a man—her first time on the range with someone else. She could swear on a stack of Bibles she had been in this very situation before: the feeling, the horses, the back of a cowboy riding just ahead of her. She felt like Dale Evans alongside Roy Rogers.

It was the most complete feeling she had ever known. *What a sap I am,* she thought. Still, she recognized it for what it was: not a crush on the client but memories from a past life. And yet part of her never wanted to leave this moment. This was it—her, her horse, and the wide-open land.

She shook herself back to attention and focused on the land around her. They had ridden about half a mile when she noticed another rider in the distance, far to the east. She called out to Yoder, who dropped back beside her.

"Do you see that rider?" she asked.

Michael frowned and pulled Buster to a halt. He reached into his saddlebag for binoculars.

"How did you even spot him? That's quite a distance." He raised the lenses. "He does look familiar—and he definitely knows we're here. He's looking straight at me. But that horse—he's riding a workhorse, a wagon puller. Why would he be out here on that?"

Dusty fired off questions rapid-fire. "Who lives on the next farm? The land he's riding on? What do they farm? How do we get over there—ride straight across? Have you spoken to him before? What's their last name?"

"Slow down, give me a chance to answer one before you throw the next," Michael said with a half-smile. "Their name's Bookman. They raise cattle. Yes, we could ride over there, but let's finish up here first—we can drive over later. Big family, all the kids grown and working on the farm. They've been here about ten years—moved in around the time my parents came to live with me. They've tried to buy my place more than once, wanted to build their herd up."

"Let's stop under that patch of trees ahead," Dusty said. "We need to talk. I want the story—and the sooner the better."

They tied the horses to a bush and sat in the shade of a stand of trees—an island in the vast grass of the high desert. The mix of forest and desert created a peace that was almost palpable. Dusty and Yoder talked for several hours, long pauses of silence stretching between them as they tried to piece together a story with nothing more than imagination.

Finally, Dusty said she wanted to close her eyes and meditate for clarity.

Michael looked skeptical. "Are you religious? How would that help?"

"There's something missing," Dusty explained. "Maybe you never knew the full beginnings of who your parents really were. I just want to let my mind help sort out the story."

"You some kind of psychic or medium?"

"No. But I've got good instincts. Let me work it through."

"Alright," he said, nodding toward the horses. "I'll be over here."

Dusty sat cross-legged on the ground, though her holster dug uncomfortably at her side. She knew she'd have to connect quickly to Wampacha. Closing her eyes, she ran the story Yoder had told her through her mind:

He had left his parents' farm in his early twenties. Winters were too harsh, and he couldn't wait for a new climate. Utah was his first stop, but after five years he moved south to Arizona's high country. The winters were cold but milder than the Midwest. He purchased 160 acres bordering the Tonto National Forest and fell in love with the land.

For years, he wrote letters begging his parents to join him, but they never answered. Then one day he received a call from Flagstaff asking him to meet them at the train station. When he arrived, they weren't there. He waited until the next train came through. As passengers filed off, he felt a tap on his shoulder.

Behind him stood a man with a long beard and black hat—and behind him, his mother. He hugged her tightly, though she looked embarrassed by the public display. His father shook his hand, all the while glancing around nervously, and told him he could ask no questions. Their life was not what it seemed, and he would never explain. The beard, the Amish disguise—that would be their story, and no further answers would come.

Over the next eight years, Michael adopted the Amish look as well, trying to blend in with his parents' strange choice. They seemed to love the farm, though they refused his offer to build them a house of their own. His sister, older by seven years, had long since moved away. They corresponded by mail when Michael first left home, but when he mentioned their parents living with him, his father exploded and ordered him never to contact her again.

His sister's last letter had been bitter. She had written him back and told him that she had gotten married the year before, and she and her husband were moving to New Mexico with his family. She said she probably would not be writing again. There was no love lost between her and the folks, and she hoped they did not destroy his life the way they had tried to destroy hers.

Michael tried to let it go. He said he never wrote to her again and that things seemed to calm down. He said he had asked his dad what was going on, and his father told him that she had ruined their lives and to just let it go.

Then, a week before the disappearance he had seen a rodent in the house while the folks were at the market, and he had chased it into their living quarters, trying to corner it. A dresser drawer was opened slightly, and the rodent darted inside. He said he quickly pulled the drawer open and started pulling clothes out, and that's when he uncovered the money—thousands of dollars, fifty banded bundles of hundred-dollar bills lining the bottom of the dresser drawer.

The bundles were two inches thick, and he knew it was a lot of money. He pulled the drawer out, got the rodent on the run again, and then put everything back as it had been—even leaving the small gap where the rodent had gotten in. He said he didn't know what to do with the situation. His parents had always been cold in nature and barely spoke to him when he was growing up. He said he had always felt like they had him just to have free labor on their farm, but as a kid he never thought it all through—it was simply the way things were.

Michael decided not to say anything to them about finding the money, but a couple of days later his father told him they might take him up on building them their own place. Michael thought it was because he had been courting a woman in Pine and was contemplating asking her to marry him. When he told his folks he wanted to bring her to meet them, his father made his mother leave the room so he could talk to him alone. His father said they did not want to meet anyone, and that was final. If Michael felt the need to marry, then they would move on. Michael asked him why they would be that way—surely they could meet her and just let it be—but again, his father said no.

Dusty's mind raced as she pieced this together. The secrecy, the coldness, the money—it painted a bigger story, darker than Michael seemed willing to admit.

She opened her eyes.

"Well," Michael said with a grin, "did you have a nice little nap?"

Dusty scowled, catching him off guard. "Is there any chance your parents weren't good people? Were they softhearted, kind to animals and children, able to see beauty—or were they dark and cruel? I don't want to speak badly of them, but the vibe isn't good. And what about the lady in Pine? Did she ever come down here? Are you still seeing her?"

"No, I haven't seen or heard from her since the folks went missing. I've been to Pine several times looking for her, but she had moved away. The landlord at her place said she hadn't given notice and that she left in the dead of night. He figured she must have been planning it, because the house was completely empty and nothing was left behind to make it look like she'd left in a hurry."

"Where did she work? Did you talk to her friends?" Dusty pressed.

"No. I just figured she gave up on me. I had too many other things on my mind to worry about that part of my life."

Dusty stood. "Did you ever think the two might be related? Your parents disappearing, and her vanishing in the same timeframe? What was her name? What kind of work did she do? Where was she from?"

Michael's expression grew strange. "I never thought one had anything to do with the other. Her name was Lily Dodge. She worked for the Farm Bureau out of Camp

Verde, in the insurance department. She said she was from New Mexico."

"How long did you know her? Did she ever come to your farm?" Dusty pressed. "And what about your sister— do you have a phone number or address for her?"

"Why do you want that? I told you she doesn't want to be involved with the family." His voice was firm.

Dusty stared in disbelief. "You mean you haven't spoken to her at all since your parents disappeared? Yet you listed her in the missing persons report—why?"

"I did try, that night," Michael admitted. "She said 'good riddance' and hung up. So I never called again. I put her name down because the report asked for family members."

"Doesn't that strike you as odd? If your parents vanished, why wouldn't she want to talk to you? Weren't you curious why she hated them so much—what her story was?"

Michael sighed. "Let me try to answer some of this— it's piling up. Lily and I went out for about a year, maybe two or three times a month. We talked on the phone often. She seemed genuinely interested in my farm and my family, but she never came here. Maybe that's why she gave up on me.

"My sister is seven years older. We were never close. By the time I was old enough to know her, she and my father were constantly fighting. When she was seventeen, he made her leave. I'll never forget that night. My mother had been canning all day, and Sarah—my sister—was helping with supper. I came in from putting the animals down for the night and went to wash up. Suddenly I heard shouting. She was yelling that she wasn't his slave and that she hated him.

"He hit her. Hard. Maybe a slap, maybe his fist. When I came out of the bathroom, he had a gun on her. Told her she had five minutes to pack and leave—or he'd kill her. I remember how defiant she had seemed. She wasn't afraid—stoic, almost. As she went out the door, she told him she knew him better than he knew himself and that she hoped they rot in hell. Then she looked at me and said something odd–I'll never forget."

Dusty leaned in. "What did she say?"

"She said, 'Get out as soon as you can, Bobby.' Then she left. About a year later she sent me a letter, and that's how I got her address. We corresponded off and on after that. She sent the letters to my one friend in town, never to the farm."

"When I moved to Utah, she said she was glad and told me to take care—and to never go back to those awful people. I never really felt that way about my parents, but we weren't close. I just thought that once I started doing well, it was my duty as the only son to invite them to live out here and not have to work so hard. I don't know why they did the things they did or acted the way they acted, but when I saw them in the Amish getup, I did wonder if they were running from something. At some point, I asked Sarah about calling me Bobby. She said I must have heard it wrong. I don't know what any of it means—I just feel like I need to put all of this to rest."

"If they are dead, or if they just left on their own, I don't really care. But since their disappearance, odd things have happened around here. I don't know exactly what it is, but Sven and I both think we're constantly being watched and followed.

"I have about ten additional farmhands who work not only my farm but others. Some of them told me that when I leave the farm, men sometimes show up asking to see me and wanting to look around the place. When the hands tell them I'm not there, the men say they'll wait. After nosing around on several different occasions, they leave before I get back.

"I don't know what's going on, but something tells me they're looking for my folks—and they think I might be hiding them. The last time it happened was right before I called your agency. My farmhand Lewy got a license plate number and gave it to me when I got home. The police wouldn't even run it. That's when I decided to do my own investigation."

Dusty said she wanted to head back to the farm and make some phone calls. Then she asked, "Do you think that might have been the rider we saw? And why did Sven follow me the other night?"

"The rider this morning was Sven, keeping an eye on us. Something must have made him wary about us being out here. And I had him follow you the other night because, after meeting you, we both thought you were vulnerable.

We thought it best until we know the whole story. We expected you to show up shouting orders and giving ultimatums about how this was going to work. Instead, you came happy and ready to get started. I just didn't expect someone so young to know so much and be so intense. Let's saddle up, get back to the farm, and have some lunch." He gave her a smile.

"You don't have to tempt me with lunch—I'm always ready to eat," she said. "Thanks for sharing the story. Now I can get started and hopefully have some answers for you soon."

As they rode up to the farm, a young man—maybe eighteen—came out of the barn to take the horses and cool them down, while Dusty and Michael walked toward the house. Dusty was already trying to guess what might be for lunch—she was more than ready to eat.

Inside the kitchen, Sven stood at the stove with an apron on. Dusty smiled. "Chief cook and bottle washer?"

"Among other things," Sven said.

Michael asked, "Why were you keeping an eye on us? What happened?"

"So much for not being noticed," Sven muttered.

Dusty smiled at him, thinking it would be a hard thing for a man like Sven to pull off unnoticed.

"Just after you left, a black Ford pickup went down the road slowly. The guy on the passenger side rolled down his window and wrote something down. I figured it was Dusty's license plate number, but I don't know for sure. I don't think they saw me—I was in the house making tuna salad, looking out the kitchen window.

"When they drove off, I saw them turn back the way they'd come. I jumped on ole Jimmy and rode through the high grass to follow them. They met up with a silver Lincoln just at the 260. They talked for a few minutes, and then the driver of the truck handed something to the driver of the Lincoln. My guess is it was the license number he wrote down. They pulled onto the highway and headed for town. I took the side road north to see where you two had gone. I rode along with you until you got to the grove of trees, then I headed back."

No one spoke for a while. Dusty went into the bathroom to wash up, and Michael scrubbed at the kitchen sink with the biggest bar of Lava soap she had ever seen.

When she sat down at the homey table—with its flowery tablecloth and pretty floral china—the smell of fresh bread greeted her. A hot loaf sat in the center of the table, alongside butter, honey, and a beautiful banded crock bowl filled with tuna salad. It had everything she loved: hard-boiled eggs, tomatoes, celery, onion, pickles, and a sprinkle of paprika on top.

"Dig in," Michael said with a laugh.

Sven sliced the bread, buttered it, and handed her a generous piece. Dusty piled tuna onto her plate and let out a sigh of pure ecstasy after the first bite. Michael and Sven both cracked up, then filled their own plates. They ate in silence, savoring the good meal while turning over all that lay ahead.

When Dusty finished, she had all but licked her plate. Looking up, she realized she had an audience.

"I don't think I've ever seen anyone eat with such gusto," Sven said. "You certainly made it entertaining. I thought you were going to start drooling."

Michael laughed so hard he nearly tipped his chair over.

Dusty grinned. "Glad I could entertain you. But I take food very seriously. Sometimes it's the only thing I have to look forward to, so I always make the most of it. Sorry if my table manners aren't the best, but honestly—how could you not show emotion over such a fine meal? Thank you, Sven. It was wonderful."

Sven actually blushed. "My pleasure. It was an honor to have such enthusiasm over a meal I prepared—and that wasn't even my best. I can hardly wait until you try my meatloaf."

"Me either! I love meatloaf. Also roast and potatoes. But honestly, there isn't much I don't like—except liver and onions. No, won't eat that. Ever." She said it firmly.

She thanked them again for the wonderful lunch and told Michael she was going to do some research and would give him a call later in the day. She asked for the information she needed to contact his sister and any old addresses for his parents.

"Do you have a picture of Lily?" she asked.

"I'll go find it," Michael said, leaving the room.

Dusty turned to Sven. "What's your story? Care to share?"

Sven looked a little uncomfortable but sat back down at the table to face her.

"Where did you come from, and how did you find Mr. Yoder?" she asked.

20

LAYERS OF TRUTH

Sven took a deep breath and said he'd met Michael in Utah and worked with him when Michael first tried his hand at farming on his own.

Sven admitted he'd been a bit of an oaf back then and didn't really know much about farming or the world in general — he'd been alone in the world. Michael had given him not only a job but a home and a bit of a family.

He told her he'd grown up in foster care from the age of eleven. His parents had left him with an aunt when he was born and never returned. Life with the aunt had been cold and isolated, and when she died when he was eleven, the state put him in foster care. He shuddered and looked as if he might cry. Dusty could feel the sadness in his voice as he talked about that part of his life, so she began asking questions about Michael and his folks.

Before Sven could answer, Michael came back into the kitchen and said, "Enough."

She tried to explain she needed as complete a picture as possible and that Sven was part of that picture. Sven told Michael he didn't mind talking about it and that he wanted to help any way he could. Dusty and Sven sat looking at Michael, waiting for him to say something. Michael sat down with them and put his head in his hands like he might fall apart.

"Michael," Dusty said, "I'm on your team. The two of you have lived through this nightmare together—no one else has a better perspective. I'm not trying to unearth hurtful things, but I look for information everywhere and then put the puzzle together with the answers I get, the lies I'm told, and the facts that come out. It's just my way. I don't want to hurt anyone, but I can be somewhat of a bloodhound and forget to walk softly.

She continued, "Sorry if I upset you. Talk about it and decide what else you think is pertinent for me to know. In the meantime. I'll start my research. I'll call you later, but if you think of anything, let me give you my number where I'm staying. We need to get moving on putting things together tomorrow. Let's take the truck around the whole property early, and then I'll head out to Pine and see what I can find on Lily."

Dusty stood. "Thanks for the day. Thank Whinnie for the ride, and Sven — thank you for the meal. If you think of anything else, even if it's just a feeling or an oddity you remember, call me." She handed him a card with the cabin number and walked out the front door.

At the truck she turned and saw Michael and Sven standing at the door like lost puppies. She waved. "See you early tomorrow for some of that good coffee." She drove out of the driveway feeling like she was leaving home. *Gosh,* she thought to herself, *she needed to put a check on getting attached to clients and their sad stories.*

On the drive back to the cabin she made a mental list of who she needed to call. The list was long and needed sorting. When she pulled around the back and went in through the back door, she hadn't seen anything suspicious on the way — no one following and no new tire marks in the drive since that morning. Still, when she walked into the kitchen she had a strange feeling someone had been in the house.

On the fridge was a note taped from Jill, the neighbor:

Dusty,

I brought over some cold chicken and potato salad. You still have stew and salad. I will skip tomorrow.

— Jill

Dusty opened the fridge and found a plate of fried chicken and a bowl of potato salad. Boy—she was being treated like royalty. She'd have to tell Jill she didn't need to cook for her; it felt a little embarrassing. She was going to end up weighing a ton if this kept up. One big meal a day was okay, but she needed to burn some of it off.

She fetched her briefcase and took it to the kitchen table, pulled out her tablet, and began writing down everything she needed help with. Iola was always reminding her to use the office resources. Well, this would be the test. She wrote for a long time, then picked up the phone and called Iola.

She gave Iola the information on the parents, Lily Dodge, Sven Johanson, the Bookmans, the license number of the truck that had been stalking Michael's house, and Michael's sister Sarah. When she finished, Iola said, "Damn, girl, this is a complicated mess. Where is your gut taking you?"

Dusty inhaled and exhaled loudly, then shared her suspicions. "At first I leaned toward witness protection, but Michael Sr. and his wife seemed a little too shifty and then there was all that money. Now I'm thinking they committed a crime a long time ago, and it's catching up with them. Is it the feds or the mob? Don't know for sure. I'm hoping when I talk with the sister and find Lily Dodge it wont be as dark as it seems. Tomorrow should make things a bit clearer."

"How long do you think it'll take to compile all of this?" Dusty asked. "Do you want me to call Clint Walker and see what he can dig up?"

She continued, "I also think there's something about the childhoods of all these people–Sarah, Michael, and Sven. It's baffling that the parents are so cold and distant. They just seem heartless. Now that I know they weren't Amish, it makes even less sense. When I thought they were in a reclusive religion, that could explain some of the mystery, but they were just using it as a disguise. I don't know. What do you make of it?"

"You might be right about a crime," Iola said. "It's far easier to follow that trail than to prove they were in a protection program."

"What do you mean?" Dusty asked.

"The program is only just getting started with the authorities," Iola went on. "It wouldn't cover a case after this much time has passed. Besides, it's not even a full federal relocation effort yet—my husband worked on relocation programs back in the '50s, and this isn't that. If they were moved, it'd be under a different, newer system, and it still wouldn't explain everything."

"Okay," Dusty said, absorbing it.

"I'll call you as soon as I know anything," Iola promised. "And go ahead—call Agent Walker and run this by him."

"I will be out and about most of the day tomorrow, so I'll call around noon and check in," Dusty said.

After she hung up, she dug out Walker's card and dialed. She was surprised when he picked up.

"Hello, Cheyenne?" she said. "I thought I'd be leaving a message."

"Just got in and sat down," he replied. "What can I do for you?"

"I'm working a case up in Overgaard, Arizona," she said, "and I'm running into some background on the missing people that seems rather curious."

As she told the story and tried to remember all the family-history nuances, she realized the case might have several layers. When she mentioned the Amish disguises the parents had been wearing, Agent Walker stopped her to ask several questions about the timeline, then told her to continue. She spun the tale with as much emotion as she could muster for Michael, and told Walker she thought there might be an old crime tied to the money.

"Do you think organized crime might be involved?" she asked.

"That's an interesting slant on the disappearance," he said, "but it does sound a little far-fetched." He told her he'd take the information and cross-check it against old cases that might be connected to the area they came from, and that he would get back to her.

She asked if he'd pass anything he learned along to Iola; he agreed. Reluctantly, Dusty gave him the cabin number and said she was there in the evenings but gone all day. "Thank you for your help—stay safe," she said, then hung up.

21

NIGHTFALL ON GREEN MOUNTAIN

She went into the kitchen, grabbed a Pepsi and some chicken and potato salad, and brought it back to the table. She sat down next to her briefcase, eating and thinking about how she felt about all of it. Suddenly the hair on the back of her neck prickled. She got up, turned off the kitchen light, and checked the doors to make sure she'd locked them when she came in.

Back at the table, she took her gun out of the holster. Until that moment she hadn't even thought about having it on—she must be pretty comfortable with the setup. As she listened to the cabin creak and the wind blow outside, she saw headlights on Green Mountain slowly head down toward the cabin and then turn off. As the vehicle's headlights went out, it stopped on the road.

She went to the front door and unlocked the inner lock, leaving the screen locked. Two car doors closed somewhere outside, and that was all she needed to run the scenario in her head. Why stop on the road and head up unless someone was up to no good? She wished she could make out the type of vehicle—she guessed a truck, but couldn't be sure. In the distance a dog barked, and brush and twigs snapped as someone approached the cabin.

Dusty stepped back in and closed the inner door, then leaned against the wall and listened. A creak on the porch told her someone was there. She took the safety off her firearm and waited in the dark. Whispering confirmed more than one person. A silhouette passed the living-room window on the driveway side—so they'd circled from the back and come up on the porch. These weren't bumbling backwoods snoops. This had all the makings of a professional surveillance and takedown. What the hell was going on?

She did not want to move and make any kind of sound to give away where she was in the house. Her breathing was even and her hands steady; she felt a strange confidence she couldn't explain. The dark figure showed against a lighter sky—the moon was her friend, and the cabin's unique glass made things visible. She watched an arm reach for the screen-door handle. The abrupt stop of the handle and the assailants' quick release told them she was probably inside. The figure kicked at the door, expecting it to collapse, but met solid iron. A scream of pain and anger filled the night; she couldn't help but smile a little.

What she hadn't expected was a round of bullets fired at the door to try to break the lock. They were serious about taking her out, and she couldn't figure out why. In her head, she saw herself as a non-threatening presence in the scheme of things, but this let her know that what she might find was of serious importance to someone, enough to kill her. She stepped away from the wall and braced, ready to fire if needed. The shaking of the handle and the door not opening held—for now.

Then they began firing at the windows. The kitchen and living-room windows took hits from some kind of semi-automatic weapon. Dusty braced for an explosion but instead heard loud voices cussing and yelling at each other.

These men hadn't expected trouble getting to her— hell, they couldn't even get inside. Before they could make another move, bright lights snapped on from both the driveway and the back of the cabin, lighting the attackers like candles. It took only seconds for the assailants to shoot out the lights and run toward their vehicle. Dusty exhaled, sank to the floor—and then gunfire erupted in the distance.

She jumped up and then listened, whoever had been out there was now silent. Who else was here? Someone had been sent to get rid of her, and then someone else had been sent to get rid of them? It was dramatic—even for her.

She wanted to go out and see what was happening but decided to stay put. At that moment the telephone rang. She didn't think she should answer, but without much hesitation she picked it up and stayed silent.

"Dusty, this is John Leatherman, the neighbor. We've just apprehended two men out on the road coming from your cabin. What can you tell me? Are you all right? Have you been shot? Can you speak? The sheriff has been called and we'll be up to get you out—if you can hear me, stay put and don't hang up."

Dusty set the receiver down, about to leave it off the hook, when a sick feeling curled in her stomach–something wasn't right. Michael didn't sound like he should know all that. Why tell her to stay on the line? Where was he calling from, and how had he gotten involved? A scenario came together that frightened her more than the gunmen had: what if he was one of them, and the other shooter was Jill? What the hell was going on?

She hung up and dialed the only number she could think of—Iola. The phone rang once. Before Iola could get a hello out, Dusty began spilling everything. "Call the sheriff's office and get me some help," she said. "Find out who the hell Michael and Jill Leatherman are. I'm in deep shit and I don't know who's on whose side." She hung up and moved back to the living room, slipping behind the couch.

Footsteps thumped onto the porch and raced to the door. Someone pounded and yelled, "Dusty — are you injured? Can you get to the door to let us in so we can help you?" The voice quieted and drifted away. Then another voice said, "I think one of the bullets hit her—she's either dead or badly wounded. Either way, we need to seal the deal. Let's just burn it down. She'll either come out or get her cremation right here."

The answer sent chills up her spine. "What if she called and gave info to someone else before we got here and they already knew her direction?" the other man snapped. "Damn—it could've been so simple if we'd just taken care of the Yoders ourselves."

Both voices were male, both had East Coast accents. Dusty realized they must have killed the neighbors and cooked up this story to trick her into coming out. If the man hadn't told her to stay on the line, she wouldn't have gone down that rabbit hole at all. Right now she had to act. One thing she knew for certain: she would not let them set fire to this cabin. That she was sure of.

She crawled to the back door as the two continued to talk on the porch. Dusty hoped there were only two of them—she could be walking into a trap the moment she stepped out the back. She eased the door open as quietly as she could, stood, and slipped outside.

She ran for the pickup and hid on its back side, wedged between the truck and the barn. She'd left the cabin door cracked so it wouldn't lock, hoping they wouldn't try it and realize she was gone. She could run into the woods and hide until the sheriff arrived, but she couldn't stand the idea of them setting the cabin on fire. This place had her future written all over it; she wouldn't let it burn.

Voices continued—one walking down toward the road, the other lingering on the porch. She could see the outline of the man on the porch against the post as he lit a cigarette, waiting. She had nothing between her and the two of them but bullets. If she tried to take one, the other would have a clear shot. She crept around to the driveway side of the cabin and waited.

She watched the second man return carrying a gas can. He told his partner to start dousing the porch while he walked around back. As he turned away, Dusty yelled, "Put your guns down and put your hands up!"

They spun, weapons raised—but she fired both guns and didn't stop. The man on the porch managed one shot, and the other fired twice. Both men ducked as they fired, but she'd drawn fast. The little .25 only made one flinch when it hit, but that gave her the opening to hit him with the .357. The first .357 round stopped the porch man instantly. Now both men lay dead in front of the most wonderful cabin in the world.

Her reaction surprised her. She should have been traumatized, but all she could think about was the cabin. She kicked their guns away, checked for pulses, and then sat on the end of the porch. She fished one of the dead man's cigarettes from his pocket, lit it, and took a draw off the sissy stick. In the distance, she heard a patrol car siren—and waited for them to arrive and take in the scene. The siren passed without turning onto Green Mountain Road and faded away. Time seemed to stop. Where was everyone?

She walked back to the cabin and went inside to call Iola, but got no answer. She went to the kitchen for the phone book to call the sheriff when a car rolled into the driveway—she hadn't heard it coming. She grabbed her boot box, reloaded the .357, slid the .25 into its place, and went back out the back door. This time she stayed close and waited for whatever was coming next.

An hour—or maybe more—must have passed. The sheriff should have been there by now. Something had kept Iola from calling, or worse—were they part of the problem? She didn't know. She repeated Wampacha's name over and over until a calm settled over her; she felt protected. She strained to hear movement but nothing registered. She wished she'd stayed inside—now she didn't know which way to go.

Peeking around the driveway side of the cabin, she saw a patrol car and two uniformed deputies inside. She could see the glint of badges; they looked like real deputies. She made a bold move: holstered her guns, stepped out with her hands raised, and the patrol car doors opened.

"I'm Dusty Roads, and I stay at this cabin," she called as loud as she could. "These two men fired on me and my property—I shot them both. I work for Abrams Investigations. My boss, Iola Abrams, called this in. May I put my hands down?"

They approached. "Put your hands down and hand over your weapon. We need to put you in the car and take a look around. Stay put."

Sitting in the patrol car, she studied the deputies. They seemed legit—that was the only certainty she had. She tried to get out when she saw lights come on in the cabin, but the doors were locked. One officer radioed in the scene;

the dispatcher's voice crackled about a helicopter arriving. When Dusty asked about it, an officer grinned. "Are you a movie star or something?" he asked.

"No—I'm a private investigator. Why's a helicopter coming in?" she asked. He shrugged and walked back to the cabin. The other deputy returned and said, "Okay, little missy, start from the beginning and tell me how this all happened. By the way, where's the other gun? Too many shots for one weapon and two different calibers."

"It's in my boot. I forgot to give it to you," she said sheepishly. "Step out." He opened the back of the patrol car and had her hand over the little gun from the ankle holster.

Then she heard the helicopter land between the cabin and the Leathermans'. She told the deputy he better check the neighbors—they might have been killed by these two thugs. "Do you know them?" he asked. When she said no, he told her to get back in the car and wait while he sorted things out.

"Why not ask me what happened? It might help. I need to use the bathroom and find out who's in that copter. You've unarmed me—I'm no threat to a big guy like you. Let me potty."

He let her out and walked her up to the cabin. She went straight to the bathroom and took a moment to thank the good Lord for keeping her safe. As she washed her hands she looked in the mirror and stared at the woman staring back. She felt like everything she'd ever wanted to be—and then some—yet she still had so much to learn and give. It was overwhelming.

She went into the living room and started to ask the deputy if she could walk over to the Leathermans' when the lifesaving screen door opened and Iola stepped in.

It hit her like a punch in the chest, the emotion that was released in her at the sight of Iola Abrams was like a tidal wave. She rushed over to her and started to grab her and hug like her very life needed it, but instead, Iola stuck her hand out and they shook hands with great enthusiasm.

"Boy, am I glad to see you," Dusty blurted. "What a surprise."

Iola's face was drawn with concern. "How did it go down? Have you given a statement yet?" she asked.

Dusty told her everything—how the night had unfolded and how unthinkable it was that anyone wanted her dead.

"They have not talked with me at all, not one question, other than to take my weapons." Dusty said in a whisper.

"Well, apparently you hit a nerve with someone—someone who might be a big deal," Iola said.

"What happened to the neighbors? Are they alive?" Dusty asked.

"No. They're both dead." Iola hung her head for a moment and wiped a tear away.

Dusty was stunned. She apologized for ever thinking the neighbors might be involved. She explained how the man on the phone, pretending to be Michael, had fooled her at first—asking her to stay on the line to keep her from calling the police. After a minute's thought, she realized he'd been part of the plot.

"What made you change your mind?" Iola asked.

"For one, if they were involved, they'd have let the men into the house and said I'd failed to lock up," Dusty said. "But when I heard the two men on the porch and their accents, I knew. They were mobsters. They'd been involved from the start."

Iola listened as Dusty relayed the porch conversation—the part about how they should have handled the Yoder situation themselves—and how that sealed it for her: these men had been part of it from day one.

Iola stayed quiet for a moment, then walked to the screen door and let herself out onto the porch. She surveyed the bullet-marred door and the chips in the glass. Even from the surface, the scene made her knees go weak. Just thinking about Dusty huddled in the cabin while they tried to get to her—God, it must have been terrifying. She looked back at Dusty. "How are you holding up? Walk me through the throw-down scene again—literally. Tell me every move."

Dusty began to describe it, but Iola stopped her. "Wait a minute—let me get one of the deputies to write this down. They're wasting time." She strode over to the deputy who'd taken Dusty's gun and, in a forceful yet professional tone, told him to do his job and take the witness statement. He pulled out his tablet—small and not nearly big enough for this situation—and licked the end of a tiny pencil.

"Go to your vehicle and get a clipboard and a statement form to go with your scribble," Iola said. "You'll need both sides of the page for this. Let me know when you're ready." She walked back to Dusty and grinned. "Might as well kill two birds with one stone while we're at it."

Dusty laughed. "No pun intended." Iola cracked up, then quickly regained her composure as the deputy returned with the forms.

Back inside the cabin, as Dusty told the story again, she realized just how close she'd come to disaster. One wrong move and she would have been dead. She did a quick mental check and felt as solid as a rock—no shakiness, clear about every action she'd taken.

It had to be Wampacha; she felt different—calm, centered, able to trust her instincts. She didn't want to sound cocky, but she felt a little cocky. She thanked the Lord and the great universe that her parents hadn't been able to make the trip—she knew she would never make that mistake again.

Then she noticed the breath leaving her in a rush. She hadn't realized how long she'd been holding it; it felt as if she'd set down a million pounds she hadn't known she'd been carrying.

22

PIECES OF THE PAST

When they finished with the report, they walked over to the Leathermans' cabin and spoke with Sergeant Adams, the lead deputy from the Navajo County Sheriff's Office who'd been on duty when the shootings occurred. As they approached, Iola called out, "Evan—do you have a moment to talk with us?"

The sergeant turned and a big smile burst across his face. "Iola—how good to see you. Why are you here? Oh—so that's your cabin next to this one. What's going on here?"

"I was hoping for an update," Iola said. "What took your officers so long to respond? Did the Leathermans call anything in? Why are they just sitting around twiddling their thumbs?"

He stepped off the porch and closed the distance, his voice snapping. "You are not running the show here anymore, and you better watch your tone. Don't think we aren't doing our job just because we don't use your big-city ways. We've got four dead bodies and your investigator sent two of them to their maker. You should be glad we haven't arrested her."

"On what charge—self-defense, defending her property?" Iola shot back, sarcasm cutting. "By the way, no one's even taken pictures. We had to damn near force your deputy to take a report. Where's the medical examiner? I don't think he has a lot of homicides on his to-do list. Not even an ambulance to pronounce these people. We're staying in my cabin tonight and I'd appreciate it if you moved this along faster."

As they turned away, another helicopter appeared in the sky and headed for the Leathermans' property. It landed just inside the tree line at the far end, and Agent Walker leapt down and strode toward them.

Dusty saw a bright aura around him and, without thinking, mentally asked Wampacha what was happening.

It is as it should be. Prepare for a dark day tomorrow before this all comes to an end. Get a good night's sleep, Little One, and know you are protected.

She thought she heard flute music as his voice drifted away.

She stopped Iola in mid-step. "Why is he here? Did you tell him to come? Do you see that pronounced aura? It's unusual to see it so clear at this hour. What does it mean—like an angel or a halo around him? It means something important, doesn't it?" Her voice quivered; a wave of sadness and fatigue hit her and she forced herself not to break down.

Walker headed straight to Dusty. She introduced him to Iola and they shook hands. "Feels good to put a face to a voice," Walker said. "Glad you're all right."

"Why are you here? Did the police call you?" Dusty asked.

"Not exactly," he replied. "Between what you told me about the Yoders and what came up at the agency, I was already en route when my office notified me of the shooting in Overgaard."

"As soon as I heard the call," he continued, "I knew my instinct was right. I radioed to find out who'd been shot—apparently four bodies: three men and one woman. Thank God you're okay. It looks like a scene from the O.K. Corral. Tell me what happened."

"How about you tell us what you found that made you fly in here?" Iola countered. "Are the Yoders mixed up with organized crime? What's the story?"

Walker scanned the scene before them. "Let me look at the bodies and read the report, then we can sit down. The deputies aren't going to be happy to see a federal agent show up in the middle of this."

He whispered to them, "This is just the beginning of unraveling the story. It started a long time ago. We need to make sure there's no police involvement—lots of gray area."

"It doesn't look like the right protocol was followed in the parents' disappearance, let alone with the money. Pieces are missing, and Dusty must have hit on something big for them to try to take her out. It doesn't make sense yet, but it will." He started walking off as he finished speaking. Iola watched him walk away with a strange look on her face.

Dusty looked at Iola. "Let's go in and take a look at the Leathermans' crime scene. We need answers of our own."

She stopped. "Oh God—we need to check on Michael Yoder and see if someone's tried to take him out. He told me he'd been watched for a long time. Did you get anything back on the license number I gave you?"

"Not yet. Did you give it to Walker?" Iola asked.

"We'll ask him later. Right now we need to check on the Yoder farm. Let's tell the deputy we need someone to check on them—or we'll go ourselves," Dusty said.

She approached Sergeant Adams and explained her concern for Michael Yoder, and the need to have his place checked. "How does Michael figure into all this?" he asked. "He's the one who hired us to help with his parents' disappearance, and this has to be connected. If someone wanted to take me out, it's because of the case I'm working on. Can you send someone, or can I go check?"

"Are you flying out in the copter?" the sergeant joked nervously. Then he relented. "Go ahead and check. We've got our hands full here—only eight people on the force and most of them are tied up. Have at it."

Dusty and Iola found Walker to tell him where they were headed. When he heard, he said he wanted to go with them and meet Michael. Dusty fetched the truck keys, went around back, and drove up to pick them up. As they climbed in, both Walker and Iola burst out laughing.

"What's so funny?" Dusty asked.

They didn't answer at first—just laughed harder— until Dusty realized she'd been sitting on the pillow she'd tossed into the cab earlier. "Real funny," she said.

The laugh eased some of the darkness settling over her. She hoped it was just fatigue and not an omen. She looked over at Iola and Walker and felt blessed to have them in her life—too bad their time together always seemed to swirl with drama and tragedy. Maybe someday it would be different. *At that moment she could hardly imagine what was to come.*

23

ROOTS AND DECEPTIONS

When they rolled up at Yoder's farm, all the lights were out except the large one on the barn. Dusty wished she'd called before they came; as she pulled up to the house, lights flicked on everywhere. Sven stepped out of the barn and Michael opened the front door a crack—both men carrying shotguns.

Dusty opened her door and hollered that she'd come to see if they were all right. "Why wouldn't we be okay?" Michael asked.

She asked if it was all right for them to get out of the truck. He asked who was with her, and she said her boss and FBI Agent Walker. "FBI agent—what's going on?" he asked.

"A lot. Can we come in?" she said, stepping out of the truck and motioning them to do the same. As she walked up the porch, Sven rounded the house with his shotgun poised and ready. "There's been trouble at the cabin where I'm staying, and we believe it's linked to your parents' disappearance. Let me start at the beginning," she said.

He invited them in and told Sven to put on a pot of coffee. Dusty glanced at the clock and realized it was 3 a.m. She couldn't believe nearly eight hours had passed since she'd left that driveway—yet it seemed like a lifetime of events had happened.

She sat in the big overstuffed chair, then quickly moved to the footstool in front of it. Michael said, "What's wrong?"

She smiled. "If I sit in that chair, I'll be asleep in five minutes. I better not get too comfortable."

"All right—let's have it. What's going on that involves my parents' disappearance?"

She started at the beginning—how the evening had unfolded and the calls she'd made. When she reached the part about the vehicle's secretive approach, both Michael and Sven seemed mesmerized. From start to finish they sat motionless.

She finished, "When it dawned on me they might have been out here first, I panicked a little. I'm glad I was wrong and that you're okay. I haven't figured out how they found me—I'd told no one where I was staying and I didn't say anything about where the case seemed to be going. So how do two thugs from the East Coast find me so fast? Any ideas?" She looked at Iola and Walker.

Before she could press them further, Michael said, "Tell me now: what are your thoughts that would include the mob?"

"I never said the mob," Dusty replied. "I just know the men had East Coast accents and acted like professional hit men. I guess you're right—it smells like organized crime. Earlier today I was thinking two lanes: maybe they were part of a relocation program because they'd witnessed a crime, or they were hiding because they committed a crime. Tonight's events could work for either scenario, but I'm leaning toward them having committed a crime against the wrong people."

"Why that?" Michael asked.

"The money," she said. "That checks all the boxes. I believe whoever's been watching you is still looking for the money—either your folks got away with it, or they didn't reveal where they hid it when someone caught up with them. Those are the only reasons they'd still be interested."

"But if they'd saved that money and then witnessed a crime," Michael said, "they might still be on the run. Maybe something scared them that day and they made a fast getaway."

"It's possible," Dusty said, "but how could they save that much money legally? You told me how hard growing up on the farm was and that your father didn't have a knack for farming. I think the farm might have been their first attempt at hiding from whoever it was. I still have lots of unanswered questions, but we'll find out who's out there looking for them." She sighed.

Then Walker spoke. "Maybe I can fill some gaps. Let's go back to 1938, when a young man and his little sister robbed a small-town bank in Lansing, Michigan. Robert and Lisa Hartman were born in Albany, New York. They lost their mother when Lisa was born in 1925. Their father took a position at a Lansing bank in 1927, hoping the move would give them a fresh start. But when the banks began failing in 1933, the pressure on him was too much. He began drinking, faced the closing of the bank, failed to support his children—and he committed suicide. The kids went to the county orphanage.

"Robert was fourteen and stayed in the orphanage until he was sixteen. He promised his sister he'd come back for her. When she was thirteen he stole her out of the orphanage; they rode the rails and lived off soup lines. They went back to Lansing to get even with the bank for what they saw as robbing their father—and to get some starter money. They didn't plan anything big, but they stumbled onto a larger robbery at a bigger Lansing bank. They saw the robbers and followed them.

"The robbers weren't ordinary desperate men. They were working for a large bootlegging outfit out of Chicago. The robbers stashed the loot in large containers and locked it in a garage on the outskirts of Lansing, planning to return in a day or two. Robert and Lisa waited until the next day; at sunrise they began loading the boxes into a stolen truck. While loading the 6 large containers Robert took the top off and realized that there was a lot more money than he had thought."

Walker continued, "A passerby stopped to see if the pair were broken down and then went on his way. Later, when the passerby heard news of the robbery, he reported it to police. The robbers came back to pick up their stash and a shootout erupted—every robber was killed. Among the dead was the only son of the moonshine king, Lucky Beal—the hammer."

"Lucky Beal searched for years. It became his obsession to find those who set everything in motion. In 1944, a few of the robbery bills began circulating in Nebraska, which pulled the FBI back into the hunt—and set Lucky Beal in hot pursuit again."

"In 1948, a couple driving to Des Moines from Lincoln, Nebraska, were killed in a crash on RR143 not far from the Yoders' farm. When police arrived, the couple were dead—and only later was it discovered they'd had a young daughter with them on that trip. She was never found. It was surmised she might have suffered severe head trauma and wandered off into the fields, but she was never located."

"Around that time the Yoders acquired a daughter. Though they said she had always been with them, no one had seen her before. Five years later, they had another child on the farm. The children lived and worked the land, and because there were no complaints, no one looked any further."

"In the early '60s, the daughter the Yoders called Sarah left the farm and never returned. The son moved away a few years later; it was reported he'd joined the military. In some ways the Yoders seemed like any other farming couple—and in other ways they baffled their neighbors. They never hauled abundant crops to market, yet somehow they had new farm equipment and kept their barn pristine."

"One day in the early '60s the Yoders simply left the farm, turned the livestock loose—and disappeared."

"I think this is your family, Michael," Walker said. "I think your parents were running when they came here. I'm not sure what made them vanish again, but I'd bet Lucky Beal has something to do with it. I believe the men Dusty shot tonight worked for him. We need to rethink this whole story."

"What did Dusty learn—something even she isn't sure of—that sent these two killers after her? How did they have ears on your place and the goings-on here? Let's get some rest and meet back at noon. How does that sound?"

Michael stood staring at Walker. Finally he asked, "My sister and I were stolen? Why—just to make the deception look real, or for free labor?"

Walker said, "It looks that way. When we get through all of this we'll try to put your past in order. It won't make it right, but it'll help. Right now we have to stop any more killings, find the money, and find the Yoders."

They drove away from the farm in silence. When they reached the cabin, Walker asked if he could borrow the truck to get a room and a few hours' sleep, then return it. Iola told him that was fine—he was welcome to stay at the cabin; there was plenty of room and a phone. "Make yourself at home," she said.

Dusty was too tired to think. She walked into the cabin, went straight to the bedroom, and was sound asleep within minutes. She needed to be lulled by the flute—and she was not disappointed.

24

TRACKING THE PLAYERS

Dusty was up early the next morning and put on the coffee. After a quick shower and getting dressed, she poured herself a big mug of courage to face the day. She went out and sat on the front porch steps, trying not to spill her overfilled cup. As she lowered herself down, her hand trembled ever so slightly and some of the dark brew landed on her shirt. She didn't let it upset her—there were plenty of other upsetting things on her mind.

Something in the back of her head kept turning over the Leathermans' involvement. Why had they been part of last night's horror? It didn't seem like they were merely innocent bystanders. Had the gunmen been there earlier?

Why park on the road if they were already at the Leathermans' cabin? It just didn't make sense, and the thought that Michael Yoder and his sister might have been kidnapped as children made her stomach sink to a new low. Life was cruel and unpredictable; if you didn't believe there was some kind of plan, you'd have no hope or faith to carry on. She needed to get a handle on all of this and find the common denominator—the thread running through each of these stories that would lead to the end of this long trail of betrayal. Poor Michael—how did he move past this and learn to trust again?

She decided to call Sarah and find out what she knew. Why had Sarah left and wanted nothing to do with her parents? If she knew, why hadn't she told her little brother? Dusty needed to know what Sarah's story was and how much she could answer.

Inside the cabin, Iola sat at the table with Walker. They both looked up and said, "Good morning." Dusty returned the greeting, grabbed her briefcase from the lamp table, pulled out her notebook, flipped to the page with Sarah's number, and made the call.

When Sarah picked up, Dusty introduced herself and said she needed to ask questions about the parents' disappearance. Sarah said she didn't want to be involved, and that set Dusty off—no one was ready for the rant that followed. She quickly brought Sarah up to date on what was happening with her brother and said that if she had to fly out to drag her there herself, she would. Dusty needed to know what Sarah knew—now.

Sarah was quiet. Then Dusty asked for names of anyone her parents may have mentioned; she wrote them down. Finally she said, "Sarah, listen to me. I expect you here tomorrow to give your brother some support. If you don't, I will find you. Do you understand? Don't for a minute think you can step away from this again. You should have been up front a long time ago—fear or no fear. Michael is, by a fluke in your life, your brother. Now step up and be a sister. I'll see you tomorrow, one way or another." She put the receiver down and closed her eyes. When she opened them, Iola and Walker were both staring.

"Well?" Iola said. "What's the story?"

As Dusty repeated the conversation with Sarah, she kept shaking her head. "In a nutshell: Sarah left when she was eighteen after seeing a flier in town about a missing girl from a car accident twelve years earlier. The family of the deceased parents were still searching for the child—who would now be eighteen. She said she went back to the farm and confronted the Yoders when memories flooded back at the sight of the flier. She knew immediately it was her, and she realized Michael had suffered a similar fate.

"She said the Yoders tried to lie, and when they saw she wasn't buying it, they locked her in a tool shed for two days with no food or water. She thought they were waiting for Michael to go to school on Monday so they could kill her and dispose of the body. She managed to outsmart them and got away. She wrote to Michael for a while, planning to bring him to her, but Michael was loyal to what he thought were his parents and wrote only everyday things. She feared for him, which is why she didn't tell him—he was so naive she thought he'd just tell them."

"After a while, she quit writing. It wasn't until Michael got out of the service that she heard from him again. He was a sweet boy, she said, and all she cared about was that he was away from them and safe. But when he wrote later saying his folks had moved in with him, she panicked and cut off all ties with him."

"She thought she might have alerted the people I was talking about when she ran an ad in the Lincoln paper trying to find the family who'd posted the flier. About a week after the ad ran, a man showed up at her home. She had no idea how he'd gotten her address—she'd used a post office box for the ad. The man was looking for the Yoders. She told him she didn't know where they were and that she never wanted to see them again."

"He asked about her brother, and when she questioned how he knew the Yoders, he said he'd been looking for a long time and would find them. He offered her $10,000 if she could put him on the right track. He left a number so she could leave a message and said he'd call back. As he was leaving he asked for a glass of water. She went to the kitchen and when she came back he was gone— and so was a stack of mail from a basket on her desk. She thinks he got Michael's address from those letters."

"She said she called to tell Michael, but Yoder Sr. answered the phone. She didn't know why, but all of a sudden every bit of contempt she'd felt for him and the woman she called "mother" spewed out. He hung up on her, but before he did, he called her a bitch and said he wished he'd killed her when he had the chance. A few days later, Michael called to tell her about the Yoders' disappearance. She thought, "Good riddance," and figured that would be the end of it. She had no idea the man who'd visited her was also a killer."

Walker asked, "What names did you get? Does she still have the phone number he left?"

Dusty tore the page from her notebook and handed it to him. Dusty went to her room to get her guns—only to find them gone. Then she remembered the deputy had taken them from her last night. She came back, looked at Iola with frustration, and said, "I have no guns, now what do I do?"

Iola went into the bedroom, came out with a .38, and handed it to Dusty. "Don't use it—I'm out of weapons to give you," she laughed, then sat back down with her coffee. Walker said, "Okay. What's the plan?"

Dusty sat with them without speaking for a long moment, then launched into a rant nobody expected.

"You know what gets me? How does a sister not contact the police about this? I get that she was scared, but how do you keep your brother safe—or at least tell someone about your own abduction? She must be as cold as the parents. Maybe she isn't quite right in the head, but I cannot imagine keeping something like this to yourself. She's right that Michael's on the naive side and wants to believe the best of his parents even after all that has happened—I don't think he wants to believe it."

Iola raised her hand to stop her for a moment. "It seems to me," she said, "when you're deprived of affection and love growing up, you create a scenario of excuses for the way things are—or you live in your own fantasy about it. Either way, those two are lucky to still be on earth. God must have had a plan to keep them alive all these years, because it seems like the Yoders would not have blinked at taking them out of the picture."

Iola paused, then asked, "Now—what's the plan for today?"

Dusty looked at Walker. "Is this an FBI case now? If so, what's next? I've got an idea where the money might be, and that makes me think the Yoders didn't go far. We might be dealing not only with the mob hunting for it but with someone working to retrieve it for the Yoders. I'm also curious about the Leathermans—last night just doesn't add up. If the thugs were there to kill them earlier, why would they come back and park down the road? If you'd already killed them, why wouldn't you wait and ambush me when I came back? Also—can we check if this phone has been tapped? Something doesn't add up, and I want to know who's on the playing field with us."

Walker looked at her, then took out his notebook and asked Iola, "Would you tell me everything you know about your neighbors and fill me in on your history up here in Overgaard?"

Iola said she'd met the Leathermans a year or so after her husband died, when they bought the Sanders' old cabin. She remembered meeting the Sanders on her first trip up with her new husband—very nice, older folks who'd been coming to the cabin for years. Mr. Sanders died shortly after her husband, and they sold the place to the Leathermans. About a year later she'd asked the Leathermans to keep an eye on her cabin; she gave them a key, and whenever she came up they'd get things ready for her. They'd been on her payroll for at least four years—she paid them a monthly fee to take care of things."

Walker asked if she had Social Security numbers for them and whether she could retrieve anything else she might have on them. "What's your husband's history up in this area? Was he from here?" he asked.

She said he'd grown up locally; his folks had owned the cabin and left it to him when they died. The story was that his grandfather had built the place into quite a fortress because he'd always been in one scrape or another with the law. That's why her husband became a lawyer—his family was always in court.

His birth certificate showed a home birth in Snowflake, not far from Overgaard. He'd gone to the University of Arizona for law school and knew people across the state. He'd built one of the best law firms in Arizona, representing high-profile clients. As far as she knew, he had a sterling reputation and was highly sought after. His passing—and the fact that he'd left everything to her—had bothered many people.

For a few years the cabin had been a source of contention among his partners; they wanted her to sell it for use as a retreat. When she refused, they became very

227

upset and even filed an illegal quitclaim deed trying to take it, but she fought them and kept the place. She told them she couldn't let it go because of all the happy memories she'd shared there with her husband.

Walker rose, went to the phone, dialed, and listened. When he hung up he nodded and said, "Yep—this line has a tap on it."

25

GRIEF ON THE FARM

They spent the next two hours on the phone and piecing together a bigger scenario of everything that had been happening. Trying to make sense of it all was overwhelming. When Walker finally got a call about the Leathermans, he learned their real names were Ron and Rita Russo from Chicago—and they had a pretty dark past.

Walker thought they'd been watching Iola's cabin not only for her but for her late husband's partners. They must have had ties to the mob and somehow been entangled with the hunt for Michael's parents. Something had linked them to the two men who'd come to take Dusty out. Iola suggested maybe the Russos had simply come over to check on why the two guys were lurking; it could have been a wrong place, wrong time thing—they might have overheard or seen something and been killed for it.

When they decided to head out to Michael's, they were all packing heat and ready for a showdown. Dusty laughed nervously at the sight as they climbed into the truck. Iola hadn't spoken since Walker's questioning, and Dusty could see how much it had drained her. Walker told them the tap on Iola's phone was a federal one, which added another dimension to the case. Dusty couldn't believe how complicated things had become—at that point she wasn't even sure who they were looking for or why.

They pulled into Michael's drive and honked a few times, but no one came out of the house or the barn. Dusty eased out of the truck and went up to the house. She almost laughed at the absurdity of having honked and then trying to be quiet.

When she peered through the front window she saw Sven lying on the living-room floor with a bullet hole in his forehead. She ran back to the truck and ordered Iola and Walker to get out and circle around to find Michael. Sven was dead, and Dusty was certain whoever'd killed him was either searching for Michael or already had him.

Iola went to the west side of the house and Walker to the east. Dusty entered through the front door with her gun drawn and moved quietly through the rooms.

She opened the basement door; it creaked as it swung all the way open. The stairs were steep and, though a light burned below, there was no sound. She stepped down two stairs and the hair on her neck prickled. She took another step and stopped.

She backed up, closed the door, and locked it from the inside. If someone was below, they'd have to leave via the outside entrance—in plain sight of her buddies circling the back.

She slipped out the back door and signaled Iola to head for the barn. Walker wasn't in sight. As Iola headed off, the basement door shook. Dusty knelt down, crawled to the door, and peered inside. Crawling was filthy and hard with a gun in her hand; she started to holster it when she heard a moan.

She pressed herself close to the rock-faced stairwell, glanced through the door window, and saw Michael tied to a chair in the lighted side of the basement—duct tape over his mouth and his arms bound to the chair. Without thinking, Dusty threw her shoulder into the door, forcing it open and shattering several small panes of glass. She ran to him, ripped the tape from his mouth, and began untying him. He babbled about Sven; she couldn't look at him. When she finished and looked up, Michael read the look on her face and knew Sven was dead.

He started up the basement stairs toward the house. Dusty asked, "Who did this? Where are they?" before she'd finished the sentence, a gunshot cracked. She bolted out of the basement toward the sound. Two more shots rang in quick succession. She quickly decided to head for the back of the barn.

A rope dangled from the loft opening where they stored hay; she grabbed it, jammed her .357 into its holster (awkwardly, and she prayed it wouldn't fall out), planted her feet on the barn siding, and started climbing. When she hauled herself into the loft she crawled to the edge and peered over.

Two men—one very short, one very tall—stood over a body. The body was Walker. Nearby lay another figure—it looked like Iola, and for a second Dusty thought she saw a slight movement of Iola's hand.

From a prone position, Dusty braced and fired. The tall man went down with a single shot to the back of the head. The short man spun and fired; the round whizzed past her and she dropped him with a second shot. She ran down the stairs and kicked the killers' guns away.

She bent over Walker and stifled a cry—he was dead. She went to Iola and pressed her fingers to the woman's neck. Iola startled, then whispered, "I think I was hit in the hip. I can't move my left leg." Michael came running through the big barn doors and Dusty told him to call for an ambulance. He ran back to the house.

Iola took Dusty's hand. "How bad is Walker?" she asked.

Dusty let out a ragged sob and the two of them wept together. When she'd regained a little control she searched the tall man's pockets—wallet, pocketknife, and a clip full of bullets. The wallet identified him as Raymond Polanski from Chicago; he carried a Teamsters card, a driver's license, and three hundred dollars. The second killer had no

ID but did have a business card for Beal Transportation Services.

Walker had it right, glancing at him, she broke down again. She mourned the loss of him so greatly that she felt as if her heart was being ripped out. Why? How did it go down? She had not even asked Iola what had happened. She only knew that he was gone.

The cops arrived before the ambulance and started asking questions Dusty didn't want to answer — not because she was hiding anything, but because Walker's death had hollowed her out and she couldn't find her voice. She didn't want them to see a weakened version of herself. Iola didn't care who heard her; she cried, cursed, and tried several times to get up but couldn't. She looked like a floundering fish hauled up in a net that couldn't breathe.

Dusty felt immobilized by grief until she heard one of the officers joke about Walker. "That shiny old FBI badge didn't help him much, did it?" he muttered.

She stood up, contempt curling through her, and walked out to the back of the barn to look at the large empty garden–two acres of prepared soil that hadn't been planted since the Yoders disappeared. She needed something to get her mind off Walker.

The ambulance arrived; Dusty went back in to be with Iola. Iola lay on her side, propping her head with her hand, trying to see what was happening. The medics checked Walker, then went straight to Iola. Within minutes they were loading her into the ambulance and heading for

Payson, probably on to Phoenix. "Do you need me to ride with you?" Dusty asked.

Iola answered in a broken voice, "No. If you're up to it, stay and finish this. Find the money and turn it over to the Feds. Sarah should be here tomorrow—don't be surprised if she knows more than she's letting on. I'll call and get another agent out here; Walker's office knows the direction he was heading and they can pick it up from there. Don't let your guard down, not for a second." She lay her head back and closed her eyes.

That was exactly what Dusty wanted to do, but she couldn't bear to see Walker placed in a body bag. She went into the house where Sven was being prepared for removal and tried to get Michael to come into the kitchen with her, but he was in no state to move. "Michael, can you tell me what happened? When did those guys show up? What did they say? Were they looking for your folks?" she asked.

He tried to compose himself but was too distraught to answer. She told him to lie down and rest while she figured out the next steps, but he sat frozen as if he hadn't heard.

The two deputies who'd been at the barn returned after the medics removed the body. Dusty sat in the big comfy chair, hoping to fall asleep so she could ignore the assholes from the barn, but her mind was in overdrive and when they got out their notebooks she was ready.

They asked why she'd been at Michael's farm and whether she knew someone had been shot before she arrived. She asked what they actually knew about the shooting from the previous night. They said they were aware of one incident and asked if she thought the two events were related. Dusty took a deep breath and briefed them on the cabin attack and why she'd come to Overgaard. When she said they were trying to piece everything together and move forward, the deputies exchanged looks of disbelief.

"What?" she asked. "Don't you have a briefing before each shift?"

They admitted they normally did, but because they were short-handed that morning they hadn't. "How did you know Walker was FBI if you hadn't been told?" she pressed.

The deputies glanced at one another and said the FBI involvement had been mentioned and they'd seen Walker's badge. They both apologized for upsetting her with their uncalled for remark; she just looked at them.

"You both will have to live a long time to hold a candle to Agent Walker. He was a fine man and a good agent. We've lost one of the best. Think long and hard before you make a joke about someone's passing — life's too precious for that."

They were silent for a few minutes until Dusty asked, "Michael, do you feel up to helping me look around, or do you need to do something else?"

Michael stood, shrugged, and said, "What do you want me to do?" She looked at the deputies and asked what else they needed from them. They said they'd check in with the station and return later. Then he smiled and said, "I will need to take your gun. We got the other gal's and the agent's but I need yours for sure since you downed them."

"What a weird expression to use." Dusty said, as she handed over the .38 Iola had given her that morning.

"Where can we find you if we have any other questions?" one deputy asked.

"I'll be here with Michael," Dusty said. "If anything changes, I'll leave word for you."

"All right," the other deputy replied. "We'll check back."

They drove out of the driveway, and Dusty collapsed into the overstuffed chair; she and Michael sat there together, stricken with grief and unable to move for the longest time.

26

THE HUNT BEGINS

When Dusty and Michael finally stood, they looked at one another and tried to take in the full scale of what had happened. The hollow feeling in her stomach and the pale pallor of Michael barely hinted at the bottomless pit they were trying to climb out of. Only putting this case to rest would set them on a course where they could begin to heal.

"Are you up to going over the morning before I arrived?" Dusty asked.

He nodded and began. "We'd just finished clearing the breakfast table when we heard someone walking around the side of the house. Sven headed for the front door to see who it was — and as he opened it he was shot. He staggered back and fell so hard it seemed unreal. I ran over and got down to help him up, and that's when the man who shot him walked in and dragged me to a chair in the kitchen."

He continued, "I just kept saying Sven's name over and over until the second guy came in and hit me so hard I lost a tooth. He told me to shut up and if I didn't want to end up the same I'd better tell him where the old folks were. I told him I didn't know where they'd gone or if they were alive. I asked why he'd shot Sven and he said, 'I'm not gonna wrestle a bear — better to remove him.' Then he laughed."

"The other guy said, 'Let's take a look around,' and dragged me around while they opened closets and looked under beds. When we got to the basement door they threw me down the steps and tied me to a chair. If I didn't help them find the old folks, he said, he'd kill me too. I lied and said I didn't know they lived in the barn, not the house–I don't know why I said it. I thought maybe they'd take me out to the barn and I could make a run for it. They went upstairs and I heard them on the phone, getting orders. They kept saying 'copy that, copy that.' It seemed like forever before they went out the back door to the barn."

"I tried to get free but couldn't. Then I heard someone coming down the stairs — you stopped and I panicked. I started kicking things, scooting the chair toward the outside door, but it wasn't working. A few minutes later, I heard you at the back of the house, talking low. I was so afraid you'd go to the barn and they'd shoot you. I kicked a big piece of wood toward the door; when it hit the glass it rattled — and the next thing I know you came crashing through and freed me. Before I could say anything, there were gunshots and you took off for the barn. I finished untying myself and just stood in the basement doorway. I heard the second set of shots, then three more, and then it went quiet. I waited a bit and then ran for the barn doors. When I got there I saw your friends were shot. You told me to call for an ambulance. I guess someone had already called the cops, or maybe that happened automatically when they heard the shooting — they seemed to roll up pretty fast."

"Michael, what kind of weapons do you have?" Dusty asked. "I need a handgun or a rifle, and so do you. One of each if you have them."

He went back into the house and returned with a canvas bag. "Rifles are in the barn," he said.

They headed to the barn, sat on a hay bale, and loaded three handguns: an old .45, a Colt .38, and a WWII Ruger. He had ammo for all of them and they loaded with the intent to put a hole in anyone who showed up to fight. In the tack shed they found two bolt-action Remingtons and a double-barrel shotgun.

Dusty thought of her mom's bolt-action and wished she'd practiced more at the range. She'd watched her mom make it look easy, but Dusty had never fired one. *Well— there's a first time for everything.* She thought as she holstered the .38, grabbed a .270, and said, "Let's go look around a bit."

She walked out through the plowed garden and paced the full two acres before Michael finally said, "What the hell are you looking for?"

Dusty stopped and looked at him. "The money."

He frowned. "I'm pretty sure they took it with them. Wouldn't they need it? Why would they leave it here?"

She met his gaze sternly. "They might've taken what was in the drawer in the bedroom, but I think there was a lot more where that came from. When they arrived, you said they only had two suitcases, but in the barn I found two large shipping tags like you use on trunks. I think at some point they had it sent to them or they'd hidden it before you even knew they were here. You said they didn't arrive on the train they claimed to be on. I think they were watching you the whole time. Sometime after they settled in, they went and got the money and buried it on your property. There's a good chance they're coming back for it."

"I also talked with Sarah. She knew from the night before she left that you and she had both been abducted as children. She left you there, knowing they'd threatened to kill her — she left you in harm's way. I don't get your sister, but I told her to show up tomorrow or I'll come get her myself. I don't know if she's behind these thugs or working with Lucky Beal, but I think she's involved. Now we need to find where they stashed the money. It could be from multiple robberies, hard to say, but I'll find out. Our friends died defending us, and with God as my witness, they'll pay for taking our friends' lives. Now, are you with me? Or do I ride alone?"

"I'm with you. Should I saddle the horses, or do you want to take the truck?" he asked. "If we find it we might need the truck to haul it—what do you think?"

"I already know where they hid the money," she said. "I just need to find where they've been hiding—whether it's your folks, your sister, or people they hired. Someone's been keeping a pretty close eye on your place for a long time. The men today were looking for people, not money—they never opened a drawer or anything small enough to hide cash in. I don't think Lucky has ever cared about the money so much as revenge for his son's death."

"Your sister, on the other hand, knows a lot more than she's saying. My bet is she's the one looking for the money if it's not the old folks. Hell, maybe she's helping them and put on a show for you so she could stay back and orchestrate everything. I don't know for sure, but she's up to her eyeballs in this. If she hated them as much as she claims, maybe she did them in before she found out the details of where it was."

"Let's get going—we're burning daylight. Saddle the horses; I need to make a phone call first. I won't be long."

27

UNMASKING SARAH

When Dusty finished her phone call she walked out the back door and stood looking at the scene, replaying the day that had just changed their world. What could she have done differently to spare Walker? Her heart ached for him—her Cheyene had come to help and had ended up dead. Tears rolled down her cheeks and a soft breeze brushed across her. A low vibration of a flute drifted in; Wampacha was near. She said his name out loud and immediately heard his deep, soft voice.

Little one, do not cry. Your friend walked to the other side with me; his destiny crossed yours, but you did not cause his passing. Remember when you noticed his aura? He was already receiving the vibrations for his transition yesterday. We each have a plan for our journey, and though you will miss him, he is needed elsewhere. Do not mourn him—this is not the end but the beginning of another road.

"So he was already going—nothing could have stopped it?" she asked. "What is there waiting for us? A ghost highway to take us to the next adventure? I'm finding this hard to believe. Why do the people we love have to go away, get sick, or die trying to do something good? Why?"

The ghost highway, as you call it, is a beautiful place. It gives each traveler rewards and memories to carry them on to a higher plane. It waits for all of us—that is the beauty of the journey. Breathe deep and remember happy times. Today you will set the course right for many and clear the old memories that have haunted them and held them back from loving and having happiness. Listen to your gut and know that pure evil awaits you on a rocky path. Go with no fear and eliminate the one who is manipulating the situation. It will come to an end today. So mote it be.

Wampacha's words were so tender she wanted to cry again.

Michael came out of the barn holding Whinnie and Buster by the reins. Dusty walked over and said a quiet prayer for them and for the day ahead. Wampacha had scared the hell out of her with "pure evil"; she only hoped she could make the bad go away or at least get through it alive.

"Which way are we heading?" he asked.

She turned halfway in her saddle and scanned the terrain quickly. "I saw some small shacks up the hill when we rode out the other day. Let's check them—maybe someone's camped there to watch comings and goings at the farm. Keep a sharp eye and stay close. Did you bring binoculars?"

"Yes—we each have a pair in our saddlebags. Those shacks are about a hundred yards apart and usually used for tools or shelter in a storm. The cattle should be over the ridge past the sheds; I have a wrangler with them. His name is Cody and he'll be riding a dapple-gray mare. He'll recognize us, but be cautious. I can't lose anyone else and neither can you." He snapped Buster with the reins and they were off. Dusty knew he'd left quickly so she wouldn't see him cry for Sven, but she felt his heartbreak.

Whinnie had an easy gait; Dusty loved the climb up the hill–if only it were a pleasure ride and not a march toward a showdown with the past. She hoped this would be over soon so she could go home and see her family.

Before they left Michael's, Dusty had checked on Iola and her father. Iola would be in the hospital a day or so, but she'd notified the FBI about Walker's death; they were sending a team, and it sounded serious. "How are you holding up? What's the plan?" Iola had asked.

Dusty told her about the outbuildings and where they were heading. She promised to call the hospital after they returned. When she hung up, she phoned her mother.

"Mom, how is it going? Are you and Daddy holding up okay?" she asked.

"We're okay—just waiting on test results. We won't make it up there this time, but maybe later this summer when we know more about Daddy," her mother said, sounding worn. Dusty promised it would be another time and mentioned she had the perfect horse for her to ride. At the idea of riding a mare, her mother's voice lit up like a little girl. "What kind? What's her name?" she asked excitedly.

"How did you know it was a mare? Her name's Whinnie; you're going to love her. I'll take some pictures before I head home to show you this place and the steed that awaits you." They laughed and said their goodbyes.

When Dusty put the phone down and looked at the exact spot where Sven had lain that morning, she trembled. She gave herself a stern little speech, forced her jaw to set, and walked out the door to meet another grieving human who was trying to get it together. She grabbed her camera bag and some snacks from the truck and moved toward the sheds on the hill.

She swept the rise with a wide scan, watching the tree line for movement. Nothing seemed out of place, though the cattle were mooing in the distance. Michael was veering left of the shed and motioning for her to join him. She angled Whinnie that way and rode up beside him. He wore a nervous, very serious expression.

"What do you see? What's wrong?" she asked.

"I see two riders by the herd, and someone's had a campfire by the west shed. I didn't feel it, but it looks like it was used recently. I'm going down to the herd to talk to Cody and see who's with him."

"I'm coming," Dusty said. "We should not separate if we don't have to. Does the second rider look male or female?"

"Can't tell from here. Let's go take a look." Michael launched his horse into a dead run and she gave chase, hoping to catch him before he reached the riders.

As they closed the distance, the man Michael called Cody on the dapple-gray turned toward them and trotted out. The other rider shoved a hat down tight and took off north at a gallop.

When Dusty reached Michael, he yelled, "Not sure who it is. Cody says she showed up at the shed and told him I sent her out to relieve him."

Dusty tapped Whinnie in the flank and took off. She didn't know exactly what she planned to do, but she couldn't let this mystery rider get away. She kept the rider in sight and rode for what felt like a long time. At the top of a hill she pulled up and looked back and saw that Michael was about a mile behind, working his way toward her. She drew the binoculars from her saddlebag and scanned ahead, searching for a flash of red flannel.

She caught a glint of metal in the trees: a pickup with a camper tucked among the trunks. Two people stood at the tailgate; a blonde woman and a short dark-haired man in a green Army coat. Both held rifles; the woman wore a sidearm. Dusty waited for Michael to reach her and then handed him the binoculars. When he lowered them his face looked bewildered.

"Do you recognize them?" she asked.

"That's Lily Dodge, and that's her boss at the Farm Bureau," Michael said. "I met him once. She introduced him as her boss when we were out for dinner. I never thought anything of it. What are they doing here? What does this have to do with any of this?"

"If I had to guess," Dusty said, "she's been spying on you all along. While your folks were still here. She got cozy with you and then when they disappeared. She removed herself from the picture for a while. I think that your girlfriend is in with whoever else is after the money. I still don't believe that Lucky Beal is looking for it; he is just looking for them. Somewhere along the line, your folks took a large sum of money and whoever knows about that is who Lily works for. We should circle them and see what they say. They shouldn't be on your land. What did Cody tell you?"

"What did Cody have to say?" She asked.

Michael was a little hesitant, but he finally found his voice and gave her the rundown. "Cody said she rode up and said I had sent her from the house to tell him about Sven being killed. She told him that the shooter was a young

247

woman who was after my parents and the money they had. She said that I wanted to warn him to be on the lookout for you and to shoot to kill. That you were a type of mercenary and not to hesitate to pull the trigger. When I told him you worked for me and that you had not killed Sven, he said that he was sure glad I rode up because if you had come alone he would have put a round in you and asked questions later."

Micheal looked concerned and mentioned,"He did not question what she said because he knew that she was a friend of mine from Pine. He said he had seen me with her before, and that she had rode up a couple times before, alone, as if she was just out for a ride. When I told him I had no idea who she was, he told me he had seen her with me at the cattle auction last year. I knew then that he was talking about Lily, but I did not want to believe it until I saw her through the binoculars. What a dummy I am. She was just using me the whole time."

"Don't be so hard on yourself," Dusty said. "These people are methodical and patient. I wonder who they work for. Let's go find out."

With that, they both rode out—attempting to get closer to the answers they needed to figure this thing out.

Dusty rode up within a short distance of the truck, dismounted Whinnie, and tied the horse to a loose pine branch, pulled the rifle out of its sheath, and began slowly walking toward the vehicle. She got close enough to make out their words.

She took the safety off the .38 and rotated a shell into the chamber. Ten feet more and she set the rifle against a tree, pulled the revolver from the holster, and dropped to the ground to listen. The first clear word she heard was the name Sarah — just what she had suspected. Michael's sister was behind all of this.

Suddenly all hell broke loose as Michael came riding in. He dismounted quickly, but any cover he might have had was gone. He found himself standing with two rifles pointed at him and stammering. "What the hell is going on, Lily? What are you mixed up in? Who sent you to spy on me and my family? Do you know where my parents are? And get that gun out of my face!" he yelled.

Lily told him to shut up and to throw his gun over to her, nice and slow. He looked startled and didn't respond. "Put your gun on the ground and step back from it. Do it now," she ordered. As he obeyed, the man with her shoved him to the ground, pulled out a pair of handcuffs, and started to snap them on Michael.

Dusty stepped out and made herself known. Lily and the man turned and aimed. Dusty aimed for the handgun the man had trained on her and fired. He went down. Lily fired the rifle, but Dusty had already lunged and rolled to the side of the truck. As Lily stepped out, another shot rang from the other side of the vehicle. Dusty thought Michael had managed to retrieve his weapon or that the man had shot him.

She stayed flat and fired at the only clear target she had — Lily's ankle. The round hit with such force it blew half the ankle out of Lily's boot. The scream that followed was horrifying. Dusty sprang up, disarmed Lily and saw that Michael had shot the man and taken his weapon.

"Put the handcuffs on him and find the key. Get it off him and stow it," Dusty ordered. Lily still screamed. Dusty ran to the truck, dug around, and came back with duct tape. She taped what was left of Lily's boot together and wrapped the injured leg as tight as she could. "That'll have to work until we get you to a doc. Doesn't look like your friend was so lucky. I guess the trip won't bother him at all. Now you can ride in the truck or you can walk–depends on how quick you start talking."

Dusty leaned back on the tailgate and stared at the sniveling blonde. "Well?" she said.

Between sobs, she finally gave the information Dusty needed to unravel half of the forty-year saga. Sarah was behind much of it and had not realized the full involvement of organized crime until Dusty called her. She'd been trying for years to get the Yoders to move the money. When Michael called to say his folks were living with him, Sarah thought the timing was perfect.

For years she'd sent anonymous threatening letters to the Yoders to make them think someone close knew about the money. When they moved to Arizona, she staked out the place with hired men to watch for the stash, and sure enough one day their vegetable wagon came back with more than vegetables. They took it into the barn — and that was the last she ever saw of it. Over the years, Sarah noticed other people spying on the place and assumed they were men the parents had hired. She planned to wait until they moved the cash and then 'rob the robbers,' but the money never reappeared."

When Dusty arrived, Sarah tightened her surveillance and planted spies as workers on the farm. She told Lily she knew the money had never left the property. Lily said she'd been in the barn when Agent Walker came in; she panicked and shot him. Iola came around another corner, and two men stepped out and shot at them both. Lily fled to the shack expecting someone to be after her, but no one chased. When Dusty heard Lily admit she'd shot Walker, she nearly pulled the trigger again. If they hadn't caught Lily, the shooter might have vanished; ballistics would have told part of the story, but Lily would've been gone.

What worried Dusty next was that Sarah had planted spies among the farm workers. She leaned in, right in Lily's face. "Now tell me, what workers did Sarah put in? How many? Names and descriptions."

Lily confessed: two of the crop workers and the cowboy Cody were Sarah's plants. Dusty's heart jumped to her throat. She was relieved Michael hadn't left earlier without knowing Cody was one of the bad guys. Michael looked shaken; Dusty wasn't sure how much longer he would hold it together.

"I think we'll take the road back and avoid confronting Cody right now," Dusty said sternly. "Let the S.O. handle the farmhands and send someone for Cody."

Michael nodded, mounted Buster, and Dusty handed him Whinnie's reins. They started back toward the farm.

Before they left, Dusty wrote down the details about Sarah that Lily had given and slipped the note into the glove compartment. She reloaded her handgun and Michael's rifle. When she slipped the rifle back into Michael's saddle scabbard, he grabbed her hand.

"I probably would be dead at the end of this if I hadn't called you," he said. "I'm such an idiot. I never imagined any of this."

She patted his hand. "Don't worry. We've got it under control, and it'll be over soon." She told him he was welcome to come with her to fetch Sarah once she'd handed Lily and her accomplice to the police.

They put Lily and the man in the camper of the truck, searched them thoroughly for other weapons, and locked the camper with the key they'd found on the ignition ring.

Dusty said she'd take the old logging road down the back way and drive slowly so Michael could keep up. She retrieved the rifle she'd left at the shrub and loaded it in the front of the truck. She slid behind the wheel, turned east, and headed back to the scene of the mess. It was going to be a bumpy ride–she smiled at the thought.

Maybe Lily would bleed out on the way down. One could only hope.

Wampacha's voice cut through the thought and scared the hell out of her.

Do not become one of the haters. Do your job and keep it a reckoning, not a vengeance you seek.

She considered it for a moment. "I'll try, but it won't be easy."

Two wrongs won't make a right. Move past your emotion and you'll know I'm telling you the best way forward, whispered Wampacha.

Dusty said, "Well, right now all I can think about is the loss of a good man and what a waste. It may never come to me, that I should not owe him and the life he lost, to seek vengeance for the insanity of it. Why did he have to die? Why?"

It was his time, little one. Let it go, Wampacha said softly.

28

WHAT'S BURIED IS FOUND

When they finally drove up to the farmhouse a patrol car was sitting there waiting for them. Dusty climbed out of the truck and motioned for Michael to take the horses to the barn. She walked slowly up to the first deputy and explained the situation. The second deputy stood inside the house listening through the screen door.

When she finished and neither officer said a word, that sick feeling started in her stomach. She was pretty sure Sarah had heard her updating the officers and now had a gun leveled at them from inside. Damn — she wished she'd waited for Michael to come back from the barn to fill everyone in. Maybe Sarah would have played along a while. It was too late to worry about it now.

Dusty stepped back and turned toward the truck. "One of you come help me unload the varmints I brought back," she said, forcing a laugh. She made it to the truck door before she heard the screen open and Sarah's voice, hard and cold, tell her to turn around and drop her gun.

Dusty kept opening the truck door as if she hadn't heard a word. She pretended to be getting the keys from the ignition while really pulling a gun from the seat. When she looked up, a hard woman stared back at her — a woman who looked like she'd been on a long trail and this was the last stop before the showdown she'd been working toward. Sarah had a handgun pressed to the back of the deputy's head and Dusty knew she would shoot.

Well, so be it, Dusty thought. But before Sarah could take the shot, a voice rang out behind her.

"Put the gun down, Sarah. The gig's up and you lose. I'll take you out and not have a minute's remorse — drop the gun," Michael commanded.

Sarah shoved the deputy forward and swung to face Michael. Her gun clicked as she chambered a round — and Michael fired the old Ruger. Sarah's shot hit the porch ceiling instead of her intended target. Suddenly everyone scrambled. The two deputies fumbled for their weapons and Michael tucked his pistol into his waistband.

Dusty smiled at him. "I hope you put the safety on — wouldn't want you to shoot yourself." He laughed, she laughed, and then they both realized how close to hysterical they were: nerves shredded, at the end of their rope. They sat on the front porch steps in silence until other officers and the FBI rolled up. There was nothing more to do today; tomorrow they would get the money and sort things out.

The FBI arrived along with Navajo County deputies, the medical examiner, an ambulance, and a lot of chaos: questions, answers, paperwork. In the midst of it, Dusty and Michael went out and did the evening feeding and chores. Dusty even took a picture of Whinnie and Buster to send to her mom. It had been a long day; now they were getting ready for tomorrow.

Dusty spoke with the FBI and told them she'd be there at daybreak to show them where the money was. "Have a way to get it out of Overgaard as quickly as possible," she told them. The commander looked at her skeptically. "So you think you know where the money is? What makes you think that?"

She gave him a weak smile. "It's the next piece of business–the money–and I can't go home until we turn it over to you. See you at daybreak."

Dusty left Michael at sunset, both of them with tears in their eyes, and drove back to her cabin to call Iola with an update. Iola answered on the first ring. Dusty walked her through the afternoon, how she'd shot someone, and how Michael had shot too. She could hear Iola gasping. When Dusty finished, Iola said she needed time to think and would talk when she got back. Dusty warned she might not be back the next day; it would depend on how long it took to recover the money.

"First you have to find out where it is," Iola said.

"I know where it is," Dusty told her. "I just don't know how much there is. I'll call in the morning."

When Dusty hung up, Iola sat holding the phone and talking to herself. *When did she figure out where the money was?* Iola smiled. *Of course, Dusty had figured it out.* The little cowgirl never ceased to amaze her. She couldn't wait for the rest of the story tomorrow. Iola would save the details about Michael's abduction and who his real parents were for another day.

Dusty dialed her folks next. A winded voice finally answered—Layne. Dusty asked about everyone and whether Dad's tests had come back. Layne said she'd just come home from the hospital; they'd admitted their daddy because of a rapid heartbeat. They'd gotten it under control and would keep him overnight or maybe a couple days. Layne was glad; until they got it regulated, the hospital was the best place. Mom and Milo would be home later. Layne had to go to work at St. Joseph's on the swing shift that night and had a clinic in the morning. "Call back in a couple hours and you can reach Mom," she said, then hung up.

Dusty sat looking out the window, thinking of her dad in that hospital bed. She wondered whether he'd heard about the shootings in Overgaard and whether that had set his heart racing. Life felt fragile and fleeting; she couldn't bear imagining her family not being there. They probably felt the same thinking of her and her line of work—every ring of the phone could bring bad news. Wampacha had said there was a plan; that everyone would be present in one dimension or another. He'd told her death was an illusion on this plane.

She took a long hot shower, washed her hair, and stood under the water until it went cold. After she put on pajamas she hunted for her slippers; the wood floor had a few splinters and she crouched to look under the bed. Her slippers were hiding there with an arsenal of weapons.

She pulled them on and examined the guns one by one. They were all loaded and ready: a deer rifle, two sawed-off shotguns, and an assortment of handguns. She couldn't imagine who'd put them there. They had no dust on them–either they'd been cleaned recently or they hadn't been there very long. Either way, she needed to know how they'd gotten there.

She called Iola immediately; Iola answered in a sleepy voice. Dusty told her what she'd found and started asking questions. Iola finally said, "Stop. I need to think a minute. Secure the premises while I figure it out."

"All the doors are locked and the windows do their job," Dusty said. "What else should I do, and who are we expecting?"

Iola replied, "At the hinge side of the doors, between the door and the wall, there are slots that five-foot-long 2x6s fit into. Drop them across the door into the metal holders. Barring the door with those will keep you safe when you're inside the cabin. Move the guns to the left corner of the bedroom you're sleeping in and lift the corner up—it's a trap door. You can put the guns down there and also use that door as an escape hatch. It won't open from the outside, so you can only leave through it. Also check the shed for fire extinguishers—the Russos were supposed to keep them up to date."

"What I think is going on, but can't be sure of, is the Russos were using our cabin to store what might be needed for a standoff, knowing their cabin wouldn't be the place to hole up. The cabin has a history in town– everyone knew it was a fortress. When I refused to sell it to the firm, they probably moved people nearby and figured they could break in if they needed to since it was empty most of the time. I know this is part of a universal plan, that these two scenarios came together as they did so you could put an end to it. There's no telling the trail of evil that will be uncovered from this disappearance. Any feeling about where the elder Yoders are?"

"I think the sister killed them," Dusty said. "I'll tell the FBI and have them check out her place in New Mexico. I think she took them there and ended up killing them, so she had no choice but to stake out Michael's farm for as long as it took to find the money. She always knew it was there–at least that's what Lily Dodge said. Sarah didn't live long enough to tell me anything. Michael meant to kill her; I don't blame him. She was as evil as the parents, maybe worse. She might have a darker past than even we're aware of. It just goes on and on–the evil we're surrounded with. It makes me very sad."

Dusty sighed as she finished her talk with Iola. The moment she hung up she broke down and cried for her

Cheyene; the light he'd brought her was gone, and life was starting to put too many holes in her heart.

She did what Iola had told her and went down into the trap door to see how it worked. She left several handguns out and put the rest in the hideaway. She called her mother back and asked about her daddy and how she was holding up. Armindia said all was well and they were going to get it straightened out soon. She worried about how Myron would handle things if he couldn't be a deputy anymore; she knew he'd hate a desk job. Dusty told her God had a plan and they had to have faith it would work out. Her mother agreed and hoped to see her soon. They said good night.

Dusty climbed into bed, said her prayers, and waited for the flute to send her to slumberland.

The next morning she woke before daylight. She dressed, armed herself, and tucked an extra handgun into her waistband to leave in the truck. She was sure the cops would want to take hers today. She called the S.O. substation and identified herself, asking for an update on Lily Dodge and whether the male's body had been identified.

She was told the FBI had taken over the investigation. Eight dead and two wounded—the numbers were growing, and Dusty felt like a one-woman gunfight moving from town to town. Maybe she'd soon be considered a gunslinger. As she thought of that and the litter of souls left behind in each case she handled, she could almost see herself wearing the old-west name like a badge–a righteous warrior who happened to be a gunslinger.

The sun was just up when she hit the road for Michael's. Today might be the end of it all, and she was ready to go home.

Michael sat on the front porch amid yellow tape. "I'm not supposed to be out here; it's a crime scene," he said with a laugh.

He told her to go around to the back door and into the kitchen; he was at the table when she came through.

"Want some coffee? It just finished brewing. I'm drinking yesterday's, warmed up. Sven's last pot."

She poured a cup and held it up. "Here's to your good buddy Sven–never a better sidekick. Happy trails, Sven. We'll see you on the other side when our journey is over." She smiled and took a big drink.

"Do you believe that?" Michael asked.

"Which part? That we'll see him again? You bet I do. If I don't, what does anything mean? I believe we've been together many times before." She said.

Michael laughed. "Sven always said we'd been brothers in another lifetime. Now you say the same. Must be something to it. May I ask you a personal question?

She looked up from her coffee.

"Were you in love with Agent Walker?" He asked, "You seem attached to him."

"I wasn't in love," Dusty said. "I didn't know him long enough for that. I did love him though. He was a kind, sweet lawman who sought justice for those who couldn't get it themselves. The world lost a bright light. He must have been needed elsewhere. I'm honored to have known him. Sven was special too. He was your protector for a lot of years—a guardian angel."

"Funny, that's what he said about you after you left that first day. He said God sent you a guardian angel tough as nails. I didn't think you'd be back, but he said you would because you'd save me. I laughed at him and said I didn't need saving. But I guess I did."

They talked over coffee until trucks pulled up out front. After chores, they planned to use Michael's tractor with the big scoop to dig in the second acre of the vegetable plot. Dusty headed to the house to talk to the FBI.

The bureau commander, Agent Dan Shaver, introduced himself with a goofy smile as he updated her. Lily Dodge's gunshot wound might cost her the foot, Cody and two laborers were in custody and being interrogated, and Lily had given up what she knew about Sarah and the payroll she'd run for years—spy duty and a string of convenience store robberies and burglaries. Sarah had told Lily the Yoders had stolen millions over the years from various bank robberies and murders. They were hard-core criminals and Sarah had followed that path.

Dusty told him she believed the Yoders were dead and that Sarah had killed them, probably at her New Mexico place. Agents had been sent to check that out and he'd know more later.

"We'll need laborers to bring up the money," Dusty said. "If you're ready, let's get started."

He said with a grin, "I am all yours, let's go."

She wanted to ask him what was so funny, but they were burning daylight, and she hoped her hunch was correct now that she had everyone here.

They headed to the barn. Dusty showed Shaver the trunk tags and the trapdoor that uncovered a dark stairway under the barn—ten to twelve feet down.

She'd gone in and seen deep drag marks. The tunnel had been shored up like a mine shaft. She thought the Yoders had found it and brought the money there to hide. She'd marked it so it could be dug later.

Shaver suggested dragging it back through the tunnel.

Dusty shook her head. "I guess you didn't notice the booby trap at the end of the shaft. If we open it from this end it's set to cave in or blow up. I thought we'd dig from the other end."

He shook his head and laughed. "Little lady, you need to come work for the Bureau. We need your insight and the comic relief."

"You think this is funny? I'm not here to entertain you. You should be thanking me for saving your ass, not laughing." She walked to Michael, who looked like a kid on that big tractor. Maybe smiling wasn't so bad after all; she'd apologize to Shaver later.

Everyone assembled at the tractor and Michael began digging. Dusty told him how far down the tunnel was and where to start.

With the first shovel full she yelled, "Do you think we should clear the animals out of the barn in case of blast or fire?" He nodded and shut off the engine.

Shaver sent an agent back toward the farmhouse. Dusty and a farmhand started putting ropes around the horses and moving them out to pasture on the east side of the barn. They ran the goats, pigs, and chickens out of the coop. Dusty wore the helmet and goggles an agent tossed her and kept working.

For two hours they watched Michael dig deeper and deeper. When the trunks finally came up it looked like a meteor hit the ground–they were huge, much larger than she'd expected. There were six of them. They loaded the trunks onto trucks to be examined and traced to their sources.

Forty years of evidence. She saw old silver certificates on the top of one trunk when they opened it. As the fifth trunk was being loaded there was a large explosion and the ground around them began falling away. She yelled for the trucks to leave and for everyone to run. The back side of the barn started to lean and she thought it was coming down, but then everything stopped moving and went silent.

The barn held; it was a miracle, and so was her ability to put this case to rest. In her mind, she knew that what had happened here would follow her in some significant way for the rest of her life. A love lost, a friend found, and yet still so many unanswered questions. Only the future held the answers, and she was ready to move into it.

29

COUNTING BLESSINGS

The next morning she packed up her stuff, cleaned out the refrigerator, locked the truck in the shed, and secured the cabin. The morning was almost as emotional as the evening before had been.

Saying goodbye to Michael was hard, and she hoped their paths would cross again. She knew she would be back up to the cabin; it was a part of her now, and being here was a comfortable old memory. She didn't know where it came from, but she felt she had to be a part of this cabin and this area again.

It was as if she had come back from a long journey and found it all waiting for her. The evil she had dealt with had nothing to do with the feelings she had for Overgaard.

This area held a part of her heart that she didn't even know was missing until she stayed in the cabin.

When she pulled the Mustang out that morning, she felt like she was storing part of an earlier life that had been good, fruitful, and sprinkled with magic. The Mustang felt good, and as she made the turn onto Green Mountain Rd., she waved goodbye to the magical cabin with a tear in her eye.

The trip down into the valley was uneventful, but not as peaceful a drive as coming up through Pine had been. After she got through Payson, she felt the excitement return—excitement to see her family and take the next step in helping with the dilemma they were in.

She also wanted to stop and see Iola and find out how she was doing. She drove to the office first, and since the drive was much faster coming down 87A, she would make it by lunch.

As she drove into Phoenix, with its hustle and bustle, it made her more aware of how being in the country had done some good for her. But the thought of a good cup of joe put a smile on her face, and she acknowledged that there was something good in every place you journey—you just have to look for it.

She went into the office, said hello to everyone, and headed for Iola's office, making a quick stop in the break room. She had coffee in one hand and a donut in the other when she realized she had forgotten to eat the day before. She had made the entire drive back with no coffee or food of any kind after her coffee with Michael. That just blew her away—she had never forgotten coffee or food. What did that mean? Surely it had some significance to her well-being. She would ask Wampachaw tonight. Right now, she was famished.

She went back to the receptionist and asked if a lunch order had been put in yet. When the answer was no, she put one in for Johnny's to be delivered. This was Friday, and she ordered the special for herself, Iola, and Missy, the receptionist. They had fish and chips, but she just didn't feel like fish today, so she ordered the Italian sub special. She was drooling just thinking about it.

She knocked on Iola's door as she walked in. Iola was asleep in the chair. They probably had her on painkillers for her injury, but she was snoring like crazy. It was pretty loud, so Dusty quietly closed the door and went to her own office.

She walked over to the window and watched people down below—they looked like ants. She stood there until the donut was gone, then she sat down at her desk and put her feet up. After a few minutes, she picked up the phone and dialed her mom to see what was new. If her dad was still in the hospital, she would stop by and see him before heading to their house.

The corridors of the hospital were shiny and quiet. She saw a doctor and her mother standing down the hall in front of her daddy's room, talking in a conference-type circle with a nurse. Her mother looked up and smiled at Dusty. She reached for her hand and then introduced her to Dr. Bowlin. His name badge said Head of Cardiology, and he gave her hand a solid shake before resuming his information to her mother. Armindia said, "Let's go in and tell Myron what you have found, and discuss what our options are." With that, they turned and went into the room with her daddy.

She hung back at the door and waited until she was called in to participate in the conversation. Her daddy looked ashen and tired. Her mother was standing tall and stern while Dr. Bowlin was earnestly telling them that the news was life-changing.

Her daddy would not be able to be on patrol anymore. He would be on medication for life, and though it would not affect anything he wanted to do, it would not be acceptable with department protocol. He was done being a patrol officer, and to her daddy this was devastating. He was pissed, ready to fight the system, but the doctor said it would do no good. He was sorry, but that was the way it was going down.

As the doctor turned to leave, he said in a very matter-of-fact way that in most cases, his life would take on a different meaning—probably more important to him than being a patrolman—but only he could move forward with the positivity that would make that happen.

They sat there listening to the doctor's footsteps fade away in the polished corridor, taking with him all of her dad's dreams that he had worked so hard for. Her heart ached for him. She sat down on the bed and picked up his hand.

"Daddy, don't be sad. This is the start of a new adventure. You know, the Universe must have a big plan for you to make a change of this magnitude, so get your strength back and take on the new challenge. I am excited for you and your future. Just you wait and see—it's going to be great."

She looked into his eyes with the biggest smile she could muster. Then she kissed his forehead, stood up, and hugged her mother.

"Just take this one day at a time. The path will be shown to you, and you will know it is exactly what you needed. Where is Milo?" she asked her mom.

"He is with Layne. They should be back here soon to take me home. They are discharging your dad in the morning. Maybe you can come and spring him out of this place, and I'll fix us a big dinner to celebrate," Armindia said, as upbeat as she could.

"That sounds like a fine idea. What are you going to fix? You won't believe it," she said, "but I went a whole day without eating, and more than 24 hours without coffee. I didn't even think about it until I got to the office. It must mean something. I never go without eating, and I hardly function without coffee." She said exasperated.

"You must have really been wrapped up in what you were doing, and then so tired you just dropped when your day was done. I've done that on a couple of occasions. It is weird to be that focused that you forget something so important.

"What was happening in the case?" her daddy asked.

269

"Well, I'm a little leery to tell you, for fear I will send your heart a-flutter. How stabilized is your heart?" she asked.

"Oh, Bippy," her daddy said, "did you shoot someone? I am okay. Sit down and tell your mother and me what went down. And where does the case stand now? Are you done, or do you have to go back up there?"

"I don't have to go back up for the case, but I absolutely loved Overgaard, and that cabin Iola has is really something. I can't wait for you guys to go up with me—you're going to love it. Iola said anytime I want to go, it's mine. Anyway, it will take a while to tell the whole story, so settle in and get ready to be astonished at what went on in the last forty years with this family." She took a deep breath and started her tale. Her folks were all eyes, and a couple of times she had to tell them to take a breath.

When she left the hospital, she went to KFC, picked up a family bucket and sides, and headed for the ranch, as her daddy always called it. She went in, set the food on the table, and then called Iola. She told her she would not be in the next morning because she was bringing her dad home from the hospital.

Iola asked her to come to her house on Sunday for dinner so they could really get caught up, and Dusty said she would be there. She hoped Iola would get some rest.

"I am worried about you, partner," she said.

"I'm a little worried myself. This hip is cramping my style. It's just a flesh wound, but it took a chunk of the muscle out, and it is very uncomfortable. The hospital said it would take a couple of weeks to get back to normal, but patience has never been my strong point. By the way, how is your shoulder doing? Has it given you any problems?"

"The shoulder was doing great until I decided to use it to open that basement door. Now it's a little sore, but not too bad. I have a lot of scrapes and bruises but nothing to complain about. My butt is sore from riding—I need to do that more often. I loved the horseback riding part of this case, but I am sore from being in the saddle. Don't tell anyone that Annie Oakley is a wuss." She laughed as she thought about the Annie Oakley part.

She wished she was that talented. When she hung up, she said a little prayer of thanks for Iola being in her life, and of course, for a speedy recovery. This case had been a rough one on many levels, and really, she had not found the Yoders, which was what she was actually hired to do. On Monday, they should get an update from the FBI on what they found in New Mexico and anything else that had turned up.

She was setting the table when Layne, Milo, and her mom came in from the hospital. They were all smiles when they saw that dinner was on the table. Milo looked up at her and said, "Thanks, Sissy, for bringing my favorite. What's to drink? Any Pepsi?"

Dusty told him to go look in the fridge and then wash up so they could eat.

"I'll wash up if everyone else has to. I'm not any dirtier than you are," he said matter-of-factly.

"Right on, bro, let's do it together," Layne said.

They sat and ate and talked until after dark. Milo had lots of questions about Overgaard—not just about the case, but about the history of the area. He loved the story of the cabin and said he wished he could have seen it.

Dusty told him there would be plenty of time for that and that she was anxious to get back up there, spend some time relaxing, and get to know the area better. When he smiled at her, she thought her heart would burst. She could only imagine how the cabin would affect him. It was magical—just like he was—and they would fit together like peas and carrots.

Dusty quizzed Layne on her schooling and how it was going, and she was pleasantly surprised to learn that Layne was at the top of her class and would graduate sooner than expected. Then she would be off to medical school. Her sister, a doctor; her brother, a Navy man; and her mom and dad, saints. Milo was still figuring it out, but it would be something the world needed more than anything—she was sure of that.

When the conversation turned to their daddy, they all said they felt terrible for him and the depression he felt about the doctor's announcement. Dusty assured them he would be fine and that his road was changing for the better. She said she was sure he had another career coming that none of them could even imagine.

Milo said, "I know what it is, but I can't tell you just yet—it's a surprise."

Layne, Dusty, and Armindia stared at Milo, and then they started laughing. They did not doubt that he just might have that information. Weird as it was, they all told him to let them know when he could talk about it.

She drove home that night happy and sad at the same time—happy to be home and sad that her daddy was facing an unknown future. She knew when he got over the shock of it all, he would dig deep, find his inner guide, and be able to set his course in the right direction.

Life was unpredictable from our vantage point, and yet from the universe's view, it was planned out to perfection.

Isn't life grand, she thought. The silver lining is always the surprise for everyone who looks to find it.

As soon as she got back to her apartment, she sat down and counted all of her blessings and said a prayer for those who had moved on—especially her Cheyenne.

30

THE COMFORT OF HOME

She was up early on Saturday and called to check in with family about her dad getting released. Her mom said she hadn't heard anything yet but figured it would be late morning or early afternoon before they knew. Dusty told her she was going to head down to St. Joseph's around 10 a.m. and would call when she had spoken with the doctors. She was also going to stop and get her daddy a strawberry malt—it was his favorite, and she hoped it would put a smile on his face.

She cleaned up the apartment, took a shower, and then had a long talk with Wampachaw about her daddy and what she could do to help his journey. When she left for the hospital, she was still awed by what she had learned was coming for her and her family. She decided that, for the time being, she was going to slow down, reconnect with them, and strengthen the bond they would need in the trying times ahead. She almost wished she hadn't asked Wampachaw so many questions—or that he hadn't made her privy to the answers.

She went to Mary Coyle's and got a malt for her dad and a hot fudge sundae for herself. She would just count it as her breakfast and not feel guilty about it.

She walked into her dad's room, said good morning, handed him the malt, and sat down to eat her sundae.

"This is the breakfast of champions, Dad—just you and me, getting ready for a creative change coming into our lives. I am so glad you're coming home today. That's the best place for you to get better, don't you think?" she asked.

He smiled and took a few sips of the malt before he answered.

"It will be good to get home and see everyone. I hope I won't have to come back here again. I do not like hospitals. We need to start making our plans to go to San Diego for Rock's boot camp graduation. I was thinking Momma, Milo, and I might go over a few days early and visit the San Diego Zoo. Do you think you and Layne can make the drive together? I know she has classes through Thursday, so you can't leave until after that. Does that work for you?" he asked.

"It works for me if it works for Layne. I'll talk with her today and we can make a plan. Are you going to be up to the drive?" she asked. "It's still a few weeks away, so you should have plenty of time to recoup—but take it easy. Don't go jumping back into work too soon." As soon as she said it, she was sorry. The look on his face was heartbreaking.

"I don't think we will have to worry about that, so I'll be ready to go when the time is here," he said.

The doctor came in and said his bloodwork looked good and that he was signing the release papers for him to go home. The new medicine seemed to be doing the trick, and he was "good as new," the doctor said. Dusty told her dad she would get the car and pull around to the front to wait until they brought him down. He agreed, and when the nurse came in to get him ready, she headed to the parking lot.

She had so many emotions swirling in her head and wished she could calm down enough to sort them out. When she got to her car, she rolled down the windows to let the heat out and just sat there thinking about the future. When she heard the flute music, she relaxed and let it soothe her—it was exactly what she needed.

She drove around to the front of the hospital and waited until the nurse wheeled her dad through the front doors in a wheelchair. The sight of him in the chair caused her to choke up and hold back tears. He was up and out of the chair as soon as the nurse stopped pushing. Dusty grabbed his bag, got him in the car, and off they went.

"Do you want to stop for something to eat?" she asked.

"I just want to get home and sit in my ole chair and hold your momma's hand. I know she'll have some good ole sweet tea and sandwiches made for us." He smiled and went into deep thought.

Dusty drove to the house and honked when she pulled up. The front door opened and a flood of love poured toward them. Smiles and hugs filled the air until they made it inside. Myron went straight to his easy chair, and Armindia quickly took a seat next to him. She reached for his hand, and they sat there just looking at each other. What a beautiful sight to see her folks still so in love.

Layne said, "Lunch is ready! We've got sweet tea and grilled cheese sandwiches with tomato soup. Any takers?"

Momma told Daddy she would fix him a plate and bring it to him, but he said no—he would come to the table. After they all sat down, Milo asked if he could say grace. Of course, they said yes and bowed their heads.

Milo thanked God for bringing his daddy home and for the food. Then he stopped and thanked God for his family. "Amen," he said, looking up with a smile to see faces with tears running down their cheeks.

It doesn't get any better than this, Dusty thought to herself, and she added a little extra prayer of her own.

After lunch, her dad went and laid down for a nap while Dusty and Layne went out into the backyard. They walked around awhile, and finally Dusty said, "Dad asked if you and I would drive over together for Rocky's boot camp graduation. He, Mom, and Milo would leave a few days early and go to the San Diego Zoo. What's your schedule like? Are you okay with leaving Friday after I get off work, or should I take the day off?"

Layne thought for a minute and said, "I have a clinic that morning that goes till 2:00 in the afternoon, so we can just leave later that day. Or you could pick me up when I'm done. I'm okay with either, so you decide."

"That will work. I'll pick you up here at 3:00 p.m. and we can get a jump on traffic. I'll book us a room and talk to Mom and Dad about where they want to stay. It should be a fun weekend. Let me know if anything changes with your schedule, and I'll adjust mine," Dusty said with a smile.

A little while later, Dusty headed home and decided to stop at Ma and Pa Clark's to pick up a sandwich for later. She loved how, the moment she walked in, the wonderful smell of garlic and steak filled her nostrils with pure comfort and love. She decided to get two.

When she arrived at her place, she was ready for a night of food, television, and sleep—and that is just what she did.

31

WALKER'S WISH

Sunday morning she watched *Oral Roberts'* sermon for an hour and tried to comprehend the fire and brimstone he spoke about from his interpretation of the Bible.

She was astounded at the way he worked his audience and talked of healings that would take place if only you purchased this small cloth that had been prayed upon.

Dusty remembered her mother telling her about being sent a cloth from Oral Roberts when Layne was very young and gravely ill. After seven blood transfusions and no clear answers from doctors, the disorder simply vanished once the cloth was laid upon her. Her mother was certain it had saved the little child they had feared they would lose—God had saved Layne and let her be Dusty's sister.

As Dusty thought about all of this while she watched the evangelist on television, she began to weep. She wasn't sure why she was crying, but she knew she was so grateful to have her sister with her. The Lord had been with her family since the beginning, leading them through the valley of the shadow of death and the shadows of darkness to do good in this world.

Dusty was overcome with the memories of her mother and the story of a personal relationship with God. She felt blessed and hoped she was doing the work of the Lord in the only way she knew how—retribution exacted for an injury or a wrong. That was the long and the short of it. Now, if she could just keep the faith, the universe would get her through it.

When she turned the sermon off, she felt exhausted. She laid her head on the pillow she had slept on and said a prayer for strength, healing, and gratitude for all her many blessings. She slept so soundly that she missed *Sky King* and *My Friend Flicka*—and almost dinner at Iola's.

She raced around getting dressed and putting away laundry, trying to finish up the chores she had overlooked by sleeping the day away.

When she arrived at Iola's she was fifteen minutes late. She apologized to Eunice and Heidi for holding up dinner and went directly to the kitchen. Heidi laughed and told Dusty she wasn't ready yet, and for her to make herself comfortable, as Iola was in her office. Dusty walked around the kitchen for a minute and then said, "I have to ask, what are we dining on tonight? I am so ready for some of your wonderful cooking."

Heidi said, "We are having wiener schnitzel and beets with mashed potatoes, and cucumber and onion salad."

Dusty turned and looked at Heidi with a sour expression. "What is that? I have never heard of it. I hope it's not liver," she said.

Heidi burst out laughing and told Dusty she would just have to try it and see what she thought. Man, the air was taken out of Dusty's sails—she had been looking forward to one of Heidi's meals. Now she was thinking about skipping dinner altogether.

She knocked on the door to Iola's office and smiled through the glass as Iola looked up from her work and motioned her in. Dusty went in and said, "A penny for your thoughts."

Iola just smiled and told her to sit down and take a load off. Dusty plopped into the beautiful old leather chair and leaned back. She looked lost in it. Iola thought she resembled Alice in Wonderland when everything was so large. It was a sharp reminder to Iola that Dusty was so young and fragile to the average observer, but in reality, she was a formidable adult. Many people would underestimate her. Iola was more concerned with nurturing her. She was always amazed at Dusty's ingenuity, yet also struck by the simple way she went about everyday things. Dusty was definitely a combination of naïvety and complexity.

Dusty kept watching Iola and wondering what she was thinking. Iola kept watching her.

"This is getting really weird. What's going on? Are you alright?" Dusty asked, concerned.

"I'm fine—just thinking about a lot. It's hard to believe what we've just been through, and I've been a little weepy. The hip is annoying and my emotions are all over the place."

She dropped her head and stared at her hands.

Dusty said, "Well, it sounds like you need something to eat. That always makes me feel better. When you don't give your stomach something to do, it just makes everything seem gloom and doom until you feed it—give it purpose."

Iola looked up and broke out into uncontrollable laughter. It startled Dusty, who jumped out of the chair and backed away from the desk. Iola just kept laughing.

When she finally gained control of herself, she stood up and said, "Well, let's go see if I can give my stomach some purpose." She smiled and then wrapped her arms around Dusty. "What a treasure you are."

Dusty laughed nervously. "Does that mean you're going to take me to the backyard and bury me?"

Iola started laughing again and headed for the kitchen.

Heidi met them with a smile. "Just in time—it's on the table. Enjoy! It's one of my favorite meals, and Iola's too. I have German chocolate cake for dessert if you clean your plate."

Dusty grimaced at the thought of missing out on the cake but wasn't sure she could make it through this meal.

When her plate was set in front of her, it already had some of everything on it. The beets were in a separate little bowl, as were the cucumbers and onions, and the meat looked delicious—even smelled good. She wasn't going to ask about any of it. She decided to take a small bite, then excuse herself by remembering a previous engagement. She took a deep breath, cut a small piece of the wiener schnitzel, covered it with mashed potatoes, and started to chew with a grimace—which was quickly replaced with surprise.

It was the most delicious thing she had ever eaten. She looked up and saw everyone staring at her with big smiles. They had known all along she would love this manna from heaven. She dug into the other delights with gusto, hoping she'd still have room for the German chocolate cake at the end. She knew she would be asking for seconds of the main course. It was the perfect ending to a really good day.

She was so full after dinner that all she wanted to do was lie down and nap. Iola had stuffed herself just as much as Dusty and wasn't in any better shape. They both told Heidi they'd have to wait awhile for dessert, then headed to the overstuffed chairs in the living room. Dusty leaned back, rubbed her stomach, yawned, and dozed off. Within a minute, Iola did the same.

An hour later they were awakened by the clanging of the coffee tray Heidi brought in. Neither wanted to wake up, but slowly they sat up and stretched. They poured cups of joe and hoped the dark brew would bring them out of their eating stupor.

Iola laughed at how silly it felt to sleep while the sun was still shining but said it was the nicest nap she'd ever had. Iola asked Heidi to have Eunice join them, but Heidi said she had also laid down for a nap and wasn't awake yet.

They both took sips of coffee—well, Dusty's was more of a gulp than a sip—and it was just what she needed.

They spent the rest of the day and part of the night talking about the events of the past weeks and making notes of the loose ends still out there. Dusty told her boss she would spend the next week tying everything up so she could attend Walker's funeral and meet with the attorney for the Sherwood case. It was only a short time before she'd be heading to San Diego for the boot camp graduation, and she wanted to leave with a clean slate.

Iola talked about the seriousness of the clients they were getting and what skills they needed to sharpen for these complicated scenarios. She was acutely aware, she said, of how out of practice she was in the field. It had almost cost her life. She told Dusty she should have seen the shooting coming when they walked into the barn—that she had let Walker down.

They both broke into tears at the thought of the man they had lost—the friend they were so comfortable with, and who seemed to feel the same way about them. Dusty tried to compose herself but couldn't.

Finally, Iola said, "Let's go take a walk out back." The fresh air helped, and they ended up sitting on the benches by the guest house.

Iola asked "Dusty, would you do something for me?".

"Of course," Dusty said. "What is it?"

"I want you to go to a six-week training course at a private facility that trains law enforcement and the private sector in security. You'd be paid your salary and come out of it with abilities to handle a multitude of situations that might be coming our way. I learned about this facility from Walker. He had been hounding me to let him sign you up. He said you had the best instincts and thought it would give you the leg up you needed. What do you think?" Iola asked, giving her a big hug.

Dusty thought about it. "Walker is behind all of this. Was this his wish for me?" she asked.

Iola nodded and closed her eyes. "What do you think? It will happen sometime soon, maybe not until fall. You have to stay for the full six weeks to graduate. By then you'll either be twenty-one or close to it. You in?"

"I am—but what about the cases we have and training new investigators? I thought we were bringing some on?" Dusty asked.

"All in good time," Iola told her. "But with the urgency of Wampachaw's conflicts and the universe sending us more and more high-profile cases, I can't send you out there without honing your skills. I believe in on-the-job training, but you've been handling things most men only step into once in a career—and you've had them one

285

right after another. We need to read the writing on the wall and take heed while our luck is still holding."

Dusty said, "I'll go and do my best, but I have to go to my brother's graduation. After that, you can send me away."

Six weeks seemed like a very long time to be away, and she wasn't sure she wanted to be gone from her mom and dad that long. But she would deal with that when the time came.

They went back into the house and had another cup of coffee. Dusty sat and talked with Eunice, who was knitting a beautiful afghan. It was so pretty, and she tried to show Dusty how to knit, but it was a brief session. Dusty found no interest in learning.

She finally left for home, eager to lay her head down again and sleep until morning.

32

GOODBYE CHEYENNE

The night went by too fast with dreams of horses, flowers, and puppy dogs. It was a restful sleep, and she woke up ready to face the day. She did a quick cleanup of the apartment and took inventory of her refrigerator. She had unpacked all of the snacks and drinks she'd taken up to Overgaard but hadn't had the time or need to eat them, since she was fed quite nicely by the neighborly bad people.

Sometimes it was hard to believe her own reality— the things that happened to her were most people's worst nightmares, yet she just rolled with them. Was there something wrong with her? Or was she simply protected by the armor of justice? It didn't matter one way or another; it all seemed to work.

The first chance she got, she decided she might need to seek a therapist. She hoped it wouldn't come to that, but she would if she needed to. Maybe church would help. Prayer, meditation, boot camp for cops—geez—it just got weirder and weirder.

She decided between the peanut butter and the jelly she had enough to eat for a while, and she was totally stocked with Pepsi. After a long hot shower, she dressed and contemplated taking the scissors to her hair—it looked pretty disheveled. She decided to think about it for a while and maybe pick up some clothes. She would ask Iola what she might need for the training course, then go shopping.

The more she thought about the training, the more she dreaded it—probably meant getting her butt kicked by a bunch of goons. Next thought was whether she should mention it to her dad—another scenario she dreaded. Well, one step at a time was all she could do.

She stopped at the office, said good morning to Rick, and gave him a check for the rent coming up. He informed her it wasn't due yet, but she said she might be out of town for a while and asked him to hold it until the first of the month. She asked how he was doing.

She worried that the loss of his father might cause him to feel depressed, and since she had been involved in all of it, she felt responsible and wanted him to know he was in her thoughts and prayers. He told her he was doing fine, that all had been taken care of, and that she shouldn't worry about him. She smiled and told him it was easier said than done.

As she walked to her car, remembering the death of her old boyfriend and the shooting at her office, she counted her blessings. It seemed a million years ago, but it had only been months. Life just seemed to roll on by.

She understood how most elderly people thought a lifetime went by in the blink of an eye. She wanted to stop and smell the roses, but that wasn't an option right now.

Work, graduations, clients, training, and her daddy's illness were filling the hours, days, and months ahead. She hoped she was up to the tasks—that she wouldn't let anyone down, get anyone killed, or have to kill anyone. But she knew that would probably not be the case.

When she got to the agency, she went into the office with a smile on her face and headed straight to the break room. Donuts awaited her, along with the smell of fresh-brewed coffee. The day was off to a good start.

She sat down at her desk with a hot cup of joe and a maple long john. As she looked through her messages, she let out a yelp when she came to one that said the Prescott Animal Shelter was going to euthanize Lizzy Sherwood's dogs, which had been kept there temporarily for Walker.

She picked up the phone, called the shelter, and explained who she was and the reason for her call. They told her they were full and turning other animals away, so they needed the room. The animals had until Friday to be retrieved or they would be euthanized. Dusty offered to pay a generous board fee, but they weren't interested. She said she would get back to them that afternoon with a plan.

She walked directly to Iola's office and told her the problem. She was beside herself, thinking they would kill those little dogs—she had to do something. Iola asked her to describe them—their size, breed, disposition, and whether they barked. Dusty told her what she remembered: that they were not barkers, small and loyal little critters who had done nothing wrong to deserve this.

She was surprised when Iola said she should go to the jail and talk with Lizzy Sherwood. Dusty said she thought Lizzy would have been out on bail by now, but Iola didn't think so.

Dusty headed out the door and walked the six blocks to the county jail, waiting two hours to see Ms. Sherwood—the last person she had ever wanted to see again.

When they brought her out and she picked up the phone, Dusty could hardly believe it was the same woman. She looked like she had aged twenty years. Dusty almost felt sorry for her.

"What do you want?" Lizzy asked.

Dusty informed her about the dog and cat situation and asked what she wanted her to do. Did Lizzy have someone who could take them? Had her husband made bail, and would he be able to take them? Dusty asked with as much empathy as she could muster.

Lizzy looked shocked, leaned into the glass, and said, "What can I do? I don't know anyone. That's the last thing I thought you were going to say. I thought you were going to laugh at me. My poor little pups and Dante are probably total wrecks after living in a cell for this long. I know that I am. What can we do?"

Dusty told her she could sign them over for adoption or sign them over to her, and she would find homes for them. She explained that she had offered to pay board but was refused, and she wanted Lizzy to make the decision.

Lizzy said, "Well, maybe that cocky FBI agent should have to figure it out. He just threw them in there and forgot all about them. I hope he's happy with himself. Why don't you talk to him?"

Dusty took a deep breath, looked Lizzy in the eye, and said, "I gave the shelter a call, and I'll make a trip up to Prescott and pick up the dogs. But you have to decide what you want to do. Your choices now will decide if they live or if they meet their maker—and it's all on you. You've got an hour. If you want to sign them for adoption, to me, or end their innocent little lives, have your attorney call my office. If I don't hear from you, I'll know you signed their death warrant. I look forward to seeing you in court."

Dusty walked out of the jail, mentally making a plan. She would give Lizzy until 3:00 p.m., then call the clinic, drive up there, and bring them all home with her. She had no idea what she'd do from there, but she would not let them go down for this.

When she walked into the office, she was met by Iola with a stack of mail and a carafe of coffee. They went into Dusty's office and closed the door. After Dusty updated Iola on the situation and her plans, she waited for her boss to chew her out for getting involved with pets—but that wasn't what happened.

Iola said she thought they would do well at her house, that Eunice and Heidi would love having the animals for company. If it didn't work out, at least they would have time to find good homes for them.

Dusty's jaw dropped, and she stared at her boss in stunned silence. Iola laughed and said, "Now let's move on to more crucial matters. On Friday we need to go to Walker's funeral to pay our respects and say goodbye to our friend, Clinton Charles Walker—aka Cheyenne. We can fly out in the morning and be back late afternoon. What do you think?"

Dusty started to tear up and just nodded. "Where is it going to be? I don't even know where he's from. Did he have a family?" she asked.

"The services are in Santa Barbara, California. The rest, I don't know. I guess we'll find out when we get there. The Bureau is conducting this one, and he'll be laid to rest in Oklahoma. That's all I know," Iola said with a weak smile.

Dusty asked what she was going to wear.

"I'm going to wear a navy-blue pantsuit with a white blouse and black pumps," Iola said.

"I guess I'll have to go shopping. I really don't have anything like that. Where do you recommend I go?" Dusty asked.

Iola told her she would take her shopping the next morning and not to worry about it.

"It has to have a western cut to it—old school but Dale Evans chic. I might even buy a dress pair of Justins. Only the best for Cheyenne," she said.

She picked up the mail and got on with it. She didn't want to think about the funeral anymore.

Iola smiled, thinking of Dusty in a dress. It didn't seem to fit her image of lil Dusty Roads, but knowing her as she did, she bet Dusty could pull it off in style. She better make some phone calls just in case.

That night she called Dusty and told her to meet her at Butler and Sons Western Wear on 27th Avenue and Northern at 10:00 a.m. the next morning. She was excited and hoped Dusty would be happy with her first shopping experience with a stylist.

Dusty spent the next morning trying on some of the best western suits she had ever seen. She had no idea what a statement you could make with clothing. She ended up with a black western suit with white buck stitching on the collar and down the buttonholes of the tailored jacket. The boot-cut pants covered the new Justin boots perfectly.

At the funeral, they had everyone talking. The Abrams Agency name was passed around, and both Dusty and Iola spoke with great admiration about their friend Clinton Charles Walker to all who would listen.

33

RESCUE ROAD TRIP

Her Mustang just didn't have the room for carrying kennels, so the animals were going to be loose in the car. Milo offered to help, and much to her surprise, her mom and dad said he could go with her. She was relieved they let him, even if surprised.

She pulled up in front of the house and honked the horn. Milo came running out with a little book bag and a lunch box that had the television show, Lost in Space, printed on it. He was so excited that he dropped the lunch box. When he stopped to pick it up, Mom and Dad came out the door telling him to slow down. Dusty walked up, gave them both a hug, and asked how their morning was going.

"Well, he's been up since 6:00 a.m. and ready to go since 6:15. The last few hours he's been a handful. We hope he doesn't drive you crazy on the way up there," her mother said with a sigh.

"He'll be just fine," Dusty said. "We'll have a great time, and I know the animals are going to love him."

She went in the house to use the bathroom, then poured herself a cup of coffee. Sitting down at the table with Layne, she asked her, "How's everything going with Daddy?"

Layne said he was doing great health-wise and was trying to make a decision about going back to work.

"What kind of decision?" Dusty asked.

"Whether he should leave the S.O. or take a desk job," her sister answered.

Dusty felt an emotional lump in her throat. Her dad must be devastated, having to even think about leaving the job he loved so much. She said a quick prayer. Dusty asked Layne if she wanted to ride along, and Layne jumped up and said "yes" before Dusty even finished the sentence. Dusty smiled and said it would be a fun day.

"Where are we going?" Layne asked.

When Dusty told her, she shook her head.

"Me in a car with dogs? I don't think so. Not happening," she said.

Dusty explained they were all small dogs and one small cat, and they wouldn't bite. Layne thanked her for the invite but said she wasn't going to ride two and a half hours in a car full of dogs. That was the end of that conversation.

Milo jumped into the car, Dusty hugged her folks goodbye and off they went.

They stopped at Rock Springs and had a big breakfast. Milo liked the western feel of the café and asked Dusty how old it was. She told him it was a historical landmark that had been serving great pies for a long time—that it was the best food you could have on the road.

Milo smiled and said he wished they could get a pie to take home to Mom and Dad. Dusty told him they would on the way back, and put it in the trunk so the dogs wouldn't get to it. Milo said maybe the dogs could have a little bit—it might not hurt them. Dusty laughed and said, "It'll give them diarrhea. I don't want to start Iola's first night with them like that."

Milo agreed and said, "Okay, I brought them treats and water so they won't feel left out." What a sweet boy, Dusty thought, giving him a big hug.

When they arrived in Prescott and located the animals, she was as excited as Milo to meet them all. She had collars and leashes for the dogs and a small kennel for Dante. She gave the gear to the workers, and within fifteen minutes she had them with her. They all looked in good health, tails wagging at ninety miles an hour, and Milo was smiling from ear to ear.

Once they were loaded—Milo in the back with the dogs and Dante up front with Dusty—they hit the road. On the way back, they stopped again at Rock Springs to pick up the pie. Dusty ran in and was back in a flash. She had left the car running, popped the trunk, and carefully set the pie down, hoping it would make the trip home safely. She felt so good to have these little critters back with people who would love them and give them a good home.

Sherwood had loved the dogs, and that was one of the things that made Dusty feel bad for her. She might actually have been a good person at one time, before she met Durant. Time would tell if she went to prison, but Dusty was pretty sure she would. She was grateful Lizzy had signed the animals over and promised herself she would do right by them.

Iola, Eunice, and Heidi would love them and give them a great home—it would all work out for the best, she was sure of it.

Milo was smitten with Poncho and said he wanted to keep him. Dusty told him he'd have to visit him at Iola's. He smiled and said, "We'll see."

When they got into town, they went straight to Iola's, where they were met with a fanfare of happy faces and plenty of "oohs and ahhs".

Heidi had cookies baked for Milo and gave him a tall glass of cold milk. He sat down in the kitchen and forgot all about keeping Poncho—for now, life was good.

34

A FAMILY PROTECTED

Dusty finished documenting her deposition in the Sherwood case. She had worked all day clearing up loose ends and filing paperwork, trying to get everything done before she took a few days off. Today at five she would pick up her sister Layne, and they would head for San Diego for their brother Rocklin's graduation from boot camp. She was looking forward to the days off and spending time with her sister and family. It was going to be heartbreaking and wonderful all at the same time.

Dusty picked up Layne at their parents' house, and they were on the road by 5:00 p.m. Dusty wanted to stop and eat, but Layne insisted on putting Phoenix in the rearview mirror. They drove with the radio blasting, singing country and rock and roll all the way into San Diego. They never stopped for food—Layne had packed Hostess Cupcakes and cold Pepsi, and they were fueled with sugar all the way there.

The time flew by, and when they checked into the motel, they were ready for a good night's sleep. They saw their parents' car in the parking lot of the Bayside Motel and were relieved that they had gotten there safe and sound. They fell asleep as soon as their heads hit the pillow—Dusty to the sound of flutes off in the distance, and Layne with Rick Nelson's *Travelin' Man* still playing in her head.

Morning came way too soon for the sisters, and both threw on clothes at 6:00 a.m. to go find coffee. It was going to be a long day.

Sending the older of their two baby brothers off to war was a hard pill to swallow. She and Layne had always protected Rocky, being the best big sisters they could be. As they watched him graduate, they cried at the passing of his childhood—their childhood—and the unknown future the military would lead him into.

They all had dinner at a wonderful seafood restaurant called *The Captain's Chest* and listened to Rocky tell them about his six weeks in hell. Dusty cringed at the thought of her brother marching in the rain with his rifle held over his head for hours. He said he'd had cramps for two days afterward and would never again make the mistake of not finishing a task in the mandated time. No one, he said, was cut any slack.

That night, Rocky went back to the motel with them and stayed in the room with the folks and Milo. Little Milo had been extremely quiet all day and through dinner. He seemed sad and deep in thought. It was hardest on him being away from Rocky—they were really close.

Though the sisters had grown up with Rocky, Milo had been right by his side, while Dusty pulled her shenanigans and Layne had married and moved away. He was having a hard time letting his big brother go, and they all felt the weight on his heart.

Dusty asked Milo if he wanted go out to the parking lot and practice with her and Layne on the CB radio she had brought. He smiled and said yes, of course. While Rocky visited the folks, they thought up their "handles" and figured out the channels, learning how to talk like truckers. It was hilarious, and they cracked each other up for over an hour. Dusty was "Calamity," Layne was "Medicine Man," and Milo decided on "Googy Boy." He told them he had handles for Mom and Dad too, but it was a surprise.

When they went back in with the family, they told their CB stories. Rocky said he wanted his handle to be "Lonely Boy." They all shed a tear at that one, but he laughed and made fun of them.

Milo got upset and said it wasn't funny—that he might never get over Rocky leaving him to fight with the Compound Brothers alone.

"What are you talking about, Milo? Who are the Compound Brothers?" Armindia asked.

"Rocky knows—and he better quit laughing at me. I don't know if I can keep patrolling the neighborhood when he's gone. That's why I need a gun and to learn how to use it. I'm the only one there to protect the family."

Myron pulled Milo into his arms and rocked him. "Don't you worry, little man. I've got your back. You don't have to take on the neighborhood by yourself. I'm with you."

They all stood there crying over the little brother who tried so hard to be grown up in every way. As Layne and Dusty started to head to their room, Milo asked, "Don't you want to know Mom and Dad's handles?" Of course they did.

He looked at their mom and smiled. "Your handle is Earhart. And Dad, yours is Blue Yodeler. Do you like them? Amelia Earhart and Jimmie Rodgers—the Blue Yodeler—your heroes. Do you like them?" he asked with such anticipation that it was hard not to tear up again.

"We love them. And we'll practice tomorrow on our way up to Knott's Berry Farm. The girls will be on their way home, and we'll put those fine handles to use. The Roads clan is now savvy on the CB radio," Armindia said.

"What does savvy mean?" asked Milo.

"It means we've sharpened our talents as much as we can to keep track of each other with our Citizen Band radios."

The girls headed to their room and talked about the day—laughing, crying, and feeling blessed to have each other.

It was two in the morning when Layne woke with a scream. Dusty jumped straight out of bed to grab her gun. Layne went back to sleep immediately, but Dusty's heart was racing. She quickly realized what had happened, then sat down with a plop to calm her pounding heart. That's when she heard a flute's distant melody. As she strained to listen, a soft, familiar voice said:

"Hello, little one. Today will be filled with unexpected confrontations. Be on your guard and protect the one that is with you. Don't hesitate in flight."

Dusty was caught off guard by the unexpected visit and just sat there like a bump on a log, saying nothing. She laid her head back down, and the soft music lulled her to sleep.

When she awoke at 7:00 a.m., her sister was staring at her from her bed.

"What's the matter?" Dusty asked.

"Who was talking to you in the middle of the night?" Layne asked.

"What do you mean? I wasn't talking to anyone. What did you hear?" Dusty asked sheepishly.

"I couldn't make it out—just that you were listening intently to something or someone. It sounded like a low humming, but I couldn't make out the words. Then, when you laid down again, I swear I heard a flute. What's that all about? Care to share?" Layne asked, then got out of bed and went into the bathroom, closing the door.

Dusty laid there trying to think of something to say. If Wampachaw was heard, maybe she was supposed to tell her sister about her spirit guide. She whispered his name and asked what to do, but heard nothing.

This was probably a test of some kind. It was too early to decide—she needed coffee. She threw on her clothes and told Layne through the bathroom door that she was going out to get them some morning joe and would be right back.

"Okay, I'll get my shower out of the way. Be safe," Layne said.

Dusty knocked quietly on her parents' door. Rocky opened it a crack and said, "What?" She gave him the rundown, then turned toward her car—when she heard Rocky say, "Hey, did you know you've got an Indian ghost thing following you?"

She swung around. "What are you talking about?"

He smiled. "I see him now and then when you're around. I just wondered if you saw him."

"Yes, I see him. Do you see other spirits?"

"Not around you—but I see them all the time. So does Layne. Probably Milo too, but he wouldn't tell us."

She was a little shaken by all of this as she got into her car and drove to the diner down the street. She ordered six coffees and one orange juice—the extra coffee for Milo, in case he felt left out.

She tried not to think about the Wampachaw thing, but she was baffled that her siblings had seen him all along. She had thought it was her special secret. Turns out the whole damn family has a special secret.

When she got back to the motel and delivered the coffee to Rocky, she returned to her room and set a cup in front of Layne.

"Drink this and I'll take my shower, then we'll talk, okay?" Dusty said, heading straight to the bathroom.

When she joined Layne after her hot shower, she thought she was ready for the conversation. Layne set her straight on the spirit guides she had seen through the years. She said she didn't have one of her own but had been helped many times by different guides since she was about twelve. She heard them and felt them often. She knew Rocky had also had similar experiences, but she wasn't sure about Milo.

Dusty explained she had only had Wampachaw since her first case in New Mexico, but that he had been with her ever since. He had led her and helped her with every case she'd worked on. Layne said it made her feel so much better about the line of work Dusty was in, and that they were all very blessed.

When they finished their coffee, they packed up their room and loaded the car, then went in to say goodbye to the family. They promised Rocky they would write as soon as they had his information on where he would be stationed. Tears, smiles, and awkwardness filled the goodbye before they finally drove off toward Phoenix.

They drove for a while without speaking, each lost in their own memories and thoughts of how exciting and yet scary life's changes could be. Finally, Dusty broke the silence with her famous words:

"I'm so hungry. Let's stop in Yuma for breakfast and gas. I think there's a truck stop there with decent food."

"How far is it?" Layne asked. "I'm not hungry yet, but maybe in a few hours I will be."

"It's almost three hours away, so it should work for you. In the meantime, I need a snack," Dusty said.

They stopped at a 7-Eleven. Layne ran in and came out with snacks for Dusty and a cup of coffee for the ride.

Dusty decided not to get gas there, since it was higher-priced in California. She'd wait until Yuma—she'd have to, because the Mustang would be empty by then.

They hit the road and played with the CB, trying to sound like seasoned road warriors. They laughed at the smooth truckers and their endless come-ons. Layne took some teasing over her handle, "Medicine Man." The first thing the truckers said was, "You sound like a woman to me." They just laughed and laughed like kids again. Dusty couldn't remember the last time she and her sister had this much fun together. She felt lighthearted for the first time in two years—like another person, without the heavy weight she had been carrying.

35

BAD ASS SISTERS

The gas gauge was dropping faster than Dusty had figured. The mountain road that brought back vivid memories of her driving the semi to bring Layne home to Phoenix seemed like a lifetime ago—and it had already taken the fuel gauge down a quarter of a tank. They limped into Yuma but couldn't make it to the truck stop. Instead, they had to pull into a Chevron just the other side of the river, where gas was still at California prices. Dusty didn't care—she was just happy they'd made it to a pump.

She got out, opened the flap, and twisted off the gas cap. A hiss escaped—nothing but fumes. She stuck her head through the window and told Layne she was going inside to pay and use the bathroom. Layne jumped out on her side.

"Let me go first. I can't hold it much longer."

"Okay, go ahead. I'll pay and fuel up, then I'll go. Why didn't you say something?" Dusty called, but Layne didn't hear—she was already halfway across the parking lot.

Dusty scanned the surroundings, then washed the windshield. As she set the nozzle back on the pump, she noticed two men climb out of a Chevy pickup—both holding pistols. She went straight to the glove compartment and grabbed her .38, double-checking her ankle holster before slipping the revolver into her jeans. Maybe this was normal for Yuma men, walking into stores armed—but their look didn't sit right.

She walked toward the east-side bathroom. Out of the corner of her eye, she saw Layne inside the station—hands raised high. *Why did she go in there? The restroom was outside.* Dusty thought nervously.

Dusty ducked behind their own truck, reached inside, and yanked the keys from the ignition. Then she sprinted to the back of the station, where another pickup sat idling by a row of oleanders. The driver was waiting. She peeked around the corner and made a dash for the back door, but it was locked. Her only option was the garage opening.

As she moved, the getaway driver spotted her. He thrust his pistol out the window. Luckily, he didn't fire immediately—probably didn't see her weapon. That hesitation saved her life. Dusty drew, swiveled, and fired. His shot ricocheted off the building, hers hit his chest. He slumped sideways.

Dusty slipped into the garage. Inside, two men were still busy—one rifling the register, the other yelling about the shots. *Where was Layne?*

She tried to sneak closer but knocked over an oil display. Both men spun, guns raised. Dusty darted behind a rack of maps and additives, but one robber came around the corner, face to face with her.

"Drop it! Hands up!" she shouted.

He let out a wild, manic laugh and pulled the trigger. Dusty fired almost simultaneously. They both went down. Her thigh burned—she'd been hit. He took a bullet to the face.

Gritting her teeth, Dusty forced herself upright and checked behind the counter. The station attendant lay dead—no pulse. She hurried to the back door. It was unlocked from the inside. The robbers had escaped that way. Layne had to be out there.

She circled back through the garage and glanced toward the pumps. There—Layne, in the passenger seat of their truck, a gun pointed at her head. The gunman was digging under the seat for the keys. Dusty's heart froze.

Then she noticed Layne's subtle move—raising her right leg. Dusty remembered: her sister was wearing the thigh holster with a snub-nose tucked inside. Thank God.

Dusty pulled a spare ring of keys from her pocket and dangled them in the air. Her right hand clutched Smitty. She and Layne locked eyes.

"Hey!" Dusty shouted. "You looking for these?"

The man on the floorboard spun, back flat, gun raised. At the same time, the getaway driver reappeared from around the building. Dusty had to pick—she couldn't stop both.

She fired first. Her bullet struck the man in the groin, then the arm. He crumpled beside the truck. The second gunman aimed—only for Layne to whip her pistol up and put a round clean between his eyes.

Dusty rushed over, kicked the gun from the wounded man's reach, and checked his pulse. Then she turned to her sister, who was sliding out of the cab.

"Let me make sure he can't fire again," Dusty said.

Layne holstered her weapon. "He ain't going anywhere. And I still need to use the bathroom."

Inside the station, the phones had been ripped out. Dusty grabbed the CB and sent out a call for law enforcement, giving a quick rundown of events. Within five minutes the lot swarmed with police and gawkers.

Statements given. Weapons surrendered. Exhaustion setting in. The officers were stunned—two young women had taken down a crew that had already robbed multiple stations across California, leaving a trail of wounded and dead. Eventually, the sisters were told they could go.

Dusty and Layne thought about grabbing a hotel, but decided to drive on. As they pulled onto the highway, the CB crackled.

"Calamity or Medicine Man, you out there? This is Googy Boy. What's your twenty? Come back."

Layne picked up the mic. "This is Medicine Man. We're flying low, heading back to the ranch. All is good. Call from your hotel tonight and I'll tell you a story. Do you copy?"

"Ten-four, good buddy," Milo's voice came back. "Over and out."

The sisters exchanged a look, then broke into hysterical laughter—part relief, part shock, part nerves. Somehow, they'd made it out alive.

What did it say about them—that they could take lives and then roll on down the highway, trying to laugh it off? Maybe it was just how they survived. Maybe it was justice. They'd think about it later.

For now, Dusty was just grateful for her badass sister.

She smiled, and flute music followed them all the way home, and to whatever would meet up with them down the road.

Acknowledgements

A heartfelt thank you to my publisher, RLA Publishing, and Editor Raynie Andrewsen for the patience and professionalism that she has shown working with me on my series of crime novels. What a gift she is.

About the Author

Rebecca Harscher writes with the sharp eye of a natural observer and the soulful heart of a mystic. Raised on tales of justice and mystery from her badge-wearing father, Rebecca developed a lifelong passion for storytelling, human nature, and the unseen threads that connect us all. Her years in sales and service deepened her understanding of people—and sharpened her instinct for the unsaid.

Rooted in her love for family, the Wild West, and a good mystery, Rebecca brings a fresh and heartfelt voice to crime fiction. A proud mother of three grown children and happily married, she now calls Arizona home, where the desert's wild spirit matches her own.

Dusty Roads: First Highway Taken is her debut novel and a testament to divine nudges, gut instincts, and the courage to follow where they lead.

Message from the Author

Thank you for stepping into Dusty's world. Writing this story has been a journey of the heart—fueled by intuition, memory, and mystery. I hope Dusty's story reminds you, as it reminded me, to trust your gut, follow your calling, and believe that anything is possible when you dare to pay attention.

We all have a little detective inside us. I hope Dusty inspires yours.

With gratitude,
Rebecca Harscher

www.RNHarscher.com

YOUR VOICE MATTERS

Dear Reader,

If Dusty's story moved you, surprised you, or stayed with you long after the final page, I'd be so grateful if you shared your thoughts in a review.

Reviews do more than just offer opinions—they help indie authors like me reach new readers, grow visibility, and keep telling the stories that matter. Whether it's one sentence or several, your voice can make a big difference.

You can leave a review on:
- **Amazon** (where most readers discover new books)
- **Goodreads** (a great place to connect with fellow readers)
- **Barnes & Noble, BookBub**, or wherever you picked up this book

Thank you from the bottom of my heart for reading *Dusty Roads: Ghost Highway*. Follow Dusty's Journey in the next book *Dusty Roads: Broken Highway* and don't forget to pick up the fourth book in the series, *Dusty Roads: Rogue Highway*—coming soon! Your support means the world.

With gratitude,
Rebecca Harscher